Quiet Mountain Press

Mr. Darcy's
Mail-Order Bride

A Pride and Prejudice Variation

J. DAWN KING

Quiet Mountain Press

Cover Design: JD Smith – Design
Interior Formatting: Sarah Johnson, Peculiar World Designs

Published by: Quiet Mountain Press

Print ISBN-13: 978-1540466976
Print ISBN-10: 1540466973

Library of Congress Control Number –

Acknowledgments

Combining Jane Austen's Pride and Prejudice with the Wild, Wild West was a huge risk for me. Even though I've lived in Oregon most of my life, I've never written about it before. By the time I typed "The End" I had fallen in love all over again with my home.

My sincerest thanks to Dr. Cynthia Maynes of Evergreen Family Medical and the paramedic staff of the Urgent Care Clinic on Edenbower in Roseburg. I've never had a compound fracture before and am not old enough to have experienced a broken bone in 1869, so their information and willing assistance was invaluable.

A great big shout of appreciation also goes to the staff and researchers at the Museum of the Oregon Territory, the Clackamas County Historical Society, as well as to those at McLoughlin House. Your exhibits helped me visualize the 1860's. I thank you.

To all the readers who left comments on both fanfiction.net and beyondausten.com – you are AWESOME!!!

Table of Contents

Prologue

Wednesday, February 10, 1869 – Baltimore, Maryland

The cowboy pulled his six-shooter from his holster and peeked around the corner of the bank building. Shattering glass along with screams of panic and terror from within sent a stream of sweat trickling down the middle of his back. Marshall Morgan Brown was over an hour away, attending the trial of the notorious outlaw Barton Solomon, the scourge of the West, a hired killer who had over sixteen notches on his pistol grip. With no lawman available, the cowboy was on his own. Only he could protect the innocent women and children of Bent Nail Creek.

He sighted down the barrel, the rays from the burning sun bouncing off the cold steel. Holding steady, he zeroed in on the front of the building. The door burst open, and two gunmen carrying bags of money…

"Lizzy!" Jane whispered loud enough to get her sister's attention. "Uncle Gardiner is here."

Elizabeth Bennet closed the dime novel and shoved it under the cushion in time to stand and welcome her mother's only brother back from his long journey at sea.

The Bennet family surrounded their favorite uncle, Mr. Edward Gardiner, to hear about his journey.

"Did you discover lovely vistas and beautiful forests, Uncle?" Elizabeth Bennet had a great admiration for nature. Living in the midst of a city on the Atlantic Seaboard gave her few glimpses of the earth's verdant bounty.

She was weary of witnessing the remnants of the war between the states. One of her father's colleagues referred to the conflict as the Civil War; an oxymoron from her point of view. Reconstruction had begun, yet a sense of hopelessness and loss still blanketed her neighborhood.

Most had lost at least one male family member to the conflict. The prospects for any of the Bennet daughters marrying and having a home of their own were slim to none. The ball they had attended the night before affirmed the sparsity of male partners as she was forced to sit out all but two of the dances— standing up with her eldest sister, Jane, both times.

"The West is like nothing I have ever seen before, Lizzy. The soil is rich, begging to be planted. Tall fir trees are remarkably thick, keeping the sun from reaching the forest floor. Bushes dripping with sweet blackberries hanging from the vines grow so abundantly I soon tired of the fruit. Apple trees, pear trees, and plum trees filled groves so the produce fell to the ground wasted. The grass was green and lush, and it felt like walking on your mother's thick rug in her sitting room. When our vessel pulled into Portland on the mighty Columbia River, we spied a snow-capped mountain shaped like an upside down funnel overlooking the bustling city. I cannot wait to sell out and return with my family. The Willamette Valley is the future for the Gardiners."

"And Indians, Uncle?" Mary, the middle sister, had wanted to be a nurse during the war, but her tender age and her father had kept her home. Now, she dreamed of becoming a missionary to the native Americans.

"How about men, Uncle Gardiner? Did you see many men?" At fifteen, Lydia Bennet felt the loss of potential suitors as heavily as her older sisters. Brash and bold, she was determined to marry first. Her next eldest sibling, Catherine, called Kitty, followed her lead. Though Lydia had been the one to mention what was on all of their minds, all five Bennet sisters dared not breathe until their Uncle Gardiner answered.

"Yes, Mary, I saw Indians." Uncle Gardiner knew his nieces well. "While there, an express rider arrived in Oregon City. In his mailbag, he had an East Coast newspaper with the headline, "30,000 Women in Need of Husbands". The ensuing uproar caused a stampede as gentlemen and ruffians alike tore at one another to read the information. Therefore, yes, Lydia, there is an abundance of single men who long for the comforts of home and good companionship."

Even Mrs. Bennet sighed at the thought.

Mr. Bennet did not find his brother-in-law's comments amusing. "You will not continue to encourage my daughters, Edward. I will not have them running to the Wild West in search of any Tom, Dick, or Harry to be their husbands. With the war over, it will soon be as it was before."

Elizabeth wanted to shake her head at her father—or shake him by the shoulders. When the Confederate army attacked Fort Sumter in April 1861, Thomas Bennet buried his head in his books and refused to look up until the surrender of General Lee to General Ulysses S. Grant in Appomattox Court House in Virginia. Their mother had taken to her room with a four-year case of nerves. Both Jane and Elizabeth had striven to make their meager funds stretch to cover the rising costs of food. Luxuries had been eliminated, to the chagrin of her mother and younger sisters, and fear had settled over most of the household at the many changes they had been required to make. Fewer young men were seeking tutorage in classic literature from her father and their coffers were almost drained dry. In the years since the war was declared over, economic expansion to the West kept the students from their door, so conditions continued to be lean.

She caught Jane shaking her head, her eyes closed against their father's attitude. His denial had intensified their hardships, and they both were weary of stretching the few coins they possessed to feed and house seven residents. Gone were the cook and housekeeper. Jane cared for the oversight of the living rooms while Elizabeth tended the kitchen chores. For the most part, it was thankless work. Nevertheless, Elizabeth's nature would not allow her to remain discouraged. She felt she owed it to her sisters to bolster their dreams for a happier future.

"Uncle," Elizabeth was desperate to hear more, "tell us of the trip itself."

As she listened to descriptions of the ports-of-call down the coast of the Americas, around the tip of South America, and northward to the Pacific Northwest, Elizabeth felt her perpetual longing stir to make such a journey. The thought of having a good, kind, intelligent man waiting at the end of the months of travel with a home, garden, and friendly neighbors was Jane's dream. As for Elizabeth, she wanted adventure—even if it meant she would never marry. But travel took money, something which was always in short supply in the Bennet household.

Later that night, after the family had retired, she was unsurprised to hear Jane's soft knock on her door.

"What did Uncle say?" Elizabeth had been puzzled when Edward Gardiner had met in private with her eldest sister. Rarely had she been excluded from their conversations.

Jane thrust a letter into Elizabeth's unsuspecting hands. "Read this." Then she sat on the edge of the bed to await her sister's opinion—something Elizabeth typically shared freely.

The envelope was, surprisingly, in almost untouched condition, showing Uncle Gardiner's care of the letter. The contents, therefore, had to contain either sensitive or life-changing information.

September 4, 1868

Netherfield Ranch

Oregon City, Oregon

Dear Miss Bennet,

Please allow me to introduce myself. My name is Charles Archibald Bingley. I am nearing twenty-three years of age and the owner of a 640-acre property outside of Oregon City. My parents moved my two sisters and myself to the Pacific coastal region in 1867, only to suffer an accident at sea. Within a month, my siblings and I relocated to the Willamette Valley. With the help of a trusted friend, I built a large home and have enough income from my land to support a family. My eldest sister, Louisa, is recently married to Mr. Gilbert Hurst. Caroline, who is just turned nineteen, attends a school for ladies in Boston and is in her final year. She plans to return to Netherfield in the fall of 1870.

Your uncle described you as beautiful, kind, and caring. These are the qualities I am hoping to find in a wife. My friends describe me as amiable. I spent enough time in Mr. Gardiner's company for him to give you an accurate portrayal as to whether or not this is the truth.

Life in this part of the country is quiet if you fail to listen to the calls of the natural world. In the spring, the air is filled with the noise of birds as they seek food for their young. From red robins plucking at the ground for a fat worm to the cry of magnificent eagles, the variety is astounding. In the autumn, bull elk bugle to call their mates and bears grunt as they fill up on the last of the summer's crop of insects and berries.

I believe the beauty of our part of the world is best described by a British poet.

"There is a pleasure in the pathless woods,
There is a rapture on the lonely shore,
There is society, where none intrudes,
By the deep sea, and music in its roar:
I love not man the less, but Nature more"

Only this morning I walked outside my home to find a doe with twin fawns. The little ones still had some of *their spots. They played by the honeysuckle arbor as their mother grazed on the newly cut grass. Serenity and joy filled me, as well as longing to share the moment with someone.*

Have you ever hoped to travel outside of Maryland? Would you, or could you, imagine yourself married to a man so far from the rest of your family?

My hope is that you respond soon so I know whether I have hope.

Most sincerely,

Charles A. Bingley

Elizabeth's eyes moved over the paper a second time and then a third. "Lord Byron," she whispered to herself. *How many modern men were familiar with Childe Harold's Pilgrimage?* Yet, he had quoted one of her favorite verses of the lengthy poem. Each word fed her soul. Mr. Bingley was a wordsmith, a man who appreciated a turn of phrase—the solace of joining adjectives and nouns—until a human heart was touched.

She looked at Jane, who sat calmly at her side. Elizabeth could not fail to see the dream lingering in her sister's eyes. Though they did not know of any females of their acquaintance who had become mail-order brides, the practice had been going on for a decade or more; being a drastic solution to an otherwise unsolvable problem. "Will you reply?" She knew before asking what her sister's answer would be.

Jane's chin dropped to her chest as a blush covered her cheeks. "I would love to meet Mr. Bingley." Then she looked directly at her sister. "But I need you to write him, Lizzy, as I could never match his elegant hand. You are much more skilled with words than I am. You even knew whom he quoted, while I did not." Jane grabbed Elizabeth's hands. "Please, say you'll do it for me. Please?"

Without hesitation Elizabeth replied, "Of course I will. Your goodness needs rewarded, sister dear. I'll do all within my power to help you along."

Jane giggled. "Oh, Lizzy. To think that I might have a home of my own. The land sounds beautiful, and I would love to be married to an amiable man."

"Who is handsome."

Jane's giggles grew louder.

"And rich."

They both laughed until their father yelled through the walls for silence.

"Does Papa know about the letter?"

Although Jane was twenty-two years of age, she was still under her father's authority because she lived in his household. As unwilling as their male parent was for change, this might be something they would have to keep from him until Jane had decided whether or not to travel to Oregon with their uncle and his family later in the year.

"He does not."

"What did Uncle say about Mr. Bingley?"

The blush returned until Jane's cheeks were as red as Elizabeth had ever seen them. "Uncle described him as six feet tall, lean of build, with strawberry blonde hair, blue eyes, and a big smile. He claimed Mr. Bingley is sociable, pleasant, and eager to learn. His home is, as the letter says, newly constructed, overlooking the river."

"You have always preferred fair coloring, so he is sounding like the ideal man for you." Elizabeth slapped her hand over her mouth as her laughter threatened to bubble over. She had not seen such happiness on her sister's face since before the war.

"Perhaps the friend he mentions who helped him establish his home is tall, dark, and handsome. He would be your ideal man." Then it was Jane's turn to muffle her mirth.

"He is probably short, round, and balding with no comprehension of how he would handle a woman like me as a wife—if he is not already wed."

They chuckled.

"Oh, Lizzy. I could not move so far away without you." Both sisters quieted at the thought. The two of them were the best of friends. To be separated by such a distance was intolerable.

"Then I'll move with you to Oregon and be aunt to your many children. I will teach them to darn socks poorly and play the piano with robust enthusiasm until we are all driven outside to listen to the sounds of nature found at the Bingley family home."

"Why did you have to write about the fawns? What if Miss Bennet doesn't like baby animals?"

"Bingley, would you want a wife who did not?" Fitzwilliam Darcy chuckled to himself as he watched his closest friend wear a path in Darcy's carpeting. At this rate, the floor covering would not last the year. The rug had survived its trip from the Eastern Seaboard when their family left Boston in 1830. He had not yet been born when his father traveled years later to attend university and obtain a wife whom he packed up and moved back to Oregon to take advantage of the Donation Land Claim Act. They arrived in Oregon to settle on his father's 640 acres of prime forestland bordering the Willamette River. In the years after he was born, his father and mother had purchased additional property until he was surrounded by four square miles of Darcy land.

"And poetry? Darcy! She will think I have mislead her to think me more educated than I am." Bingley raked his hands through his hair as he walked, making the top stand up in a spectacular disarray.

"You are educated." Darcy had met the Bingley siblings soon after they had arrived at Oregon City. Within a week, Bingley's eldest sister had married the owner of the local livery and stable. Since then, they had sold their business and moved to Portland so Mrs. Hurst could enjoy the benefits of city life. After a month spent pouting at the rustic conditions and attempting to bind her seventeen-year-old self to the wealthiest single man in the area, Will Darcy, Caroline had been returned to the East Coast to polish her education and, as Darcy hoped, dispose of her bold ways.

"Yes, but I didn't pay that close of attention in school." Charles Bingley's father had sent him to two years at the College of New Jersey. The older Mr. Bingley felt this was enough learning for a landowner. He pulled his son out of university to bring the family west.

"Bingley, I wrote it in the same manner I wrote to my sister, Georgiana. The letter will be fine."

"But, you aren't wanting to marry your sister." Bingley shuddered. A horrified expression covered his face. "That came out wrong!"

Darcy rolled his eyes.

12

Bingley continued, "I *want* Miss Bennet to want to meet me as a potential husband. I don't want her to be disappointed when and if she gets here by the man I truly am."

"She won't be. You're a fine man." Darcy took a sip of the strong black coffee—his typical morning beverage. "Maybe next time you should write your own letter."

"I can't." Bingley finally sat opposite him in the tall leather chair. "My penmanship is so bad, she would immediately know someone else wrote the first letter. You'll have to continue the correspondence until I can get her to say "yes" to my proposal."

"I told you this wasn't a good plan." Darcy well remembered Bingley pleading with him to pen the letter.

Again, Charles ran his hand through his hair, taming the top part a bit.

"There is too much to lose. When Mr. Gardiner told us he was going to move his family out to the Goulding ranch, along with his eldest niece, I felt this was my best chance of getting ahead of the crowd. If she is as lovely as he claims, the men will come from a hundred miles around to court her. I could not take a chance of not attaching her to me before she left Baltimore. I had to have your help."

"I understand."

"You do?" Bingley looked closer at this friend. "I am surprised you did not want her for yourself. You don't, do you?"

Darcy could hear the concern in his voice and was, therefore, quick to reassure him.

"No, I'm not necessarily looking for a wife at this time. Don't worry, Miss Bennet is all yours."

Relief flooded Bingley's face.

"The real test, Charles, will be when she writes back. Through her words you'll know if she has any intelligence. Imagine the horror of being stuck with a woman who has a pretty face and an empty head."

While Darcy shuddered, Bingley smiled. "I wouldn't mind at all."

Elizabeth rested the end of her pencil on her chin. She had re-read Mr. Bingley's letter so many times, it was indelibly imprinted in her memory. She felt the weight of replying in a manner consistent with Jane's personality. However, each sentence describing the young man and his home resounded in her heart until she found herself pouring her own emotions onto the pages.

February 11, 1869

Baltimore, Maryland

Dear Mr. Bingley,

With pleasure I received your letter of September 4, 1868. Our uncle Gardiner delivered it to my hand only yesterday. Please be reassured of his safe arrival to our home.

Our family listened with delight to the account of his travels. I cannot imagine the adventure of sailing from one ocean to another, though my dreams are to one day do that very thing. Combined with the descriptions of your part of the country, I am intrigued to learn more.

My father is a tutor of classic literature, so I easily recognized Lord Byron's words. I would share with you a favorite portion of a story on the same theme, which describe my desires and goals, and wonder if you know its source.

"A quiet, secluded life in the country, with the possibility of being useful to people to whom it is easy to do good, and who are not accustomed to have it done to them; then work which one hopes may be of some use; then rest,

15

nature, books, music, love for one's neighbor —such is my idea of happiness."

We live a simple life, sir. Due to circumstances far beyond our control, my next younger sister, Elizabeth, and I have managed our household since the beginning of the war. My heart aches for the loss of your parents. Though ours were traumatized by the news of battles and the death of the sons of many of their peers, they are still present with us.

My uncle could not clearly recall the details he shared with you about myself and my family. Since you introduced me to your sisters, I will do the same. I recently turned twenty-two and have four younger sisters. Elizabeth, whom we call Lizzy, is twenty. Mary, the middle sister, is nineteen and has a deeply-embedded passion for spiritual edification. Catherine and Lydia are the youngest at seventeen and fifteen respectively. Lydia has a zest for life, and Kitty follows her wherever she goes. All of us have fair hair and blue eyes apart from Lizzy.

Mr. Bingley, my uncle has invited me to travel with him and his wife to Oregon later in the year to winter with them at their new home. He has said it is in fairly close proximity to your own property of Netherfield Ranch. I would be pleased to accept an introduction. In the *meantime, my hope is that you choose to write again as I found much enjoyment in your letter.*

As always,
Miss Jane Bennet

Four weeks later, Bingley burst through the door of Darcy's home. Pemberley had a housekeeper and a foreman to see to the outside chores. Bingley had managed to evade them both.

"She wrote." He waved a letter at his friend. "You have to write her back."

Darcy had not had the chance to rise from his chair behind his desk, so held out his hand to receive the letter. His cursory glance revealed fine, even handwriting. By the time he reached the second paragraph, his curiosity at this young woman was piqued. *She yearned for adventure?* When she quoted *Family Happiness* by Leo Tolstoy a few sentences later, he realized his own heart was in danger. Horror at the thought had him carefully placing the letter on the surface of his desk. This document had not been intended for him. He was surprised at the disappointment filling his heart.

Breathing in deeply, he picked up the paper and finished the letter. Before he could speak, Bingley interrupted his thoughts.

"She is an angel, is she not?" Bingley barely paused. "I'm determined, Darcy. Miss Jane Bennet will be Mrs. Bingley before she has spent a week on Oregon soil. I can't wait. I mean, I'll have to wait, won't I, though I don't want to."

Bingley leaned over the top of the desk until he could read Miss Bennet's letter upside down. "You'll write her right away, won't you? Please, Darcy. Don't delay. I'm all anticipation of hearing from her again."

Darcy blew out the breath he had been holding. *When had his life gotten so hard?*

Two months later – Oregon City, Oregon

"I believe she is practically perfect." Charles Bingley handed the well-traveled letter over to his closest friend. They had checked for mail as soon as they arrived at the post office, and the latest note, the third response, had been waiting for Bingley.

Fitzwilliam Darcy quickly scanned the letter and then leaned back on the front porch railing to read it a second time. The words danced off the page straight into his heart. Miss Jane

Bennet was both articulate and intelligent. Her choice of expressions and use of a precise script painted her as a woman Darcy longed to know. However, it was to his friend she had written. The letter was not his. *"No, Bingley,"* he thought to himself. *"I believe she is not practically perfect. She is perfect."*

Chapter 1

Even though trains had been crossing from the Atlantic to the Pacific Ocean for almost a month on the tracks of the Transcontinental Railroad, the trip was not without its hardships. The cool morning air seeped through the thin panes of glass in the compartment windows along with ash and soot from the steam engines. Benches made from hardwoods ran down each side of the railcar, swaying and bouncing in a never ending fight to unseat the rider.

With each clang of the metal wheels against the rails, the two sisters moved closer to their destination—San Francisco, California. They would remain in the city long enough to acquire transport via ship to their future home in Oregon City. Elizabeth couldn't wait.

Her intention had been to keep a journal of her adventure to later share with her father. However, the movement of the passenger car made the task impossible.

Elizabeth and Jane were currently watching two sets of twins belonging to the couple seated in front of them. At eight years of age, Timothy and Markus Pedersen were as active as every other boy they had known. Christine and Whitney, though two years younger, had enough vitality to keep up with their brothers. The effort to keep them from running up and down the center aisle was a monumental task for the parents; one they routinely failed. Another part of Tolstoy's book came to mind as Elizabeth watched the boys launch themselves out of their seats for the millionth time that day.

> *"I wanted movement and not a calm course of existence. I wanted excitement and the chance to sacrifice myself for my love. I felt it in myself a superabundance of energy which found no outlet in our quiet life."*

The parents were exhausted and fell asleep as soon as they left the post stop where the Union Pacific railroad gang had met the Central Pacific team at Promontory, Utah.

By far, the majority of the train travel was behind them. They had been fortunate when the days were dry. Dust through the windows was preferable to being soaked with rain water. They could brush off the debris at each stop, but would have had to sit in the dampness until the air temperature dried them out in a downpour.

Elizabeth Bennet loved each and every minute of it. She had seen her first buffalo while on the Mid-West plains. In her excitement, she had drawn everyone's attention to the massive animal. She had done the same for the second and the third, until finally realizing that once you saw one buffalo, you pretty much had seen them all. Even so, the sight still thrilled her.

When crossing the Rocky Mountains, she spied the oddest looking mammal she had ever seen. At first she had thought it was an elk, similar to what Mr. Bingley had written about in his third letter. Almost immediately after, Elizabeth saw a majestic beast with narrow horns extending to the sky and realized the first animal must have been a moose. She wondered if they had moose in the Willamette Valley—something to ask Mr. Bingley when she finally saw him.

When Jane had finally herded the twins to their bench, she flopped down onto her designated seat at the end of their row. Both she and Elizabeth took turns keeping an eye on them for their parents.

"How much longer, Lizzy?" Jane brushed a strand of hair away from her face.

Elizabeth smiled broadly, but then closed her mouth quickly so she wouldn't get gritty sand inside.

"We shall arrive soon enough." Digging out the picnic hamper from under the seat, she passed around the canteens of water they had refilled at the last train stop. The children drank as if they had spent the past eight days on the desert.

"Jane, might I re-read Mr. Bingley's letters? I can't seem to keep my attention on my book." She recognized it to be a paltry excuse. Her sister did not hesitate to hand them over.

As the children finally fell asleep, the sisters used the last of the evening's light to select a letter from the pile. There were four altogether. The first had introduced Mr. Bingley. The second had richly described his daily life. The letter was sprinkled with words and phrases from Shakespeare and other British writers. She had to wonder at the gentleman's extensive education. *Possibly he had gone overseas to attend either Oxford or Cambridge?* Jealousy at his being able to do so filled her chest, until she realized how ridiculous she was. Possibly, he had been educated at home by his father as she had been.

Letter number three provided more information about Bingley's area of Oregon, yet it was number four which was her favorite. When she wrote to Mr. Bingley of the sameness of her daily existence, he replied by speaking of the intrinsic value of a woman and how he yearned to provide a home worthy of her. He spoke of his mother in a way that reflected his deep love and respect for the woman responsible for his birth. The tender manner with which he wrote of his younger sister made her feel the need to be equally as cherished. Elizabeth could not contain her sigh.

Aunt and Uncle Gardiner's plans had fallen through, and Elizabeth had not wanted Jane to traverse the country on her own. The sale of Uncle Gardiner's business enterprise was taking longer than he had planned, so he and his wife would not be able to leave Baltimore until Gardiner's Import and Export Service belonged to someone else. There was no guessing how long it would take.

It was the paragraph at the end of the final letter that had spurred Elizabeth to insist she travel with her sister. Mr. Bingley's neighbor, Mr. Will Darcy, had apparently decided it was time for him to seek a wife as well.

> *Your letters have had a positive influence on my friend, Fitzwilliam Darcy, whom we call Will. His property abuts mine on the northern boundary. Should your sister, Elizabeth, be inclined to travel with you to Oregon and become your closest neighbor, he has offered his hand in marriage as I offer mine to you.*

Therefore, Elizabeth had retrimmed her best dress, packed it carefully, and accepted one of the tickets the two men had included with the letter.

By the time Bingley concluded with "deep affection", Elizabeth felt the chambers of her protected heart melt. With this re-reading of letter number four, Elizabeth Anne Bennet felt the

25

danger of, for the first time, falling in love…with her favorite sister's suitor.

Shame and guilt settled upon her like a heavy cloak. She glanced at Jane and felt relief at finding her head bent over letter number one. When pink started rising from her neck to her forehead, Elizabeth realized her sister was reading the part where Mr. Bingley said he hoped she would find him the husband she always wanted. Elizabeth's sigh was borne of immense pain. *She needed to stop this foolishness now!*

Folding the letter, she waited until Jane had finished and then handed it over to her. She was resolved to read no more. Suddenly, she wished the train crawled slower, or that it was going in any direction other than west. She was determined to conquer these feelings before they reached the California coast. Mr. Darcy would be her husband, not Mr. Bingley.

Charles Bingley looked in the mirror for at least the twentieth time since they had arrived at the hotel, Oregon House. Both men had bathed and changed into their finest clothing before riding into town. Unfortunately, Oregon weather in every month of the year was typically rainy, and this day was no different. Fortunately, Darcy had thought to pack extra clothes in his saddle bag and had encouraged his friend to do the same.

The steamship's captain had sent a rider from Portland to let them know they would be sailing up the Willamette once the main cargo was unloaded. The two Bennet sisters should be arriving at the dock only a few blocks from the hotel sometime that day unless there was difficulty with the wind, current, or the cargo. Darcy had stationed himself by the front window of the second story room to best watch for incoming marine traffic. He had reserved rooms for the ladies in addition to the rooms he and Bingley occupied.

As was his nature, he had arranged for the young women to have an excellent view of the best Oregon City had to offer. Built in front of a large park-like square, each room inside the Oregon House had a fireplace, a cozy bed, and facilities where they could wash up after the trip. The day promised to be warm as the breeze had blown the early morning rain clouds from the sky. The walk from the docks would be lovely.

Deep inside he prayed Bingley would find Elizabeth Bennet much more attractive than the beautiful eldest sister. Although Darcy's intention had been to look for a wife after his sister, Georgiana, was married and settled in her own home, the letters from Jane Bennet had thawed his cold reserve until fledgling feelings of affection had filtered into his heart.

From the receipt of the first reply, he had often found himself walking the hallways of his home in the silence of the evening unexpectedly wishing he had a lovely companion to share it with. He had never before felt lonely. With each successive letter, the feelings had grown with intensity until he did something so out of character it still surprised him. He offered marriage to a complete stranger—not even the stranger he actually desired. He would marry Miss Elizabeth Bennet—not her sister, Jane.

The eldest Miss Bennet was not his. She would never be his. He needed to stop this attraction immediately.

"Do you think she will find me attractive?" Bingley asked for at least as many times as he had looked in the mirror.

"I am not going to comment on your appearance, my friend. You can change nothing at this point, so calm yourself." *What a hypocrite!* Darcy had packed his finest linen shirt and tie, shined his boots, stopped by the barber to have him trim his wavy dark hair, and made sure he waited to shave until just before the steamship arrived. His treacherous heart had him grooming himself to his best for Miss Jane Bennet. He wished Bingley to take one look at Miss Elizabeth and decide she was the one for him. He huffed aloud.

"You can be impatient with me all you want, Darcy. I am soon to meet my bride. You are as well."

Will Darcy wished he hadn't been so unchangeable in his ways when he spoke with Mr. Gardiner. Being a cautious man with a set plan for the future, he had not responded as quickly as

Bingley. Had he done so, it would be him waiting for the woman he held in his heart, instead of second best.

From a distance, he could see a vessel as it rounded the last bend before it would glide quickly into port. The river ran rapidly before the horseshoe falls, so it took a skilled mariner to deliver the passengers safely. He waited until it was much closer before he informed his friend. They both grabbed their hats and walked out the door.

San Francisco, California, had been a marvel to the weary travelers. Brimming with gold-seekers and foreign workers, Elizabeth and Jane had found lodgings at the Occidental Hotel, rejoicing at the luxury of having a bed which was soft and unmoving. Once in their rooms, the waiting bath and laundry had been worth the extra days they had spent before gaining passage to Oregon.

Jane had chosen to remain behind to rest, while Elizabeth accompanied the Pedersen family to points of interest around the city. They sampled Chinese fare, each of them craving the small dumplings filled with seafood of some sort as well as Dungeness crab on the waterfront. It had been a wonderful coincidence to discover the twins were traveling to Oregon City, Oregon, on the same ship.

By the time they crossed the violent waves at the mouth of the Columbia River, they were, all of them, ready to be back on solid ground. The rain and wind had not stopped the whole time they were at sea, and both Jane and Elizabeth worried they would be wilted and ragged by the time they met Mr. Bingley. Nonetheless, the sun appeared as they sailed upriver, and they were fully dry from the wind by the time the ship made its first stop in Portland, almost a day's journey west of their intended destination.

Again, they sought comfort in a dockside hotel. When the travelers reboarded the vessel the next day for the remainder of their journey by water, the ladies were attired in their best.

"Look, children!" Elizabeth pointed to the evidence of a community in the distance. She stood at the bow of the boat with both sets of twins. Jane and the children's mother were seeing to the last minute packing of the items they had used in their quarters, while the father conversed with the captain.

The children jostled to be in front of the other for an unobstructed view. Their movements accidentally shoved Elizabeth to the side. She did not see the coiled rope or the hook which would be used to tie the boat to the dock. She landed in a puddle of water on the tar covered surface after losing her bonnet and some of her hair to the hook. Pins popped from her coiffure and heavy ringlets dropped over her eyes as she struggled to right herself before anyone could witness her graceless fall.

Too late! The pier was lined with men of all ages pointing in her direction. Somewhere in the small crowd was Mr. Bingley and her own husband-to-be. *Surely they would be disappointed with the sight of her.* Brushing the hair from her face, she was resigned to not making the dignified entrance she had planned.

Knowing the only dress not packed in the stowed trunks below deck was the salt-air coated one she had worn from San Francisco, Elizabeth's heart sank to her feet. Rather than arriving to Oregon City to meet Mr. Bingley and Mr. Darcy in her finest, she would look worse than a ragamuffin from the streets. She wanted to sob, but the children looking at her with guilty terror on their faces needed her reassurance far more than her anger.

One of the boy twins was the first to act. He pulled from his pants pocket a shiny pebble, a penny, a piece of lint, and a well-used handkerchief. His offering the unsavory cloth with the air of a gentleman made her smile.

"Miss Wizzy, you can use my hankie if you want to." Timothy Pedersen was unable to say his l's and r's. "I might have had to use it a wittle, but thew's a wittle bit that's cwean on one of the edges."

Elizabeth endeavored not to smile. The little boy's heart was in the right place.

"I am a mess." She tried shaking the dirty droplets from her skirt.

"You aw a mess." Four little voices proclaimed at the same time.

By the time Jane and the other adults approached, Elizabeth was laughing at her own vain ridiculousness.

Darcy, at almost four inches taller than Bingley, saw her first. He almost lost his ability to breathe in and out. Jane Bennet was as glorious a woman as he had ever seen. Beauty accompanied by an intelligent mind and kind heart made her unparalleled—far above all the young ladies of his acquaintance.

When his friend pushed ahead of him, he mourned the loss of such a woman. Irritated at his own lack of self-regulation, he sought to be tough with himself. Charles Bingley had first claim, so he would step back and accept that—although he would most likely not find her equal—he would have to settle for her sister.

Crewmen assisted a young family down the gangplank. Bingley rushed to offer his hand to his beloved Jane. To Darcy's eyes, she fairly floated down the walkway. Tall and slim, her grace and serenity made him feel his loss even more. He could not keep the frown from his face. The crewman turned to help another young woman from the ship, Darcy was horrified to see the other Miss Bennet. She looked like she had been in a waterfront brawl and had come out the loser.

The younger Bennet hung back during introductions and kept her head bent. Darcy forgot her as soon as Miss Bennet said her name.

"Welcome to Oregon City!" Bingley offered his arm to Miss Bennet after greeting the whole family of fellow travelers. Darcy watched his friend and thought he had never seen him so tall. Pride at having such a woman on his arm was evident in the set of his shoulders and the tilt of his head. Darcy wished it was his arm she held. Resolved that he would think on it no more, he walked slowly behind them, his shoulders slumped and his eyes to the ground, completely forgetting the presence of Miss Elizabeth Bennet.

Several hours later, the two men waited for the ladies to return downstairs for the evening meal. As each minute had passed, he had to listen to Bingley praise the woman of his dreams. For the first time, Darcy wanted to hit him squarely in the mouth. Clenching his fists, he decided to put an end to his friend's speech.

"You are, indeed, fortunate in your choice of wife, Charles."

"I say, Darcy. The younger Bennet sister, Miss Elizabeth, is uncommonly pretty as well."

"How could you tell? She was covered in mud and filth like a hellion let loose in a mud bath."

"Now, be fair." Bingley tapped his friend on the shoulder. "I am sure she is as pretty as her sister when she is cleaned up."

"Pretty?" Darcy was appalled. "She may be tolerable when bathed, but she's certainly not beautiful enough to tempt me."

How dare Bingley try to pass off an inferior woman to him. His heart belonged to the writer of those remarkable letters, not some misfit who probably did not even know one book from another.

Elizabeth cleared her throat. Standing in the doorway next to her was Jane Bennet, with her chin to her chest and an uncomfortable flush of red covering her cheeks. From the lift of Elizabeth's head and the fire shooting from her eyes, Darcy knew he had been overheard.

Darcy felt a moment's regret at his rudeness, but he soothed his inner guilt with the knowledge that she would gain much more from their marriage than he would. Few landowners had a home as grand or a property as productive as his. On the other hand, he would be wed to a misfit who could not present herself appropriately in public. She would be an embarrassment to the Darcy name.

He wanted to bellow aloud at the unfairness. If he could not have Jane Bennet, he wanted no Bennet at all.

Chapter 2

In her lifetime, Elizabeth could not remember despising another human being as much as she did Mr. Bingley's arrogant friend—her future husband. She refused to look anywhere but at him directly. While he had the right to his own opinion, he was wrong to express it so publicly. For a certainty, she had wished to appear to the present company—Mr. Darcy excluded—in a more dignified manner, but it could not be helped.

"Miss Bennet, Miss Elizabeth." Bingley cleared his throat while a red hue flooded his face in, what Elizabeth assumed was, embarrassment at his friend's words.

Elizabeth turned to observe the fair-haired gentleman. He was everything he had claimed to be—friendly and approachable. She was extraordinarily happy for her sister. No single person on earth deserved the level of happiness that Jane did. Elizabeth moved from her sister's side to stand next to Mr. Darcy. She would take no chances that Bingley's companion might unleash his bitter ire on her sweet sibling. The thought of being wife to this lout made her stomach churn. *How could two such opposite personalities be the best of friends. Life was not fair!*

Jane was overcome with shyness, so Elizabeth responded to the gentlemen. "Mr. Bingley, I thank you for your kind welcome upon our arrival. You have been all that is gracious. We appreciate your reserving such fine rooms for us." Elizabeth looked closer at the only other man in the room. "Mr. Darcy, I will not pretend we did not hear your words when we came into the room. My family is unused to blatant unkindness and ill manners."

"I am sure that is so." Bowing towards her, he offered, "I beg your pardon."

He could not move his eyes away from Jane. Yet Darcy knew, then, that by his own abominable words, any chance he might have had to win her was gone.

"Humph!" Came the disbelieving response from Elizabeth.

Darcy did not blame her. Even to his own ears his apology sounded insincere. He glanced at the younger Bennet sister to find she had bathed and changed into a clean dress. At least she was presentable and would not embarrass him by being seen in public with her.

"Well, now that that is settled…" Bingley smiled, and offered his arm to Jane. Darcy looked at Elizabeth for a long time, then finally extended his elbow. Uncomfortably, Darcy walked with her into the dining room. He prided himself on being an honorable man. In spite of the fact that he knew he should not have made such a comment, it was done. He could not wish it unsaid. His apology was sufficient.

Once they were seated and the food ordered, Bingley bent his head towards Jane and whispered, "I am delighted to finally meet you. Since your uncle first told me of you almost a year ago, I have thought of little else but being in your presence. Now that the time is here, I can only believe that each second was worth the wait."

The muted noise of the rest of the diners did not block out the soft sounds. *When had Charles become so verbose?* For the hundredth time, Darcy wished he had told his friend 'no' when he asked him to write and then read the letters that had traveled back and forth between Baltimore and Oregon. Having no knowledge of Jane Bennet's character would have made his circumstances more palatable. And it would have meant he would not be marrying her sister in the morning. *Blast!*

Boldly, Jane replied. "Though I have only known of you for the past five months, I have done the same. Your letters…they kept my hope of being introduced to a fine man alive. I will keep them and cherish them forever."

Bingley blushed a brilliant red.

Darcy felt his heart break in two. *He had written the letters!*

He was so intent on his own roiling emotions, he paid no attention to Elizabeth.

Darcy's instinct was to retreat—to return to his home to lick his wounds in private. But he didn't run from anything. He would never be able to convince Bingley to accept Elizabeth so he could marry Jane. Despite his intense disappointment, he would do as he had promised. The die had been cast. They would be tied permanently to each other by morning. He would return to Pemberley hopelessly married to the wrong woman.

By the time the food arrived, Elizabeth had gained a measure of control over her own innermost feelings. She abhorred Mr. Darcy and could feel no empathy for him that he failed to capture Jane's attention. *What a travesty to have to marry a man who was in love with her sister!* She could see it in his eyes. He was entirely besotted.

Elizabeth, on the other hand, could not fail to appreciate the goodness of his friend, the man giving Jane his full attention. *How could she do anything other than rejoice in her sister's good fortune?* She endeavored to find out more about Mr. Bingley, not for her benefit, but for Jane's.

"Mr. Bingley, the land along the river was lovely with its lush forests. Did we, by chance, pass your favorite overlook of the water in our travels?" Elizabeth longed to hear the beauty of his speech to soothe her battered heart.

"Oh, no, Miss Elizabeth. I rarely look at the water or the trees. They are a common sight; something we see every day. You will get used to them too."

His reply surprised Elizabeth, though it seemed to have no impact on Jane, who was looking at him adoringly. Elizabeth became aware her sister could care less what he had to say.

"Mr. Bingley, you shared in your letters your love of the land and the nature surrounding us." Elizabeth's curiosity had been piqued with his reply. "Then, if not the trees and water, what does hold your attention and appreciation?"

Bingley reluctantly took his eyes from Jane as he turned to answer Elizabeth.

"Well, to be honest, I am not sure. I guess I like it all." He shrugged his shoulders and moved his eyes back to where they longed to be.

Elizabeth tilted her head and narrowed her eyes almost to a squint. *Where was his loquaciousness? Where was his depth?* Suddenly, she wanted to chuckle to herself. Of course, he was befuddled by the beauty in front him so he was unable to speak in the same manner of his writing. She wanted to laugh at her own foolishness.

Turning, her eyes accidentally met Mr. Darcy's. Instantly her anger flamed to an intensity she had never felt before.

"Mr. Darcy, do you have a sister or a close female relative you are particularly fond of?" Her voice had a snap to it that even she could hear.

"I beg your pardon?" He glared at her, insulted she had addressed him directly.

"Twice now you have begged my pardon, and we have only just met. How odd." Again, she refused to look away from the piercing intensity of his blue eyes. "My question is valid, sir. Do you have a beloved female family member you cherish?"

He hesitated before answering, wondering what this wild woman was about.

"My sister is much beloved by me."

"I am pleased to hear this, sir." She smiled at him and lowered her voice. "Do you believe your sister's value is solely based upon her appearance?"

Darcy saw the trap and knew it was his own fault for being in a position where his integrity was endangered.

"I do not." The way he saw it, he might as well willingly step into the trap before she pushed him into the snare.

Only, she did not. With a little smile, she turned away from him and addressed Bingley, unsettling him far more than had she attacked. *What was this woman about?*

She appeared to give him no more thought for the rest of the meal. Instead, she turned her attention back to his friend.

"Mr. Bingley, from our current location, do you continue to travel via boat until you reach your home?"

Darcy could tell that Elizabeth was ready to depart the current company—his. Her eager questions whenever she spoke to Bingley, indicated her heart was as attached to his friend as his was to Jane's. Until that moment, it had not occurred to him that the woman he married would be in love with his best friend. However, Bingley had clearly made his choice, and it was not Elizabeth.

"No, Miss Elizabeth. From here we will transport your sister's belongings by wagon. If we get an early start and the weather continues to hold, we should arrive at the edge of my property before noon."

"I am extraordinarily pleased you will do so." Her smile was genuine, though restrained. "Jane will be able to turn the house into a home as well as explore the land she will grow to love."

From the fact that Mr. Darcy had not been able to take his eyes away from her sister, Elizabeth assumed the man had fallen in love at first sight. His disappointment with having another so thoroughly claim his lady's attention, had to be challenging to a man who gave the impression of being used to having his own way.

Their uncle Gardiner had spent far more time with Mr. Darcy than the younger man when he was last in Oregon. He had been impressed with the efficiency of his operations, his honest approach to business, and his kind generosity in readily offering him hospitality. Once the decision had been made for her to accept the arrangement to become his bride, her uncle had shared with her as much as he knew of the man. When compared to the reality sitting next to her, she wondered at her uncle's opinion.

She also had to wonder how Mr. Darcy felt about losing the upper hand to Bingley. It had to frustrate Darcy to no end to have been completely disregarded by Jane and out-maneuvered by his friend.

Before the empty plates were cleared from the table, to make amends and reestablish Miss Bennet's—Miss *Jane* Bennet's— good opinion, Darcy sought to make peace. This meant conversing with her sister. "Miss Elizabeth, you appear to have great interest in the outdoors. Is there some aspect you particularly look forward to seeing while you are here?"

Elizabeth looked at him closely as if she could detect whether or not his question was sincere. When she shrugged her slim shoulders, he rejoiced he had been successful at needling her even though it meant no peace.

"I want to see it all, sir."

Her direct stare unnerved him, and he scrambled for something to say to regain the upper hand.

"So you hope to spend your time in exploration? How very unusual for a lady." With her older sister lost to him, he looked at her closely for the first time. She was a petite woman. Her dark hair was pulled back into a serviceable knot, her skin was clear, and her lips were full. What finally drew his attention were her eyes. They were an indeterminable shade of brown with gold flecks that sparkled in the lamp light. Her dark eyelashes were so thick and heavy that he wondered how she was able to keep them up.

"To sit in the shade on a fine day and look upon verdure is the most perfect refreshment, I find."

"You are a reader of Jane Austen, then?" He wanted to chuckle at her surprise. "My sister loaned me her copy of *Mansfield Park* and encouraged me to read it." He kept his tone light so she would not believe him to be condescending. It was past time for him to quit looking at Bingley's fiancée and pay attention to his own.

"Then tell me, what is your opinion of Fanny Price? Would you describe her as an accomplished woman?" The corner of her mouth lifted, and her eyes twinkled in mischief.

He did not think he had ever seen such life in a woman's eyes before. *Not that he had much opportunity to study a woman's face that closely. How could they be piercing and full of humor at the same time?* The angle of her chin gave him the first clue of her confidence in the subject. He comprehended the need to choose his words carefully.

"I believe all women have their accomplishments." Darcy suspected she would not be satisfied with his neutral answer.

"I am astonished you think so, sir." He heard her disdain, and suddenly he felt like squirming on the hard chair.

He had been confident in his own character; that he was the man his father had raised him to be. Yet, a few minutes in this woman's company had proved to him that his prideful attitude and self-esteem earned her ire. He vowed to be a better man or

44

he feared to meet the wrong end of her cast-iron skillet during his sleep.

The dessert arrived, and the four of them gave attention to the warm apple pie. Darcy observed the differences between the siblings. Miss Bennet was tall; Miss Elizabeth was short. Miss Bennet had clear blue eyes, while her sister's eyes were dark. Miss Bennet exuded elegance and poise, when Miss Elizabeth…well, she had looked like a vagrant at the dock. Darcy waited until she bent her head to her plate and examined her current state. Her dress was a soft yellow and white muslin which highlighted the warmth of the honey tone to her skin. Miss Bennet was extraordinarily wise, while Miss Elizabeth…had been able to hold her own against him.

A sickening dread began to fill his stomach. *Could it be possible?* He decided to find out.

"Pardon me, Miss Bennet." Once he had the full attention of all at the table, he continued. "Your sister and I were discussing the qualities of an accomplished woman. What is your opinion of this sentiment from a book I recently read? It says, in part:

"I can't praise a young lady who is alive only when people are admiring her, but as soon as she is left alone, collapses and finds nothing to her taste-- one who is all for show and has no resources in herself."

Jane was quick to respond. Waving her hand as if it was completely unimportant, she said. "Oh, you will have to ask

Lizzy. Most likely she has read the same book. I am unfamiliar with the text."

Darcy was stunned. The quote was from the same book she had referred to in her letters—twice. *Was it possible?*

He looked across the table to Elizabeth, where she sat with a look of mock innocence on her face. *No, it could not be!* Then he spied the twinkle and fully discerned the situation. To make sure, he asked her, "Do you have an opinion on the book?"

"Mr. Darcy, in our short acquaintance you must surely be aware that I *always* have an opinion. Whether or not you agree with my opinions is, in my *opinion,* unimportant."

He saw the truth on her face. Just as he had written Bingley's letters, she had written Jane Bennet's to his friend. *Had she figured it out yet?* With the events of the past hour, Darcy became aware that he would need to be on his toes with this young woman, so he decided then and there to keep his secret to himself.

That night, Elizabeth and Jane were snuggled under the covers of the hotel bed. For years, they had shared the same room, so the closeness was familiar. In fact, it was a convenience as it easily allowed for sisterly confidences.

"What did you think of Mr. Bingley?" Elizabeth was grateful Jane hadn't yet snuffed the candles on her side of the bed.

Jane sighed through her smile. From the look in her eyes, her vision had to be covered with dreams.

"He is just as a young man should be."

"Handsome. Wealthy. Besotted?" Elizabeth chuckled as her sister's giggles danced around the air.

"I've never met a man so suited to me, Lizzy." Her soft smile showed her pleasure. "Do you know that he told me the most shocking thing. Be prepared, Lizzy, as you will truly be surprised."

"Mr. Darcy wrote his letters."

Jane turned on her. "How did you know?"

"Is it really important?" Elizabeth did not want her sister to be disappointed in Mr. Bingley. "How did Mr. Bingley happen to mention something of such weighty significance so soon upon acquaintance?"

Jane could barely control her giggle. "I asked him about an expression he referred to in his first letter." She covered her face with her hands. "Apparently, in the west the 'call of nature' refers to something entirely different from animal sounds as he, blushing profusely I might add, pointed the way to the water closet."

Elizabeth burst into laughter and soon they were both in tears.

Jane wiped her eyes with the sleeve of her nightgown. "Needless to say, I was mortified when I understood his meaning. He was as well." Jane gulped. "At that point, he confessed to me that he had asked Mr. Darcy to write the letters. His sole motive was not to deceive me, Lizzy. He feared making a poor impression. Thus it was easy for me to admit the same to him."

"I believe Mr. Bingley is perfect for you." Elizabeth was relieved to let go of even a smidgeon of attraction she felt for him based on letters he, in fact, had not written.

"But what about Mr. Darcy? His pen crafted the sentences you absorbed as much as I did. Now that you know this, aren't you happy you are to marry him?"

Elizabeth was horrified at the thought, and it must have shown on her face because Jane started laughing again.

"Don't even think about it, Jane. Mr. High-and-Mighty Darcy is the last man on earth I would ever have chosen to marry." Squeezing her eyes closed, she shuddered at the thought. Unfortunately, she would stand next to him in front of the Justice of the Peace in less than twelve hours, promising to love, honor, and obey him. She shuddered again until she feared losing her equanimity. By tomorrow morning, Jane would be Mrs. Charles Bingley and she would become Mrs. Fitzwilliam Darcy.

Chapter 3

The two men had loaded their lady's possessions in the back of their wagons and returned inside the hotel to escort them to the official's office. Bingley almost bounced as he walked next to Jane, while Darcy, resigned to his future and resolved to make the best of the situation, stepped alongside Elizabeth.

The ladies wore the same dresses as the day before, however their faces and hair were lovely and fresh under their bonnets. Jane Bennet carried a parasol to shade her fair complexion from the rays of the early July sun. Elizabeth wore white gloves and held a well-used Bible in her hand. Darcy wondered if she prayed the marriage would succeed or if something could be done to stop the wedding from being performed. *Was she praying for a hero to rescue her from her fate?*

He was fairly sure the ceremony was not what Elizabeth had hoped for, but it was the way it needed to take place so they could make it back to their homes before the heavy rain started falling.

Less than ten minutes after stepping in front of the Justice of the Peace, the two couples walked outside as husbands and wives.

Darcy had not kissed his new bride. He had not been willing and she was not welcoming. It was a poor start to their union.

If there had been any other option, Elizabeth would not now be Mrs. Darcy. However, after spending the night coming up with plan after plan, they were all rejected as impractical for a female with no funds and no real knowledge of the area. In spite of knowing Oregon was short of ladies, she would have no means of comprehending who was an honorable, honest man and who was not. At least with Mr. Darcy, she had the hope that, being Mr. Bingley's friend, he had at least a few redeeming qualities.

The one constant thought that kept cycling through her mind was that the situation could not get any worse.

Darcy assisted Elizabeth up to the seat, using only his fingertips. He looked to the wagon behind them in time to see Bingley lift Jane into his arms to place her on a bench the same height as the one Elizabeth currently sat on. The new Mrs. Bingley giggled. His own wife seemed to lose all of her color at the sound. It was a dismal beginning.

Two wagons, both filled with an abundance of trunks containing personal items, pulled away from town, the men's horses tied on behind.

There was much to inspire interest in Elizabeth. Neighborhoods filled with solidly built houses bore witness to the existence of families who had been living in the area for several decades. As they moved up the steep incline to the bluff above, the land became much more sparsely populated.

Once past the hilltop, the road was lined with heavy timber so tall it filtered the sunlight, chilling the air and darkening the sky. Elizabeth pulled her shawl tighter as she contemplated this new land she would now call her home. Occasionally the trees would part and she could catch a glimpse of the river below so the roadway was somewhat parallel to the Willamette.

"Shall we be silent for the length of the journey?" Elizabeth refused to allow the man to stew in the quiet. Before dessert the night before, she had been aware of his longing gaze on her sister. Apparently, it had been much as she had felt towards Mr. Bingley when she read his first letter. Yet, the affection was based on a falsehood, that of misrepresentation as to who the authors of the letters were. Or, possibly, he was enthralled by Jane's ethereal beauty. Elizabeth had no idea and no desire at this point in time to discover the truth.

"What would you like me to talk about?"

She caught his look as he briefly pulled his eyes from the road. "We could speak of the number of families in the neighborhood or the distance we need to cover," she offered.

"Do you always need to hear the sound of your own voice while traveling?"

"Not at all. I am needing to hear yours or anyone else's, as a matter of fact." Though his words carried a bite to them, she was determined not to fight on her wedding day.

"Then you do not enjoy the sounds of nature?"

"I hear only the jangle of the harness and the clopping of the hooves muffled by the muddy road." She looked at him closely, in time to catch his grin before his mouth settled back into its unyielding position. It was the first sign from him that he was not completely dissatisfied with her company. "What is it you hear?"

Darcy looked around them and then up at the sky. Taking one hand off the reins he extended his arm and swept it from left to right in front of them. "See what surrounds you and listen. Don't you hear the gentle breeze in the treetops and the twigs of the undergrowth tapping against each other? The rustling of the leaves as the branches are swaying to and fro sound like a symphony of soft whispers in a large room. I hear a distant woodpecker knocking his beak against the hollow of a tree and the caw of the crows circling over there." He moved his head to the left as he again clasped the leather straps in both hands, his chin pointing towards where the birds flew around and around. "You don't hear the same?"

Who was this poetic rancher to whom she was married for better or for worse? Was his rudeness of the night before or his brusqueness of the morning an anomaly?

"Yes, I hear it." And she did. The smell of damp earth and wood pitch filled her nostrils with an earthy fragrance pleasant to her senses. Various shades and hues of green covered the long branches standing stiffly from the sides of each tree. Occasionally a twig would snap as an animal moved across the forest floor.

"When you have lived in Oregon for a while, you will learn to smell the rain coming hours before it arrives. You will learn that dampness does not stop the need for chores to be done or for enjoyment to be had. Most Oregonians will tell you that 'anything you can do in the sunshine can be done in the rain'."

"Except hang out the wash?"

He chuckled. "No, even that can be done in the rain. It just takes a while longer to dry. Sometimes days."

"I will have to remember that for when the winter rains set in." She laughed at his wry expression. She was used to hard work—if that was what worried him.

As she looked closer at her surroundings, Elizabeth pondered their life in Maryland in comparison to her new life here. Jane's dreams of having her own home and a marriage to a man she admired had been fulfilled. Her dreams? They ended as soon as she had said, 'I do.' She had no one to blame except herself. She had been the one to accept his marriage proposal and his ticket to Oregon.

Again, she endeavored to reach out to this stoic rancher who was now her husband. She was not borne for unpleasantness. One of them would have to begin this marriage and if it had to be her, then so be it.

"Have you always lived in Oregon City?" Curious about the man beside her, she thought there was no time like the present to inquire.

"No. I spent two years at university in New Haven, Connecticut."

"Did you like it?" Knowing he had written the letters, she was not surprised.

"There were aspects of my years there I particularly enjoyed. Unlike Bingley, I don't make friends easily. Most likely, it's due to the isolation we faced from not having close neighbors and being schooled at home when I was young. There, I was forced to learn to get along with others from a variety of social and economic levels."

"Hmmm."

"The forests surrounding Yale were made up of deciduous sugar maple, beech, birch, and hemlock trees. Where the evergreen trees here retain their color year around, the changing of the leaves from summer to fall painted the hillsides with vibrant oranges, yellows, and reds. I have never seen the like in all my travels back and forth."

"So we have both crossed the country."

"And I have crossed the sea."

"You have?" One of her most long-standing ambitions was to see other parts of the globe.

"Yes. Before war was declared in 1861, my father decided I needed to finish my education at Oxford in England."

"I am aware of the university's location, sir."

He smiled at her defensive response. "I am not surprised."

"You aren't? Why not?" He puzzled her exceedingly.

"Because of the content of Bingley's letters. Each time he received one, I had to read it before I could write the reply. I thought Miss Bennet one of the most intelligent women of my acquaintance. Now that I realize you were their author, I will try to keep in mind that I am not in company with an ignorant miss."

"Do you even know how condescending you sound? I may not have been educated at Yale or Oxford, but I know better than to refer to anyone as ignorant. The word is judgmental and patronizing. Do you know, there is a man who used to wander the streets of

Baltimore knocking on back doors in search of shoes to repair. His clothes were ragged and his own shoes desperately needed new soles." Elizabeth watched his hands as they adjusted the reins in his hands. Control and power. "Old Elias appeared to me to be the most uninformed man I had ever seen. I thought of the differences that education would make in his life, so I offered to show him how to read and write."

"And did you help him?"

"I did not." She scoffed. "Years before, he had been a barrister in London, so, yes, he knew better than I how to read and write. He was the second son of a disreputable and dissolute nobleman. His older brother followed closely the pathway of their sire." She shook her head.

"He lost his parents and his sibling in a reckless carriage race. When the legalities cleared, he lost his family home and its assets to debt." Elizabeth sighed at the memory. "Unfortunately, it was not enough. They still owed a considerable amount. Since Old Elias was now the earl, the debts became his own."

"Taking the only ready money he had, he purchased passage to the Americas and settled in Baltimore. Though the war with the British had ended more than a decade before, attitudes towards his citizenship made it difficult for him to find work. So he decided to try his hand at a trade others felt was too humble to perform— fixing shoes."

Darcy frowned. "He was an educated attorney. Surely, the better choice would have been for him to set himself up with a law practice. He would've been far more able to support himself had he done so."

"I had that exact same thought, Mr. Darcy." With the depth of the conversation she had forgotten he was now her husband and she could call him Will. "He laughed when I shared the same with him. Then he helped me see the value of a simple life. Old Elias would have been constrained by society's expectations and his family's debt had he returned to England. Had he established a law practice in Baltimore, he would have had to remain in that one place until he retired or died. By repairing shoes, he could travel and roam, working only when needed, which was his heart's desire. No debt encumbered him. Neither did a surplus of possessions. He was truly one of the most contented people I have ever met."

She looked at the man beside her. "Was he ignorant or wise?"

He took a long time before he replied. "Though it was not the decision I believe I would have made, I can't condemn him for his choice of employment or his manner of life. I am not the judge, Elizabeth."

"Then I pray you remember that thought as I settle into the role of wife, sir."

The couples rode for another half an hour before they stopped by a stream to partake of refreshments packed by the hotel kitchen. The fork in the roadway was a mystery to the ladies. Nevertheless, as soon as they inquired, they were informed that Pemberley was to the left while Bingley and Jane would take the right.

After the horses were watered and the bread and meat consumed, the sisters hugged tightly and said their goodbyes. They would not see each other until Sunday services in town. For three days, Elizabeth would be alone with Mr. Darcy. She shivered with worry, her mind swirling with imagining what those seventy-two hours would bring.

Twenty minutes of silence passed until they rounded a bend and the house came into view. To say it was glorious would have been an understatement. Pleasantly settled on a bluff overlooking the horseshoe-shaped waterfalls in the distance, the front of the house was lined with windows allowing a view from almost every room. A wide porch ran the full length of the house with several groupings of chairs and small tables inviting a person to sip their coffee to enjoy the panoramic vista. Elizabeth had never seen such a home.

Heavy logs rested on top of each other, nestled into notches at the corners. The chinks were filled with material that retained the color of the aged wood so a visitor was first impressed by its solidness and then by its beauty.

The approach curved to the east, which afforded a view of the area at the back of the house. Behind the home was a large garden filled with tall cornstalks, bushes of beans, hills of potatoes, and the tops of carrots and beets swaying above ground. A grassy field extended across a large meadow-like area bordered by a barn bursting with baled hay. Next to the back of the house was the largest stack of wood Elizabeth had ever seen in one place. It rose to the roof of the shed and filled it from wall to wall.

"You have ice and snow during the winter months?"

He nodded. "And rain. Lots of rain."

Pulling the wagon close to the back of the building, he set the brake and helped her down. Again, he touched her hand as briefly as possible. She was relieved.

Walking alongside him, he opened the door and waited for her to enter ahead of him. Once they moved down a hallway, the walls opened to a large living area where comfortable over-stuffed furniture, beautifully carved tables, and chairs were arranged around an enormous fireplace built from huge stones. The burning fire told Elizabeth before her husband could that they were not alone at Pemberley.

"Maggie." Darcy greeted a gray-headed woman wiping her hands on a flour-sack apron as she walked into the room. "I would like to introduce you to my wife, Mrs. Elizabeth Bennet."

At the raised eyebrows of the older woman, he quickly corrected himself, red rising to burn the tops of his ears. "Mrs.

Elizabeth Darcy, Mrs. Margaret Reynolds is my housekeeper. *Our* housekeeper. Pemberley's housekeeper."

It was a rough beginning, and Elizabeth speculated if it was a portent of her future. If it got any worse, she would have to beg to infringe on the other set of newlyweds for a small room in their home, even sleeping in Bingley's barn, if necessary.

"Elizabeth? I thought you told me your bride was named Jane." The housekeeper shook her head as all of the color left Darcy's face. "I must have heard wrong. My mistake."

The implication of her comment made Elizabeth's stomach churn. Even though she had suspected her husband was attracted to her sister, having it confirmed by a party completely unrelated to them was alarming. And appalling. And incredibly disheartening.

Two men carrying her trunks past them finally brought her attention back to the present. As they turned to climb the grand staircase, they asked. "These go in the boss's room?"

Before either the housekeeper or her husband could reply, she stated firmly. "No. They go into a guest room." Without looking at either Mr. Darcy or Mrs. Reynolds, and uncaring that any of them would know this was not a regular marriage, she stepped away from them and walked out the front door, closing it quietly behind her.

Chapter 4

Muted light drifted through the window glass and woke Elizabeth the next morning. The smell of freshly brewed black coffee permeated the hallway when she stepped out of her room after washing and dressing for the day. For the first time since she left Baltimore, she was homesick—missing the normality of her life as she had grown to know it.

Leaning back against the wooden walls, she was reluctant to join Mr. Darcy or Mrs. Reynolds. The evening prior had been uncomfortable. The housekeeper had served over-cooked venison with un-seasoned boiled potatoes for supper. When Elizabeth had asked what animal venison came from, she was shocked to find it was the graceful, delicate deer that Mr. Bingley, no, Mr. Darcy had written about in his first letter. Eating was much more difficult with the knowing.

Normally, her life's motto had been to think of the past as it gave her pleasure. However, the events leading up to her decision to accompany Jane and marry a complete stranger were fairly grim. As each day passed, the struggle to feed the Bennets had been more and more difficult. Pleas for assistance from her father had fallen on deaf ears. Elizabeth looked to the ceiling and squeezed her eyes shut. *How could a man, a father, ignore the needs of his family?* If she thought on it a million years, she would never understand his indolence. With her and Jane out of the household, there were two less mouths to feed.

Mr. Darcy and Jane's husband had been generous in providing funds for their trip. After tallying up the actual cost of the journey, a small amount was set aside for Jane's trousseau and the rest was given to Uncle Gardiner to stretch as far as he could for the Bennets remaining behind. There had been no time for Elizabeth to procure new garments as they had boarded the train within days of receiving the last letter. Until that letter, that unexpected offer of marriage from Mr. Darcy, Jane would have had to travel alone.

Elizabeth took in a deep breath and opened her eyes to her new reality. Squaring her shoulders, she turned to descend the stairway, taking two more deep breaths as she walked. She was a married woman who was now responsible for the running of her husband's household. Uncle Gardiner had said western men missed companionship and the comforts of home. Resolving in her heart to find a measure of happiness before the day was over, she entered the kitchen to the sight of burnt toast piled on her husband's plate. She immediately knew where to start.

"Good morning." It took as much effort to smile as to frown. Her pleasant greeting was met by Mrs. Reynolds' wry grin. Mr. Darcy looked up from his coffee and nodded his head. If a man desired companionship, she was determined to be the best he could hope for. She started again.

"Good morning, Will Darcy. Are you well?" She had stopped across the table from him and stared until he finally looked up, her smile pasted on her face.

He slowly lowered his cup, a frown on his face, his free hand tapping on the tabletop.

"Good morning." His voice was gruff, like he had not yet used it.

Taking it as a good sign that he responded, she walked to the stove to see that the toast was not the only food with charred edges. Thickly cut bacon filled the cast iron skillet in layers. Eggs were frying in a second skillet and were dark brown on the bottom.

The housekeeper kept an immaculate home, but the woman could not cook.

"Good morning, Mrs. Reynolds. I appreciate your rising early to care for our needs." Elizabeth put her hand on the frazzled woman's shoulder. "If you do not mind, I would like to prepare breakfast my first day in my new home."

The woman looked at the pans filled with the meat and eggs and the platter of cold toast on the table before looking back at the new lady of the house.

Elizabeth, though at first startled by the elderly housekeeper's gaff upon her arrival, had later found her to be a gentle soul who cared deeply for the Darcy family. She offered Mrs. Reynolds her biggest smile as she plucked the spatula from the housekeeper's hands.

After lifting the eggs out of one skillet to a stoneware plate resting by the side of the stove, she shifted half of the bacon to the empty pan. Spreading it thin, she moved the pans to the side of the stove to cool the temperature as she asked for flour, salt, baking powder, butter, and buttermilk. Within minutes she had biscuits rolled out and in the hot oven.

Turning the bacon, Elizabeth kept the flour bin handy as she requested a pitcher of milk and black pepper. When the items were procured, she shooed Mrs. Reynolds away and prepared the rest of the meal. Within twenty minutes, a platter of steaming, puffy biscuits rested alongside a pile of crispy bacon, eggs fried until their whites were done but their yolks were still runny, and a large bowl brimming with country gravy.

After refilling Mr. Darcy's coffee, she poured her own and sat at the table across from him. Mrs. Reynolds still stood in the same place she had been since Elizabeth had taken over, a huge smile on her face.

"Come, sit. Enjoy breaking your fast." Elizabeth waved the older woman over.

Mrs. Reynolds grabbed six plates and the accompanying utensils and placed them around where the couple were seated.

"Breakfast smells and looks wonderful, Mrs. Darcy."

"Thank you." She smiled back at the housekeeper, whose gentle voice spoke of her Georgia roots.

At that moment, the shuffle of booted feet was heard at the door to the kitchen. The same two men who had carried her trunks to her room entered along with an older gentleman. Washing at the kitchen sink, they stopped cold as they approached the table.

Elizabeth thought their concern was that they would have to sit on either side of her, so she stood and moved to the right side of her husband. Mrs. Reynolds sat next to her and the elderly man took the chair at the opposite end of the table, where Elizabeth had been.

Once seated, Mr. Darcy said a prayer of thanks, and the men dug in. Only a few minutes passed before the older man spoke, his Southern drawl much more pronounced than his wife's.

"Maggie, you have outdone yourself this morning. Perhaps ole' Darcy here should have brought him home a bride sooner."

67

Mrs. Reynolds rolled her eyes. "It wasn't me who cooked."

Elizabeth looked around the table and found smiles on everyone's face except her husband's. Her first inclination was to spitefully pour a large heaping serving of black pepper on his biscuit, however, she refrained. Slowly breathing in through her nostrils, she charted her course.

She was not made for discouragement.

"Welcome to our table. I am Mrs. Elizabeth Darcy." Until she knew the circumstances better, she would be formal with the introductions. She asked the names of each man. The eldest, John Reynolds, was married to the housekeeper and was Darcy's foreman. The other two men, who looked to be in their late twenties or early thirties, were brothers, Dan and Melvin White. "Please help yourself and eat your fill. There's more where that came from." She waved towards the stove.

For a long while, the only sound in the dining room was the scraping of forks on the plates as the bowl and platters were soon emptied until not one crumb remained. The sense of accomplishment Elizabeth felt warmed her insides.

When she stood to help Mrs. Reynolds clear the table, she was waved back to her seat. "No, ma'am. You cooked, so I'll clean."

Sipping the hot coffee, she absorbed the talk of the men. It was soon apparent how respected her husband was by the men who worked for him. Darcy listened to their suggestions carefully before nodding his approval, then he spoke without ordering so they all knew how their time would be occupied for the day.

Chairs slid back from the table as the men rose to leave. A chorus of, 'Thank you, ma'am,' came from the men—excepting her husband—before they walked out the door.

He hadn't said a word. Not a nod. Not a mumbled expression of appreciation. Elizabeth wanted to lift the sixteen-inch cast iron skillet and whack him upside the head with it. She breathed in deeply to settle herself. It shouldn't matter.

Resting her elbow on the table and her chin on her hand, her eyes followed the one man she should know better than any other human, except she did not.

"Mrs. Darcy, are you well?" Mrs. Reynolds had poured boiling water over the dishes and left them soaking in the sink. Bringing the pot over, she refilled both of their coffee mugs and sat directly across from Elizabeth.

"Hmmm. I thank you for asking." With one last look at the door, she turned her attention to the housekeeper. "Please call me Elizabeth or Lizzy and, if you don't mind, I'd like to call you the same as my husband does."

Maggie chuckled into her cup. "When Will was little, he had the hardest time saying his "R's and "L's". After trying for several years, he finally started calling me by my first name as his father did."

"You have been here a while then?"

69

"Since right before Will was born." In a pose similar to the one Elizabeth had been holding, she looked out the window opposite the kitchen. "His mother was heavy with child when George Darcy came to town. He went door-to-door asking if there were any women willing to work for good wages to help his wife. My John and I had claimed our 640 acres as soon as we had arrived from Atlanta, but we hadn't yet built a home."

"Just as now, women were scarce and those who were here had their own families to tend. When we were offered a large cabin with all the furnishings by Will's father, we jumped at the chance. Our new home had been built by Will's grandfather. Mr. Josiah Darcy lived there until the big house was built. Then he went back east and came home with his wife and son. The cabin sat empty until years later when old Josiah's son, George Darcy, was old enough to be on his own. When he was at university, he met Anne Fitzwilliam. They married and returned home, thinking they would stay in the cabin the whole of their married life. However, Will's grandfather was killed in a logging accident. His wife had not adapted well to frontier life, so she returned to her family, leaving her son and daughter-in-law the ranch. It was Mr. George Darcy who offered us the cabin."

"And Will's parents?" Elizabeth had thought he was going to tell her of them the day before when he spoke of his time spent away from Pemberley.

"Will's mom was always frail. She had spun-gold hair and the bluest eyes I've ever seen. She was tall and slender and one of the kindest ladies I've ever met."

Elizabeth was stunned. It was like she was describing Jane. No wonder her husband constantly found his eyes drifting towards her sister.

"After your husband was born, the doctor recommended they not try for another child. Nonetheless, Anne insisted she had enough love to give a herd of young ones. Sadly, she was unable to carry any more children to birth. Until Georgiana."

"My new sister?"

"Yes." Maggie looked down at her cup as if the answers to the world's problems could be found amidst the grounds at the bottom. "Anne died giving birth to her daughter. Will was twelve years old and I was afraid, as close as they were, that he wanted to curl up and die with her. Then he saw that little red-faced bundle of miniature squalling female, and his heart was lost. He has been the best brother a little girl could have."

Elizabeth nodded. Her youngest sister, Lydia, was born making noise and she had never stopped. She wondered if her sister-in-law was the same.

"Would you tell me about Georgiana?"

"George Darcy mourned the loss of his wife to the extent that he allowed little emotion to be shared amongst his children. He became a hard taskmaster to young William and an indifferent

71

father to his daughter. Will hated leaving her here when he left for school. However, it was not long before Anne's brother and his wife offered to raise her with their young ones. Though they were all older than Georgie, they showered her with attention and affection.

"Georgiana Darcy is quiet like your husband. She is now sixteen and looks very similar to her mother. Will takes after his Pa."

"Why do you refer to my husband's father by both his first and last name? You do it for no other family member."

Maggie sucked in a breath and Elizabeth immediately knew she had trespassed into private territory. "Never mind. I do not need to know."

The housekeeper reached over the wood surface and placed her hand on Elizabeth's forearm. "You had no way of knowing, but Will's Dad took in the son of a friend of his named George. The man…."

They were interrupted by Maggie's husband running back inside the house, yelling, "There's been an accident."

Both women jumped up and grabbed their jackets hanging on hooks. Before they had their arms in the sleeves, they were running out the door.

Mr. Reynolds quickly explained the cause of the accident as they ran across the yard. It was a widow-maker, a heavy broken limb entangled in the surrounding trees that falls randomly on unsuspecting timber workers. This one hit Darcy on the shoulder, knocking him to the forest floor before landing on the back of his lower leg. A jagged piece of bone ripped through his denims and blood flowed freely onto the ground. Elizabeth wanted to vomit at the sight.

Falling to her knees where the side of his face lay in the dirt, she touched his cheek where his dark eyelashes rested. His chest rose and fell with regularity, but he was out cold. It was the first contact she had had with the man since he had helped her in and out of the wagon. She was surprised at the smoothness of his skin. He must have shaved right before breakfast.

Shaking her head to clear it of the random thought, she looked to the men standing by and realized she was as scared, if not more, than they were. The wound looked wicked, and his stillness frightened her more than the pool of blood accumulating by his leg.

In spite of the fact that she was unhappy at being married to him, she did not want harm to befall Will Darcy. She would need his help settling into her new life as a frontier bride.

The thought shamed her. *How could she be so selfish?* The pain her husband must be suffering humbled her.

"Is there a doctor close?"

"It would be hours before he could get here, ma'am," one of the men answered.

Elizabeth glanced at their surroundings. She saw the limb that had caused the damage where the workers had apparently moved it and wanted to walk over and kick it—hard, frustrated at the obstruction to her transition.

Again, she was acting more concerned over how this was affecting her than the injured man on the ground. *Stop it, Lizzy!*

"We need to stop the bleeding and set his leg while he is still unconscious." She stood and moved around to his head, dropping again to her knees. "Would someone bring a knife, towels, and some blankets we can put under him when we roll him onto his back? Enough blankets that will bear his weight." One of the workers ran back to the house with Maggie. Elizabeth did not remember the man's name, but was grateful the housekeeper was with him. She appeared to be a woman of sense.

Her younger sister, Mary, had fallen and injured herself many times before the doctor figured out she needed glasses. Steep, narrow staircases in their home had been the bane of the family as the middle child suffered from sprained ankles and a broken bone in her arm. However, moving a young girl to her room was far easier than a tall well-muscled man who was several inches over six feet. She was grateful for the men standing by.

Without thought, her slim fingers threaded through his hair as she bent to whisper her plans into his ear. There was no response, and she was thankful.

When they returned with the blankets, she spread them out and rolled the edges like the doctor had showed her the last time Mary had fallen. Taking the sharp knife, she moved to his leg and started to cut his pants to move the fabric from the wound, but her hands were shaking so badly, she was unable to make the first cut.

One of the men stepped up and took over. The bone protruded almost an inch above the torn skin. They had to act quickly.

"Let's move him now. On my word." The foreman grabbed Darcy's shoulders while one of the men was at his waist and the other at his good leg. Elizabeth held his bad leg in place and Maggie had replaced her at his head. "Now!"

The move was over in seconds. A groan came from her husband's lips and sweat broke out on his brow. In one fluid movement, Elizabeth clasped his boot and pulled it off. Then she grabbed his sock and did the same. An odd thought ran through her mind that it was the first time she had ever seen a bare male foot. It was as thick and large as the rest of him. She clutched his ankle between her two hands and fell backwards, pulling at the same time as one of the men pushed the bone through the skin back into place. Darcy's scream reverberated from one stand of trees to the next. She wanted to cry. Or throw up.

Wiping her eyes with her sleeve, she shook out the towels and wrapped them tightly around his leg, stopping the bleeding as much as possible.

"Let's go." Elizabeth stood and stepped back as the men rolled up the other side of the blanket and grabbed hold. Elizabeth and Maggie were by his feet. It took all five of them to navigate through the trees with their burden to the house. They continued to move as rapidly as possible until they were in his bedroom. Maggie threw off the blankets as they deposited him carefully on the clean, white sheet.

"Someone ride for the doctor, please. Hurry." Elizabeth did not raise her voice, she kept her tone nice and even to engender a sense of calm in the room. Panic threatened to rise and stick in her throat, but she tamped it down each time it made its ugly presence known.

Both the foreman and she were covered with sweat by the time they cleaned the dirt off Darcy and covered him with the blankets. She was too fearful to be embarrassed at glimpsing the parts of a man she had never been exposed to in her lifetime, but she also knew beyond a shadow of a doubt that what resided under his long underwear would eventually become as familiar to her as her own form. He was her husband and the separation of rooms would not continue forever. With all that had occurred, it was that particular thought which finally made her blush.

Chapter 5

Over the next few hours, Elizabeth learned that the quality of patience was vital to those who live so far outside the city. Maggie was a treasure as she unearthed carbolic acid to cleanse the wound and laudanum for the pain. She kept Elizabeth supplied with a continual supply of clean bandages, fresh water, and hot coffee for her to drink.

Elizabeth had been studying the man she was now tied to for her lifetime. With his face relaxed from the scowl he normally wore, he was remarkably handsome. He had striking eyes, high cheekbones, and a cleft in his chin—all the features she had dreamed of since the time she learned that boys grew to be men whom you married. Even at rest he looked powerful.

She *had* seen him without the scowl. Unfortunately, it was when he was mooning over her sister. Elizabeth wanted to throw something—preferably, at him. She did understand his unrequited love. After all, hadn't she done the same with Mr. Bingley? Yes, she had fanaticized over Mr. Darcy being a twin of the perfect man, but she left those wishes behind the instant she witnessed Bingley falling head-over-heels in love with Jane.

Had Mr. Darcy done the same? Not at all. That he continued to long for something so out of his reach showed a lack of character which made Elizabeth uncomfortable being his wife.

Darcy woke suddenly, not long after they had him settled in his bed. He lashed out at the first person his eyes encountered—Elizabeth.

"Just what do you think you're doing in my bedroom?" Anger dripped from his tongue.

"You really want me to answer that?" she snapped back. Truly, it would have been better for her to have remained calm, but he had irritated her from the first time he had looked at her with disgust. Had it only been two days before?

"Why are you here?" he demanded.

"Sir, believe me, when I woke this morning, the last place I ever desired to be was in this room with you." She restrained herself from poking him with her finger—in the eye. "Since you had the largest part of a tree fall on you, breaking your leg and bruising your shoulder, someone needed to set your bone, mop up the blood, change your clothes, and clean up the mud. Since the doctor has not yet arrived, Maggie and I have been dripping small amounts of laudanum into your mouth so you would not feel the fullness of pain when you awoke. Is this a thorough enough explanation for you or would you like me to send for

Maggie to help you comprehend the mess you have gotten us both into?"

His growl sounded similar to what she assumed a grizzly bear would sound like.

"Wait!" He pulled the blankets up under his chin, a look of sheer panic on his face. "You changed me from my work clothes?" His eyes grew round and his breathing quickened. "You?" A look of terror crossed his face as he suddenly lifted the blankets and looked down only to tuck them right back under his chin. His fists were gripped so tight on the covers that his knuckles were stark white. "I have no clothes on!"

"I know." She could not keep the left side of her mouth from lifting into a half smile. Equity at having him just as mortified as she had been lightened her heart and she chuckled at his expression, entirely grateful that he had not seen her initial reaction. Elizabeth was more than pleased that he was the one squirming under the knowledge that she had the upper hand.

"Please do not be concerned. Since yours is the first naked male body I have ever seen, I have no way of knowing whether you compare in a favorable manner or if you are lacking in some way."

When his face flamed beet red, she realized the justice from delivering an insult as painful as the one he had flung at her when she arrived was bitter. So, she softened her tone and stood from the chair next to his bed, and asked, "Is there anything I might provide for your comfort? Do you need more laudanum or some cool water?"

"I can help myself."

"I am unsurprised you think you can." Pouring a glass of water, she offered it to him, holding it just out of reach. "Nevertheless, your shoulder and back are already dark with bruising from your neck almost to your waist. Your right leg is splinted and cannot be moved. Purple, in the shade of an overripe plum stretches from above your knee to the top of your foot. So, please, tell me how you plan to 'help yourself'?"

He huffed and rested his good arm over his eyes. Since he was brought to the room, she had ample time to come to terms with their situation. To him, this was new.

"How bad is the break?" He spoke much softer. She could hear his pain.

"When my sister Mary had the same type of break in her arm, the doctor called it a compound fracture. She had to keep still for several months. Because the skin is broken, the risk of infection in the skin and bone is of primary concern."

"Two months!" He glared at her.

"Did you hear me say two?" She sat back down beside him and reached behind his head to lift it far enough for him to drink. His need for water had to be massive.

He sipped greedily, making sucking noises from the unnatural angle. Pulling against his damaged neck and shoulder had to increase his pain, though he said nothing.

"It was actually three months before her arm healed enough to bear weight." She wiped the water dribbling from the corner of his mouth. His humiliation brought her no joy.

"I'm angry," he huffed. "Three months. How can I be laid up that long? I have a ranch to run."

She said nothing. *What was there to say?* He was having to come to terms with some very unpleasant truths, and she knew nothing to make it any easier.

"I'm sleepy." He closed his eyes.

"I imagine you are. However, before you close your eyes, might I give you a bit more medicine for your pain? Since I know little else I can do to help, it might be best if you sleep until the doctor arrives."

Darcy nodded his head and then winced from the pain. Within minutes he was sleeping deeply, his soft snores filling the room.

Elizabeth felt bad for his situation. She would need to consult with Mr. Reynolds so the ranch ran smoothly during her husband's convalescence. Sighing, the weight of her situation settled on her shoulders. The responsibility of tending a man who had married her in spite of himself would be a challenge she had never faced. *Wouldn't it be lovely to turn back time?* She could have stayed with her family in Baltimore with problems she was used to solving. Rubbing her temple, she closed her eyes. Wishing did no good. Valid reasons had moved her to head west and accept Darcy's proposal.

Moving to the window, she looked down to the river. Boats drifted in the current as they left the small town. If only she was on one of those vessels, sailing to adventure beyond the horizon. Shaking her head, she touched her hand to the cool glass. Sprinkles of rain flecked the pane. The wet would slow the doctor. She sighed.

Glancing back at the bed, she worried about her future should she lose him. Ashamed at herself for, again, only thinking of her own comfort, Elizabeth guiltily walked back so she could wipe his brow. The day that had started so pleasantly in the kitchen, had taken an ugly turn.

Upon reflection, neither of them had acted in the best interests of the other. She had no power to change him, but she could adjust her own attitude. She vowed to do so immediately.

The doctor was an older man with gentle hands and a soothing voice. Darcy was still asleep when he arrived and stayed asleep through the whole of the examination.

84

"Mrs. Darcy, you are correct. Your husband has a compound or open fracture to the fibula. Using carbolic acid and water to wash his wound was a good choice. However, he shall need several more pillows to elevate his leg to help with swelling."

Maggie, who was standing behind her, left immediately to retrieve the requested items. The doctor tucked them all the way from behind Darcy's thigh to his ankle, adding more as he went.

"If I might speak privately with Mrs. Darcy?"

Once the housekeeper left, he continued. "I've known this young man since his birth, as I delivered both Will and his sister. He's been a healthy lad, but the few times he's been ill, he's been a terribly restless patient. I do not envy you the next several months, ma'am."

Elizabeth was resigned to her future.

"The most critical aspect of his healing will be keeping him still for the first few weeks. This means, and I apologize for having to be so blunt, that he will be unable to care for his normal bodily functions on his own."

Elizabeth's hand flew to her chest, and she felt her eyes grow as large as bugs. The thought had not crossed her mind at all. She wanted to stomp her foot and call someone else in to help.

"As his wife, though I know you to be newly wed, these matters are best tended by someone he is close to and can trust. Just as a mother can best tend the wounds of her son, a wife's

85

ministrations are both soothing and acceptable. What will cause you both some discomfort and chagrin at first, will soon become a matter of course."

Elizabeth heard his words, though in her deepest imagination she could not believe they could be true. *How could she ever become used to…well, how could she…?* Her mind screamed at her to walk out the door and not return for the next three months.

"You might think of sending word to the Fitzwilliams, Will's family in Portland. Mrs. Reynolds will know how this is best done. Georgiana would be a great help in keeping her brother distracted. Will is very tender towards her, and though he will most likely be a growly bear with you, he would never raise his voice to his sister."

Elizabeth recognized the sense in his suggestion. "If you do not mind posting the letter, I will write immediately. Might you take the note with you when you go?"

"Of course." He started rolling down his sleeves. She took that as a sign that she could leave.

The house was so new to her that she had to ask Maggie to help her locate paper and pen. A room at the back of the house was apparently used by her husband for a study. She seated herself in his worn leather chair and crafted the bad news to a young woman she had only ever heard of. *Would Aunt and Uncle Fitzwilliam bolster her and ease her worries?* Elizabeth hoped so.

The surface of the desk was cluttered with correspondence, notes, and randomly stacked books. This surprised Elizabeth, as every other aspect of her husband's life she had seen thus far had been quite orderly.

Folding the envelope, she thought to write to the Bingleys. It would keep them from worrying about them not appearing for worship on Sunday if they heard from her of the accident. They would be protected from the gross distortion of rumors passed from one well-meaning neighbor to the next with the note.

By the time she finished, Dr. Henderson was coming down the staircase. He accepted the letters, and he walked out to his waiting horse.

"Mrs. Darcy." He tipped his hat after mounting. "I will return tomorrow to check on our patient—and you."

She raised her hand as he rode off, wishing he could stay. Wrapping her arms around herself to ward off the chill, she turned back inside. *Had it been only yesterday that she had first walked out to the front porch after hearing how her husband had hoped to bring Jane home with him instead of her?*

Shaking her head, she puzzled at how capricious life could be.

Darkness had settled in the next time Darcy woke. The skin of his face was clammy, though his cheeks were flushed. Occasionally his body would jerk, and Elizabeth recognized his suffering was intense.

The minute his eyes opened, she held a spoon of water to his mouth. Most of it headed down his chin as a chill settled over him, causing repeated spasms. When she covered all but his leg with the quilts Maggie had brought, he threw them off, complaining of the heat.

Elizabeth kept her eyes on his as she again tried with the water. Finally, the first few drops passed into his mouth and his eyes closed in relief. He said nothing when she lifted his head to drink thirstily from the cup. Twice she had to refill it before he finally signaled to stop. Within seconds, she heard the first retch. He emptied his stomach into the pan she had waiting.

Her left arm ached from holding his shoulder up as best as she could until he finally was able to lay back on the pillow.

Not a word passed between the two of them as she left to empty the basin and refill the pitcher that had been on the table next to his bed. Maggie waited at the bottom of the stairs.

"The doctor…he said…he said I would need to care for my husband's personal needs. I am not familiar enough with the house to know where everything is, Maggie."

"You poor dear." Walking to the back of the kitchen, the housekeeper opened a door to a room just inside the back porch. "I apologize I didn't show you this last night."

Elizabeth blushed. The night before, she had stayed outside on the porch until dark. Maggie had left a pitcher of water and a cloth in her room along with a pot to use for her personal needs. Elizabeth was grateful the housekeeper did not mention her sullen behavior.

"When Will returned from England, his head was full of ideas for improving the house. The first thing he did was to build this bathing room. With all the rain we get, it is easy to heat the water so it can shower over you." She showed her how the handles and levers worked. "He installed what he called a toilet." Again, Elizabeth was instructed as to its operation. The basin was quickly taken care of, and Maggie stepped outside so Elizabeth could take care of her own needs.

"He brought home gas lamps and candles made of materials that are slow to burn and put off little smoke. Each time he picks up a newspaper when he's in town, he searches the columns for any new invention that would make our home life easier. Your husband is a smart man who is forward thinking."

"Thank you for telling me. Do you think he would mind if I borrowed some books from the library to read to him? I do not know if he would have an interest in the few I was able to bring with me."

Maggie looked her directly in the eye. "This is your home too, Elizabeth. He vowed yesterday that what is his, is yours. Feel free to make use of anything on the ranch, especially if it aids Will to be comfortable and heal faster."

She continued, "Elizabeth, you need to eat something."

"I am not hungry." The smell of the vomit had turned her stomach. Not since her sisters were little had she had to tend someone so ill.

"Of that I am well aware, dear girl." The housekeeper planted her fists on her broad hips. "You will need to keep up your strength."

"Then I will accept a piece of bread…no more." Washing her hands at the sink, she nibbled on the crust as she leaned against the counter.

Breathing deeply, she thanked the housekeeper, picked up the full pitcher and empty basin and walked back upstairs.

The room was dark when she stepped inside. Rain pounded on the window in a rhythm that soothed her. Darcy was sleeping even harder than before. She sat beside him and watched his chest rise and fall. He had thrown off the covers again, so she carefully drew them back until he was covered. Dan—or was it Melvin—had entered earlier to start and tend a fire in the stone fireplace next to the window. He followed that task by bringing in a prodigious amount of split firewood to keep the hungry flames alive. Though it was the middle of summer, the heavy clouds cooled the air.

The fire's glow flickered on Darcy's face, lighting up the side of his nose while throwing the rest in shadow. Again, she wiped beads of perspiration from his brow and ran her fingers through his hair to move the waves back from his face. The strands were thick, and she suspected he would never be like most men who had shiny pates from the loss of their youthful tresses. Bingley had thin, reddish-blond hair. Jane would eventually have a bald husband.

She chuckled at the thought. In their girlish dreams, they insisted their future husbands would be tall and well-formed, brave and strong, with thick hair, and a love of dancing. She had no clue whether her husband had two left feet or could dance to the rhythm of the music. With his current state of health, there would be no need for her to find out for at least the next three months.

To pass the time while he slept, she calculated how many days it might be. *Was the doctor figuring an average of thirty days a month?* If so, it would be ninety more days until Darcy was up and about. If he used actual months, then July and August, each with thirty-one days, plus the thirty days of September would be a total of ninety-two days. She would hope for the shorter term, and she was convinced her husband would feel the same.

By the time he woke again, she had counted the stripes on the two sets of curtains covering the windows, calculated how many dark blue squares were on the pillow cushion of her chair, and measured the length of candle that had burned since it had been lit. Truly, it was one of the longest nights of her life.

Chapter 6

During the next few days, the couple had fallen into a routine where Elizabeth wordlessly tended to his needs, and he accepted her care in silence. He had never felt such mortification in his whole life as when, for the first time in his memory, she casually lifted the covers while holding a pan in her other hand. There were a multitude of days yet to be spent in his bed, and he thought not speaking to her during those private times made it easier for both of them.

For the most part, he slept. The first two days after the accident were the worst for pain. There didn't seem to be enough medication in all of Oregon to ease his misery. Gradually, the laudanum worked to dull the pain so he could sleep restfully with only a few drops at a time. He looked forward to getting rid of the fuzzy feeling he felt when under its influence.

That particular morning, he woke to find John Reynolds in the chair by his bed instead of his wife. He immediately missed her presence and wondered if she had abandoned him.

"Where's Elizabeth?" He hadn't meant to sound so irritable, but he was.

"Your bride spends almost as much time outside as you did."

"It's raining." Tilting his head, he could see the raindrops sliding quickly down the window glass.

"That it is." The foreman was not one to speak on someone else's personal business. "I do believe you have found you a woman worth her weight in gold."

Darcy huffed.

"After she made the boys some biscuits and gravy and some of the best applesauce I've ever eaten, she hightailed it out to the front porch. The rocking chair overlooking the gorge is her favorite spot. She reads there or writes letters to home, I imagine."

Darcy was pleased she had found something about Pemberley to enjoy. Being newly married and having to care for him had to have been a challenge. A random thought flickered through his mind. A vision of a yellow-haired woman bending over him had teased his mind for the past several nights. She had not shown her face so he knew not whether it was his mother he was wishing for or Jane Bingley. He shook his head to rid himself of the thought. Mrs. Bingley had not even written the letters so he couldn't imagine why he allowed her so much time in his dreams.

His foreman cleared his throat and shifted in the chair.

"What's on your mind? Just spit it out." Darcy knew the man as much as he had known his own father. John rarely said much, so when he did, it carried weight.

"Maggie says I talk in my sleep."

"Hmmm. I'm sorry to hear she has to put up with such trouble from you." If Darcy's marriage turned out half as good as the Reynolds', he would be a happy man. He scratched at the whiskers on his chin. Having Elizabeth shave him would have been too much to ask of her. By the time he was able to get out of his room, he'd appreciate a heavy beard for the winter's cold.

"Well, the thing is, Will. You talk in your sleep too."

Darcy thought back to his dream. *Had he spoken aloud of the woman?*

"You have mentioned a woman named Jane enough times that both Elizabeth and Maggie heard—repeatedly."

Covering his face with his hands, Darcy groaned. This had to be the worst news a husband who prided himself on being honorable could receive. He deserved Elizabeth's anger and scorn.

"Maggie told me of her blunder on the first day you brought the missus home. When she apologized to your wife, Elizabeth explained the confusion of the letters and that her sister, Jane, was now wed to Bingley."

95

There was no anger or disgust in his foreman's voice—merely a plain statement of fact.

The hollow in the pit of Darcy's stomach churned with nausea generated from revulsion at his behavior. "Oh, Lord in heaven. What am I to do to fix this mess I've made?"

"I know you aren't asking me directly," Mr. Reynolds offered. "Yet, I've been giving this a lot of thought." He scooted the chair a bit closer. "Will, if you think back to all the times your pa showed preference to George Wickham, you will be able to remember how bad you felt at not seeming to measure up, no matter what you did or how hard you tried. "

"The scoundrel!"

"That he is." Still keeping his voice calm and even, John Reynolds continued, "Now think of this from Elizabeth's standpoint. Hear tell, Mrs. Bingley is a beautiful woman. Your wife would have grown up in her shadow. To listen to her talk, she loves her sister with her whole heart. She would easily believe everyone else would feel the same."

The foreman continued. "Like George Darcy, your giving favor to someone other than your own wife, can only be seen as disloyal. The one person who owes allegiance the most is a father and a husband. I've been wed a long time, Son, and I said the same vows you uttered only a week ago. The danger of thinking upon a woman other than your wife is serious."

Darcy again rubbed his hands over his face. "I am *not* in love with Jane Bingley. After reading her letters, I became fascinated with the woman I thought her to be. Yes, I was disappointed when she took to Bingley like a kid to candy. Then, I was almost sick to my stomach when I found out she hadn't even penned the words I'd held so dear."

Darcy swallowed as he gathered his thoughts. "From the first letter, I knew she couldn't be mine. I originally offered for her sister in hopes that they were two peas in a pod, and I could at least have a wife who was close to being as knowledgeable and full of grace as Jane. Instead of getting someone like I remembered my mother to be, I ended up with Elizabeth—who is in every way opposite to the one woman I held as the best example of womanhood I knew. I have to make myself remember that the letters came from my wife, not her sister. I've. no clue why I'm so slow on the matter."

John watched him until Darcy started to squirm on the bed. "I believe you have some thinking to do, Will. And some apologizing and some humble pie eating as well. And speaking of the Bingleys, they came straight away after hearing about your accident. Elizabeth was pleased to welcome them to her home."

"I imagine she was." Mr. Gardiner had explained the family's circumstances enough to know that Pemberley would look like a paradise to any one of the Bennets.

"Now that's enough of that, young man. Your wife has taken to running this household like a calf to its mama's teat. My Maggie spent quite a bit of time with Elizabeth and her sister, and she found Mrs. Bingley to be a pleasant woman, though quiet. After the Bingley's left, my wife was pleased it was Elizabeth who was left in your home."

"I am sure Bingley is pleased with his bride." Darcy waited for the bitterness to overtake him, but, other than a little hint of the emotion, to his pleasure, it failed to appear.

"If anything, I believe Bingley's smile is even bigger."

"That is good to hear." Darcy was genuinely happy for his friend. Apparently, unlike his own marriage, there had been little dissension in Bingley's.

Darcy waved his arms around the bed. "Well, I have plenty of time on my hands to consider my attitude, and I promise I will do so. I'm grateful Elizabeth is settling in fine without me." He was ready to change the subject. "Now tell me, how have you managed with one hand short in getting the last of the timber in?"

For the first time in almost an hour, the foreman would not look him in the eye.

"What are you not wanting to tell me?"

John hemmed and hawed until Darcy became equally as unsettled. The matter had to be sufficiently serious to disturb someone as tranquil as the foreman.

98

"Just spit it out."

"Well, you see…um, early yesterday when I took Elizabeth to town to meet her sister at the café, I saw Bingley, though I didn't see his wife as she was already inside out of the damp. Your wife is politeness itself, but she jumped out of the wagon before it could stop, so anxious was she to commence visiting. While the sisters talked, I picked up the supplies needed for the ranch." He took a large gulp of air and Darcy's trepidation increased. "When I returned, your wife was standing with two men she had hired to help out in your place."

"But you do the hiring. Surely she would not have done something so foolish as to not ask you first."

"Well," the foreman rubbed the back of his neck. "You see, I had tried to talk you up a bit about what a hard worker you are—that it would take at least two men to replace you. She thought it a kindness to find those two men to make the load lighter for me."

"Of all the crazy things to do."

"Well, actually, that's not the crazy part." Again, he hesitated.

"John!"

"Alright. Alright. I'll just say it." Uncrossing his legs and dropping his booted foot to the floor, John Reynolds sat erect in the chair. "She hired Bert Denny and George Wickham."

"Wickham!" Darcy wanted to jump out of bed and grab his rifle. Then he either wanted to shoot George Wickham or hit him over the head with the butt end of the weapon.

"She was just being helpful," the foreman offered. "And you should know, Elizabeth asked the Fitzwilliams to bring Georgiana back home. They will be here later today."

"Oh, my word. Say she didn't, please?"

"I'm afraid so." John had to know what was coming.

Darcy growled, then told the man to get out of his room.

As soon as John left his bedroom, Darcy wanted him back. He needed to know where Wickham was and whether or not he had told his favorite sob story to garner sympathy from his wife. Would he try to approach his young sister again in another attempt to run off and marry?

Not being able to have the answers he needed caused such inner turmoil that he was almost beside himself with anger. *How dare Elizabeth invite that man to Pemberley! She had no right, no authority to do so.* A smidgen of reason returned, and he knew she would have had no way to know how dangerous Wickham could be. *But she should have known—somehow.*

The Bingleys would be leaving to head east before the week was over. It would be a long hard trip, but they needed to collect Miss Caroline Bingley and bring her home. Though the young lady had planned to remain on the East Coast for another year, she had written requesting that her brother fetch her immediately. Jane spoke of the upcoming journey with stars in her eyes, completely forgetting the discomforts they had experienced on their way west. She was also pleased to welcome Charles' sister and looked forward to having another female in her home for companionship.

Elizabeth was equal parts thrilled for Jane and jealous for her at the same time. There had never been a time in Elizabeth's life when she didn't have a sister in her home to talk to, to dream with, and to share confidences. Maggie Reynolds was a wonderful woman who had proven herself diligent in caring for Pemberley. However, she had a husband she hurried home to each night, so she was very much unlike a sister. Elizabeth hoped Georgiana Darcy would fill the void. The Fitzwilliams would be bringing her today. Time would tell if the two would grow close. If the sister was like the brother, Elizabeth would continue to feel alone in her own home.

Despite the turmoil and stress at Pemberley, Elizabeth found peace the instant she stepped out onto the front porch. Sitting in the rocking chair, the back and forth movement soothing her, she could survey the scene with a measure of contentment. Often,

Maggie would join her. Today, it was Mr. Wickham who came around the side of the house.

"Mrs. Darcy, it pleases me to no end to see you enjoying the very view I have missed for so many years. Pemberley is one of the finest properties in all of Oregon."

"I find it as lovely as you say, Mr. Wickham."

Elizabeth had been impressed with the man as soon as she met him. He had approached her in the café after Bingley had arrived to collect his wife. Jane had bubbled with happiness in her effusions of married life, and Elizabeth was feeling anything but happy about her own.

George Wickham was a charming conversationalist and almost as handsome as Will Darcy. When Wickham told her how Mr. George Darcy had trained him in every aspect of operating a ranch the size of her new home, she realized the benefit to having him on the property while her husband was laid up. She had hired him and his friend immediately.

"Might I ask, how is Darcy?"

Again, Elizabeth found pleasure in his fine manners and genteel behavior.

"I thank you for asking. He is doing as well as possible under the circumstances." Elizabeth had always felt discomfort when her own father spoke disrespectfully of her mother, calling her silly and speaking down to her in front of others. Although she did not get along with her new husband, she would not display such disrespect and disloyalty to share that information with others.

"Well, Darcy always had a strong constitution. I doubt he will be able to remain in bed long."

Elizabeth looked up at him. She had already told him the break in her husband's leg was serious. Had the man not listened, or was he so overcome by being restored to Pemberley that he spoke without thought? Time would tell.

"Have you settled into the bunkhouse? Is all comfortable for you and Mr. Denny?"

"It's just like coming home, Mrs. Darcy. Or, can I call you Elizabeth like Reynolds does?"

Elizabeth recognized the boldness of his question. Somehow, she didn't think her husband would be pleased with the familiarity. That decided her.

"Yes, please call me Elizabeth." His smile was pleasing, and his countenance open and engaging. "Have you spoken with the foreman yet about the tasks you will be responsible for?"

"There's plenty of time to see him yet today. He's with Darcy right now."

When she stood, he was slow to step back, placing her closer to him than she felt comfortable being. Looking directly into his clear blue eyes, she raised a brow in question. He smiled charmingly and stepped back, allowing her to walk by.

He was cheeky, Elizabeth had to give him that, but so was she. Her countenance lifted at the compliment of his attention, and she returned to care for Darcy with a smile.

"Welcome to Pemberley." Elizabeth's first impression of her husband's cousin was pleasing. Richard Fitzwilliam was equal parts Will Darcy and Charles Bingley. He was as large as his cousin and as friendly as Elizabeth's brother-in-law.

"You must be the new Mrs. Darcy."

"Was it by process of elimination you figured that out, or was there a clue helping you reach your conclusion?"

Easy laughter burst from his chest as he stepped inside the house.

"I believe it was the gold band on your wedding finger that gave you away. As a single man in a land with a dearth of unmarried women, it tends to be the first place a man looks when he spots a lovely female."

"I see, Mr. Fitzwilliam." Elizabeth smiled into eyes as brown as hers. "I am wondering, sir, if you forgot something in your haste to travel to Oregon City. We were expecting Miss Darcy to be in your company today."

"I am Richard to you, Elizabeth, as we are cousins now, please."

"Thank you, Richard. In truth, I was not sure which brother you were."

"As to my young cousin, she came down with a malaise the day we heard of Will's accident and became more distressed when she realized we would not be able to leave immediately to return her home."

"Yet, she isn't here." Elizabeth puzzled over the type of young lady who was so emotionally fragile that she could not withstand a trip by boat or stagecoach from Portland to Oregon City.

"No, she is not." He hesitated, which only served to increase her curiosity and a gut feeling that all was not right with Miss Georgiana Darcy. "My mother, who is a strong-willed woman and used to the oversight of her two, as she calls us, rambunctious sons, determined that the best course for Georgie was to keep her away until Will has improved considerably."

Elizabeth put her hand to her chest. "I cannot imagine." And she could not. Elizabeth could not begin to understand how keeping a sister away from a sibling who was under distress would be beneficial. Nevertheless, she was new to the family and did not yet know all the particulars. With Darcy laid up and uncommunicative, she was likely not to learn for a long time.

"You lucky dog!" Richard walked into his cousin's room with a smile.

Darcy was pleased to see his closest friend and even more pleased he had left Georgiana in Portland.

"Since most people shoot dogs with a broken leg, I'm not getting your meaning."

"Your wife, Will. She is quite lovely with a quick wit. Good for you for latching onto her as soon as you were able."

"My wife hired Denny and Wickham yesterday, and they are here now. *That* is not the mark of an intelligent woman."

His cousin stared at him until Darcy started to feel uncomfortable.

Richard raised his hand, his palm facing Darcy, and tilted his head to the side. "I spoke with Reynolds before I came to the main house and he already told me. I'll see that they are gone before I leave, don't you worry."

"Thank you, Rich. I appreciate it." Darcy hated being powerless, and he hated being confined to his bed when there was work to be done and a ranch to oversee.

"So how is married life treating you?"

"I…I don't know to be honest." Darcy rubbed at the stubble on his cheeks. "Elizabeth…she has a way about her that is far different from the women I've been around. She has a fierce spirit that refuses to be intimidated, no matter the circumstances."

"Reynolds says she cooks better than his own wife."

"I adore Maggie, but anyone cooks better than she does."

Both men chuckled at the truth.

"And he said she has taken on your care as well as the administration of the ranch. I'd say that's a pretty special woman you have there, Will."

"I suppose."

"Cousin, she's a pretty little thing I would marry in a minute if she wasn't already yours." His cousin was growing angry, and Darcy wasn't pleased with the subject or with his response. "This is completely unlike you, Will. I've never known you to feel sorry for yourself. What is caught in your craw that's making you act like a caged polecat?"

"My leg is broken, and I'm stuck in here for the next three months. I'm unable to oversee the harvest, the timber operation, and my investments. I have a new bride who has to bathe me, hold a pan while I spit in it after cleaning my teeth, and tend to my most personal needs. She grew up in a house full of people in a city surrounded by parks and shops and things to do. I've isolated her so that she was unable to attend church and has only been to town one time since our marriage." Darcy's frustration grew with each word. "Before we married, she wrote the most

107

beautiful letters to my closest friend outside of you, Rich, letters filled with intelligence and kindness and everything sublime. Yet, other than sitting alongside my bed to read aloud to me, she says nothing. Absolutely not one word."

"Do you speak to her?"

"About what?"

Richard dropped his head and ran his hands through his hair. "Are you truly that clueless, cousin?"

"Well, apparently you think you know it all, so out with it." Even he heard the sarcasm. He was not in the mood for this and wanted to be left alone to ponder the mess that had become his life.

"Okay, fine. I will tell you." Richard looked at him without blinking. "The men you hold in esteem and seek to emulate, our grandfather and your father, were both hardworking, ambitious men. Yet, neither of them were good husbands nor were their homes happy homes. They solely sought their own desires and didn't give a hoot how their wishes affected their families."

Darcy started to speak and Richard, again, held up his hand to stop him.

"I can see you are angry and that's too bad. If you step back and look at things as they really were, you would realize I'm telling the truth. Your dad spent more time and attention on Wickham than he did with his own two children. Like his dad before him, he ignored the fact that his wife came from a

108

situation just like Elizabeth. Your mother was one of the loveliest women I ever knew, Will, but her melancholy from loneliness and isolation, in my opinion, hastened her death. Even at fourteen, I noted her sorrow."

Darcy felt like he had been slapped. He had spent a lifetime trying to be just like his father. It was expected of him. Yet, Richard's comments about Anne Darcy were accurate. As a young boy, he had striven to ease her way and bring her joy. She did find delight in her child, he had no doubt. But he remembered the look of hurt on her face when Wickham was constantly thrust to the forefront and when George Darcy chose to spend his time with the boy rather than his family.

"I…you have given me much to think upon."

"I could only say it because you can't run after me and beat me to a pulp."

Both men appreciated the humor. They had always been evenly matched when they had wrestled as youngsters.

Richard stood and extended his hand. Darcy readily shook it.

"I'll see that Wickham's gone from Pemberley."

"I appreciate it."

"And I'll kiss your wife for you when I leave."

"Richard!"

Chapter 7

George Wickham seemed at his most pleasant when surrounded by others as he laughed and joked in a manner his fellow ranch hands easily responded to. She enjoyed listening to the flow of conversation at the table from her position at the stove. Talk had been jovial until Richard walked down the stairs and entered the dining room.

"Wickham!" Richard rudely interrupted the conversation. "As soon as you are done, gather your belongings. You too, Denny. Neither of you are needed here."

Elizabeth watched the color drain from Wickham's face as the color rose to a bright red in Darcy's cousin's. Since Richard had just come down from her husband's room, it was evident that this was a decision both men had discussed.

John Reynolds nodded his head once, and Elizabeth knew she would be losing the only friend who had shown an interest in her personal happiness. She swallowed back her tears, sadness enveloping her at the loss. Then, she became angry. Bitterly so.

Once the men resumed eating, Richard moved to the head of the table, Darcy's normal chair, to share the meal.

"Excuse me, Mr. Fitzwilliam, but you are sitting in my chair." For the past five days, she had been caring for Darcy, she had cooked the meals and taken a tray upstairs. After Darcy consumed his hot food, she served herself from the little that remained. This would be her first time at the table since the accident. It may have been petty of her to enforce her authority, and he may be her husband's favorite relative, but Richard Fitzwilliam was not in charge of her home.

She carefully set the platter of fried chicken on the table and then moved her hands to rest on her hips. Her gaze didn't flinch when he looked at her in surprise. Tilting her head, she indicated a chair to the side of the table, directly across from Wickham. Then she seated herself, leaving Maggie to bring in the bowls of string beans, mashed potatoes, and gravy. The hot rolls, fresh blackberry jam, and churned butter were already in front of them.

No one said a word. Dan, Melvin, and Denny loaded their plates and bent their heads to their meals. Wickham glared at Richard, who refused to look anywhere but back at him. John Reynolds' eyes glanced between the two men as Maggie stood next to him, one hand resting on his shoulder.

"Enough!" Elizabeth spoke quietly, yet the force of her tone was enough to draw all eyes to her. "We will eat at this table in a civilized manner, am I understood?"

Everyone nodded and quietly passed the food until each person had their fill. Maggie sat in the only vacant seat next to her husband, and she too served herself.

Until the plates were cleaned, the only noise was the scraping of forks, as it had been on her first day at Pemberley. She sighed in frustration and then stood and headed back to the kitchen. When she returned with a warm blackberry pie and ice cream she had spent the morning churning, Elizabeth plopped them down onto the table, shoving the empty bowls and platter aside.

Even though the men's stomachs had to be close to bursting, the looks on Dan and Melvin's faces made her smile. They were like hollow logs that constantly needed refilled. Using her knife, she marked the top of the pie into seven slices, six large pieces and one narrow slice. Dan, Melvin, Denny, Wickham, and the Reynolds' received the fat portions heaped with vanilla ice cream which immediately started melting in the warmth. The final piece went to Richard.

"You will never disrupt my table again, Richard."

A multitude of emotions flashed in his eyes as she stared him down from where she was standing. She would not bend. This was her house and these people needed to know her rules.

When dessert was done, the men seemed to want to sue for peace as each one gathered his plate and utensils to take them to the sink. Wickham stopped by where she was standing as if he was going to address her.

113

"Do as my husband demands, sir. Pack your things and leave," she whispered quietly to him. Never would Elizabeth go behind Darcy's back and disrespect his authority, especially in front of others. However, she quickly loaded a tray with the food she had held back from the meal and headed upstairs, determined that what she would not say behind his back would be said directly to his face.

Darcy must have heard her coming up the stairs as he was attempting to sit up and lean against his headboard as she came into the room. He was a grown man so she would not remind him of the strictures the doctor had given against any movement during the first week. A full seven days had not yet passed.

Waiting for him to settle, she impatiently tapped the toe of her right foot on the rug next to his bed. Beads of sweat gathered on his brow as Darcy grunted and grimaced from the pressure he was putting against his injured shoulder to wedge himself into an upright position. She refused to help him disobey Dr. Henderson. His efforts were all his own.

Thrusting the tray into his hands, she raised the blankets at his feet to readjust the pillows so his broken leg was still elevated. Once finished, she moved the bedside chair until she was directly facing him.

"Did Richard leave?" he asked.

"As far as I know."

"Did Wickham and Denny go with him?"

114

"As far as I know." She wanted to cross her arms and lift her chin, but somehow knew he would not appreciate her defiance. Nevertheless, this did not keep her from getting right to the point. "Why is your sister being kept from you?"

Apparently it was not the subject Darcy had thought she would take up. His startled reaction almost upset his tray.

"Georgiana is not your concern."

"You truly believe that to be so?"

"I do." His voice was firm and Elizabeth had no doubt he was unused to his decisions being questioned.

"Am I correct in assuming it was your idea to keep her from her home? Did you do something to keep her from me?"

Darcy rebalanced his tray and sighed. "I asked Reynolds to write to my uncle to keep her in Portland. And it's a good thing I did with you inviting Wickham to Pemberley. What in the world were you thinking, Elizabeth? You had no right to step in front of my foreman to hire ranch hands. That clearly falls under my authority and the only one on this property I've approved to act in my place is John."

"I refuse to address my action to hire Mr. Wickham and Mr. Denny, as it was done with good intentions."

"How can bringing those two outcasts to my home be a good intention? You have no idea what kind of men they are. There's a reason no one else has taken them on."

"You are correct. I have no idea because you don't talk to me. You don't speak to me of your plans for Pemberley, you don't talk of your concerns and dreams, and you don't even thank me for cleaning you up and emptying your bed pan. You do and have done nothing for me, Will Darcy, except entice me from my home and the people I loved and who loved me."

Her voice rose with her anger. "Oh, I am not saying you don't make noise. In the in the middle of the night as I sit here to see to your comfort, it is my sister's name you murmur, not mine." By then, Elizabeth was standing, leaning over his bed, one hand fisted on her hip and the other fist waving in front of his face. Ire filled her chest until it threatened to rob her of her ability to breathe. "If I were any other woman, husband dear, I would wrap you in your sheet while you slept and beat you with my broomstick until your brain started to function properly. If I didn't have enough self-respect to know my own value, I would have walked out of here the first time it happened and never looked back. As far as I'm concerned, you could lay in your stink for the next three months. I don't care."

Color filled her cheeks and her eyes were on fire. Darcy had never seen a woman as vibrant as his wife. Images of both his foreman and his cousin flashed through his mind, and he knew it

116

was time to start making amends. Unfortunately, no instant solution came to him so he sat in stunned silence.

"Eat. Just eat." Elizabeth moved away from the bed and walked to the window. Flicking aside the curtain, she put her hand on the cool glass pane. "I don't have time for this."

"You are disappointed you married me then?" For some reason, the thought hurt. Then it made him mad. *How dare she be upset and bring up circumstances he had no control over?*

"With every single breath I take, I wish I was still Miss Elizabeth Bennet."

"Elizabeth Bennet did not own enough property to support ten families and a house that is the envy of all our neighbors. You were lucky the day you accepted my ticket west." He was proud of his position in the community. Businessmen and community leaders respected him. She was married to him. She should feel no less than others who had known him far longer.

"Lucky?" Her laugh was bitter. "You call it lucky to be attached to a man in love with my own sister? To someone who has no integrity or honor?" She turned back to him and swept her arms from side to side. "All of this is nothing. It is no more than a roof over my head and a pile of work and responsibility to benefit a man I do not respect. In every way, I wish I was not your wife."

Had she plunged a knife into his gut, it would have hurt no less than hearing her regret at being attached to him. His pride in being the owner of prime timber holdings and one of the wealthiest men in Oregon City as well as the master of all you could see for four miles around meant nothing to the woman in front of him. *Integrity? Honor?* Completely forgetting the comments from John Reynolds, he eased his conscience knowing he had both in abundance. Surely, he could admit to himself that he had held onto his feelings for Jane Bennet—no, Jane Bingley, far too long. He was over it now.

"You have said enough, Elizabeth."

"Do you really think so?" He flinched from her caustic tone. "For I believe I have only started. You see, Mr. Darcy, *I* kept my word. *I* kept my promises. Fool that I am, I vowed in front of God and my sister as witness that I would love, honor, and obey you. Neither of us were in love, at least with each other, when we wed, but, again, fool that I am, I assumed we would both work together until an acquaintance could become a friendship and friendship would grow to affection."

Her emotions were so stirred he almost heard her growl.

"In the past six days, you have responded to my questions with a grunt or silence. You, Will Darcy, are…you are…never mind. No good will come from me saying aloud the things I desire to say." She spun and returned to the window.

"Let me tell you something, Elizabeth Darcy…"

Before he could continue, she interrupted him.

118

"If I were you, I would be very cautious with your choice of words." She moved back to the side of his bed. Her calm, emotionless statement was far worse to hear than her anger. "I will leave you to your meal and return in an hour for the tray. You will have opportunity to think upon my opinions and figure out how to calmly express your own. Are we agreed?"

When and how had he lost control of his wife? And his life? Discretion seemed to indicate that acceptance of her request was the wisest course, so he nodded his head. When the door closed behind her, he dropped his chin to his chest—a sigh ripping from the depths of his soul. His father never had this kind of trouble with his wife. *Why had he chosen such a recalcitrant female?* Covering his eyes with his hands, the scent of crispy fried chicken, gravy, and blackberry pie drifted up from the tray until it filled his nostrils.

He tossed his head back in frustration, forgetting he was against the heavy wooden headboard.

"Ouch!"

For better or worse, and at the moment it appeared they were facing the worst head-on, they were bound together. He sighed again, picked up his fork, and cleaned his plate until not one crumb remained.

She knocked softly on the door before she opened it. The hour had been spent fiercely scrubbing the kitchen until the polished surfaces shone. When she peeked inside, she found her husband scooted back down in the bed sound asleep. The tray lay alongside him, and she was pleased to see all the food was gone. *At least he appreciated one accomplishment she possessed.*

Richard, Denny, and Wickham were no longer on Pemberley property and, at this point, she was pleased, wanting peace more than a friend.

Lifting the blankets, Elizabeth repositioned the pillows under Darcy's leg, gathered the tray and left the room. Once the dishes were cleaned and stacked for later use, she poured a cup of hot coffee and took it to the outside porch where she sat in her favorite rocker to look out over the land.

Lush beauty filled every inch of her vision. Summer smells of the fruit trees behind the garden wafted on the breeze as she watched one white puffy cloud after another move across the July sky.

What had she hoped to hear from Will Darcy? That he was appreciative of her efforts? That he esteemed her? Admired her? Elizabeth chuckled to herself. She was as bad as her youngest sisters, wishing for the impossible.

Thinking of Lydia, Kitty, and Mary made the loss of her home weigh heavily on her shoulders. Forgetting her original motive for leaving Baltimore would be easy under these trying circumstances and that would not do. Life in Maryland had been hard and would only be more difficult for the family as time wore on. Tears threatened when she thought of the faint hope she had of eventually bringing her whole family to live in the vicinity. Having the Gardiners at Goulding ranch, which was across the river to the west, the Bingley's alongside their property, and her parents and sisters in a house in town, would have eased her concerns and given her plenty of loved ones to fuss over and enjoy. She could almost see her dream of a happy future drift away in the wind.

"Elizabeth." The housekeeper lifted the coffee pot. "Refill?"

"You are a queen, Maggie." Elizabeth was surprised she had not retired to her own house, now that the main meal was done. The men gathered at her table for both breakfast and lunch. After the chores were done at the end of the day, the men settled in the bunkhouse with a loaf of bread, a jar of jam, whatever bounty came from the garden, and enough strong coffee to keep Elizabeth up for a week. She normally didn't see the housekeeper again until early the next morning.

Oregon City housed a large flour mill, so twice since her arrival, Elizabeth had used the finest flour for a layer cake, sending it home with the men and the Reynolds couple. She found joy in feeding appreciative, hungry people.

There were many reasons for happiness in her new life, though at the moment, they appeared buried by the troubles with her husband. Already, she loved the rich dirt that grew fruits and vegetables in abundance, the smell of wood pitch as it slowly dripped from the trees, the scurrying of squirrels and chipmunks as they sought to gather their winter stores, and the occasional bear growling as it broke apart an old stump seeking worms and grubs.

She adored sitting on the porch and watching the distant river flow, the variety of birds soaring above the canyon looking for fish swimming near the surface of the waters below to capture and take back to their nest to nurture their young. She loved salmon, and she loved Dan and Melvin for using their Sunday after services to sit on the banks of the river until they brought four of them home.

And she cared deeply for Maggie's quiet strength of purpose and her gift of calm.

"Are you settling in?" asked the housekeeper.

Elizabeth wanted to give an unladylike snort. "I suppose."

"Richard asked me to tell you what a fine man he is." Maggie chuckled. "He's incorrigible, that young man. Yet there's not a mean bone in his body. He's a trusted friend to your husband, and you couldn't have a better man standing by your side when there's trouble."

"He asked you to say all that, did he?" Her snicker matched the housekeepers. "I am sure you are correct. I am also sure that it's been far too long since a woman has been in charge of the

122

household, and that Richard has come and gone as he pleased. How long did you say Mrs. Darcy has been gone?"

"Will is twenty-seven almost twenty-eight, so it has to be fifteen years—almost sixteen." Maggie set the pot down on the table and sat in the rocker next to Elizabeth. "In truth, I can't say that Anne Darcy ran the house. She quietly went about what needed done and focused all her attention on her son."

"Well, I'm certainly not quiet." Elizabeth hoped she knew her strengths and weaknesses, what her true character was like.

At that, laughter burst from both women. It was several minutes before they could speak again.

"And I am very glad of it," were Maggie's final words before she stood, picked up the coffee pot, and went back inside, leaving Elizabeth to ponder all she was learning.

Chapter 8

Possibly it was a result of the opium drops he was still taking, but whatever the cause, Will's dreams were imprinted on his mind to the extent that he could remember the smallest details long after he woke.

In the latest, Elizabeth had the foreman haul a hot barrel of tar up the stairs while Maggie followed with a pillowcase overflowing with feathers. His wife's hair had been down, the chocolate waves reaching to the small of her back. Fire was in her eyes as she wielded a broomstick like a sword held by one of King Arthur's knights of the round table.

"Tell me the truth or you shall live the rest of your life with my broom handle lodged between your ears," she chanted as she walked around his bedroom. "Tell me the truth! Tell me the truth!"

Each time he tried to speak, all three characters surged towards him, and he hated to admit even to himself that he cowered in fear. Finally, Richard rode his horse through the door with his pistols drawn and a gleam in his eye.

"Don't worry, Will. I'll protect you. I'll take this wild woman away from your home and install her in mine."

"You can't, cousin. We are man and wife," he replied to the tall man on the horse.

"Ah, but you haven't consummated your marriage, so she is free to claim a husband worthy of her."

"And you think this is you?"

"Of course it is. I'm the one with the pistols."

His own screams of "NO!" had woken him as he swiftly surveyed his room for any company who might have been lurking in the corners waiting to pounce. He decided then and there that, no matter the pain, he would be taking no more laudanum.

Before his heartbeat had returned to normal, Elizabeth came rushing into his rooms.

Her eyes moved from his head to his toes before she lifted the blankets from his foot to determine that his leg was still where it had been when she had walked out of the room an hour before. His covers were half on the floor and his pillow had been flung into the far corner.

The afternoon sun filtered through his window and he noted dust particles dancing in the beam. Maggie would not be pleased to see them when they finally settled on whatever surface they landed upon. *What an odd thought.*

"Will, what has happened?"

"I am not sure, to be honest." He clearly remembered their hasty words and then eating his lunch. He must have fallen asleep soon after. He took a mental survey of his body and realized the nightmare had been only that, nothing more. In the aftermath, he felt foolish.

"I was on the front porch when I heard you. Do you need anything?"

She was graciousness itself, this woman who was his wife.

"I dreamed my cousin came to take you away so he could marry you instead of me." He couldn't believe he said it out loud and wished to take the words back as soon as they crossed his lips.

"Richard?"

"Yes."

She snorted. "Highly unlikely."

It was not the response he'd expected.

"Elizabeth," he ran his hands over his face, wiping away the rest of the dream. "I'm sorry for being grumpy and taking my frustrations out on you. I'm sorry for saying your sister's name in my sleep, though I am absolutely sure I was not imagining romance when I said it."

"Then what were you imagining?" Elizabeth was still standing next to his bed, but stood poised to leave, as if she was unsure of the man addressing her now. "Can you recall your dreams?"

He felt the heat on his face and knew a tale-tell blush covered his cheeks.

"Yes, I remember." Thankfully, rather than blurting out his nightmares, he considered his words carefully, but honestly. "In truth, your sister is very similar to my mother and Georgiana in looks. When I read the letters to Bingley I had assumed were written by her, she became even more like my mom in my mind; someone fair in coloring, brimming with kindness, with an intelligent mind. As I struggled in the first days after my accident, when I was receiving large amounts of medicine, it was easy to confuse the two women."

He could see she was stunned.

"You thought Jane was your mother?"

"In my dream I did and I didn't, if that makes any sense." Darcy cleared his throat and reached for the mug of water next to his bed, realizing Elizabeth had to have put it there for his comfort. "As to how I reacted at the hotel—I don't know why I said and did what I did."

"So that we are perfectly clear, you are aware that I wrote each of the letters Bingley received. Correct?"

"Yes. I am aware."

"And you wrote all four letters to Jane?"

"I did."

"Then I believe we are two of the stupidest people on the planet, Will Darcy."

To say he was shocked would have been an understatement. "I fully comprehend why you would think that of me, but why include yourself in that statement?"

Elizabeth finally sat down next to his bed.

"Because we both allowed our disappointment to color our reactions." Elizabeth sat back in the chair and crossed her arms over her middle. "Why is what we did any different from imagining ourselves in love with a fictional character in a book whose dialogue touched our heart?"

He thought over her words and quickly concluded she was correct.

"Will you forgive me?" He couldn't keep the pleading tone from his voice. Her response would, in a great way, determine how they would go on from there. If she shunned his efforts to wipe that particular slate clean, then it didn't bode well for all the other errors he'd committed against her.

A long time passed before she responded, and his nervousness and anxiety increased with each second. This was a turning point in their relationship—a beginning.

"I am not one to hold onto anger, Will, but your comments were demeaning, and they hurt me deeply. My life changed much with our marriage, but yours changed only with your accident. I went from being a second daughter with many freedoms to a wife who is waiting hand and foot on you in the manner of a servant. I have been ignored by you as I go about my tasks and am left to wonder what you would have done had it been me hurt and bedridden a day after we wed."

"I find it embarrassing to have you…well, you know." He couldn't recall ever being so disconcerted.

"And I don't?" Elizabeth was incredulous. "I'd never seen a naked man before your accident, and I was quite unsure how a man's body functioned. Being raised in the city, I didn't even have boy farm animals to learn from."

"Boy farm animals?" He couldn't keep from smiling.

"Oh, do not laugh at me. You understand my meaning." She reached over and straightened a fold in the top blanket. "My parents suffer in their marriage from a lack of understanding of each other. I always wanted… I always dreamed… I hoped my marriage would be much different; that I would find a man I could respect and hold in affection."

"I am not that man, am I?"

"No, sir, you are not." She stood to leave, and suddenly he didn't want her to go. Then his bodily urges hit him and he could have cursed himself for his bad timing. How could she not conclude that his sole reason for desiring her company was to help him ease nature?

He had never felt so low about himself as he tilted his head towards the bed pan.

Elizabeth lifted her shoulders and dropped them with a sigh. Grabbing the pan, she lifted the covers and helped him situate himself.

In his mortification, he regressed to his earlier conduct and said nothing.

Late that night he woke to find her sleeping in the chair next to his bed. It was a new moon. The only light in the room came from the candle she had left on the table she had pulled away from his bed. Beside the flickering flame was the book of poetry she had been reading to him. Tucked underneath was a dime novel. He was surprised Elizabeth was so inclined. He hadn't read one in years, though he had enjoyed them when he had.

Her hair draped in waves over her stark white gown and robe. He felt a chill in the air on the back of his hand and wondered if she was warm enough. No fire had been started, and he recalled the day had been warm with no rain since the morning. None of the men would have made the effort. He hesitated to wake her to find out.

Her lashes were thick against her cheekbones, and her skin glistened with good health in the firelight. For the first time, he felt shame at insulting her looks. Not only was she a pretty woman, she was stalwart when under trial. He had an idea she would be fierce in protecting those she cared for.

Would she ever care for him? He scratched at his almost week old beard, surprised at himself. Under normal circumstances, he thought through every decision. Richard had long accused him of worrying every little matter to death. Yet, by the third letter written to Bingley, his treacherous heart moved him to act in a manner quite unlike himself so that by letter number four, he offered marriage to a complete stranger.

He'd never stopped to consider the qualities he'd wanted in a wife before. *What a stupid fool he was!* Elizabeth knew clearly how she wanted her marriage to go, and he found he genuinely wanted the same.

Richard had been right, or was it Reynolds? His father had not shown attention to his family, and both he and his mother had suffered for it. *Was he destined to be a chip off the old block?* No. If he acted like his father, it would be a choice he made. He was determined not to follow in the footsteps of a man who shoved his children from his life.

"Will, what has you so disturbed?" Elizabeth whispered into the quiet.

He looked directly at her and knew she deserved the truth.

"Women are strange creatures."

"And men aren't?" she automatically defended.

Well, that hadn't started well.

"I meant that women are different from men."

She giggled. "You say that like it's a bad thing."

He rolled his eyes and wondered at being unable to speak clearly to the woman sitting next to him. Then he realized—that was the crux of the matter.

"Until I went back east to university, I had not spent much time around females other than Maggie and my sister. Occasionally my Aunt Catherine de Bourgh, my mother's eldest sister, would come to Pemberley to tell my father and me how to live our lives and run our ranch. Father soon ran her and my cousin Anne off, and I haven't seen them in years. Richard's mother had a much easier manner about her, but she also was determined to have us under her control. Therefore, I was quite unprepared for the ladies I met in Connecticut. England was no different. The young women seemed to have a set of rules I never understood."

"How so?"

"I wasn't as polished as the city gentlemen, and I couldn't seem to understand when they were serious or teasing. Because of this, I was called to account several times for speaking too plainly and apparently I caused offense often enough that I finally avoided your sex altogether."

Her soft chuckle moved him to continue.

"You see, I could tell my mother absolutely anything, and she would listen. If I found her crying in her room, I always seemed to know that putting my arms around her and later bringing her a flower was the right thing to do." He huffed out a breath. "With any other woman, I am tongue-tied."

Again, she chuckled. "You have certainly given me reason to believe you, Will, but I wonder at the man who was able to craft such winsome words to my sister. Your letters…they gave me hope that someone in the world would understand me and would desire a woman like me."

He closed his eyes and pondered his reply. Finally, he spoke. "During the four years I was gone to school, I wrote almost daily to my sister. Yes, it would have been easy to share only the basic details of my activities with a six-year-old, to skim the surface of my life. However, I wanted her to remember me, to come to know the real me. Therefore, I learned to write from my heart. My father never replied to my letters. I thought by writing the way I did, he would also come to know the man I was becoming by reading everything I'd written to her. When I heard Georgiana

134

had been moved permanently to live with the Fitzwilliams, I kept it up and lost hope of ever hearing from my father.

"He lived only four months after I returned home. I'd hoped during that time that he realized I was a better man." He took in a deep breath. "Yet within minutes of my arrival at Pemberley, I was relegated to the same position I had held before I'd left. Later, Maggie told me that she and my aunt had been the ones to read my letters to my sister, not my father."

"Why is your sister not here, Will?" Elizabeth kept her voice soft and even. He appreciated her consideration for his feelings. "Is something wrong that she can't return home to you?"

"There is nothing wrong with Georgiana." Now it was he who was defensive. "My sister is as sweet as my mother ever was. But she's sixteen years old, and I know nothing about helping a girl her age along."

"Does she like living in Portland?"

"I believe so. She never complains."

"Does she miss Pemberley?"

"She has said so on occasion." Last summer, she had suffered from a bad decision that if found out, could bring reproach on her good name and the Darcy name. Her letters since had been cryptic and she no longer expressed her opinions easily. He hadn't actually been in her company for over a year. *How had it been so long?*

135

"Then let her come home, Will." Elizabeth's voice was firm, though she had cloaked her words so they didn't come out sounding like a command. "The Bingleys are leaving to bring his sister back to Oregon, and I am desperate for a sister. You and I, we can do this together. Time passes so quickly and, within no time at all, Georgiana will be looking for a home of her own. Then she will forever be the concern of someone else."

He thought to tell his wife about Georgiana's disappointment, but he didn't want her to think ill of his sister—not if they were going to bring her to Pemberley.

"I will ask that you write to the Fitzwilliams and to my sister so they know our desire to have her move back home. Maggie has the address and Reynolds can see it goes out either on the stagecoach to Portland or on the steamboat. She should have it by the day after tomorrow at the latest."

Up to this point, he had not witnessed a smile that bright on his wife's face, and he was amazed at how it transformed her. *She is beautiful!*

The next day the Bingleys arrived for a visit.

Bingley went right up to his friend while Jane joined Elizabeth in the rocking chairs on the porch.

"Are you happy, Jane?" Elizabeth needed no answer as her sister radiated joy.

"Deliriously so. And you?"

Elizabeth struggled with how to answer. On the off chance they spent any time with the Bennets or Gardiners, she didn't want her family to worry.

"Having Will's accident happen so soon after we wed has been a challenge, I will admit. However, I spent several hours with him yesterday making plans for our future. His decision to bring his sister to Pemberley makes me very, very happy."

"I am so delighted for you." Jane was everything good. She had never understood meanness and longed for everyone to love everyone else. In her mind there was no one who deserved any less.

"Come and say hello to Will, sister. I'm certain he would find pleasure in your company."

In truth, Elizabeth wanted to see how her husband reacted. Although some progress had been made the day prior, it was minimal and there was still no basis for trust.

As for her seeing Charles Bingley? She was completely unaffected, which was as she'd expected. The man was apparently a good husband to her favorite sister. That was his most attractive quality in her mind.

When they walked into the room, Charles stood from the chair and moved towards his wife. Elizabeth watched Darcy closely, but saw no evidence of discomfort or desire on his face. She was immensely grateful.

"Mr. Darcy, you don't need to stand in my presence," Jane sweetly insisted.

Darcy shook his head slightly and looked to Elizabeth, who raised her shoulders and tilted her head to the side. He would not be able to try getting up on his legs for at least another two and a half months. He'd assumed Jane would understand.

"Thank you, Mrs. Bingley." He had no clue how else to reply.

"Please call me Jane. After all, that was my name before I married Charles. Well, actually, that is still my name even after I became his wife, isn't it?"

"Yes, my dove." Bingley replied, both halves of the couple lost in each other's smiles. "Sweet pea, would you like to tell your sister how you have spent the past few days?"

"Of course, my love." Jane beamed with accomplishment, and Darcy could see how Elizabeth was every bit as proud of her sister as Bingley was. "I copied all of the recipes in Charles' last housekeeper's recipe box so we can have a good variety of dishes at each meal. Then I planned menus for the first month after we return."

"Good for you, Jane. The kitchen has never been your area of expertise. I'm pleased you are willing to take on this task." Elizabeth fairly glowed with pleasure.

"Oh, no, Lizzy. You misunderstand." Jane was quick to reassure her. "I've not actually tried any of the recipes. I merely copied them into my own handwriting."

Darcy looked at his wife, knowing he should understand what was happening and failing miserably.

"Then who is doing the cooking, Jane?" Elizabeth queried. "Did you find a new housekeeper?"

"Oh, no. There is not another female within miles available to help us. Charles and I drive the buggy into town each day and eat at the hotel. Then we have them prepare enough to take with us for the evening. It is a splendid arrangement as we are able to bring the serving dishes back the next day. When Miss Bingley returns home, we can do like we did in Baltimore, Lizzy. I'll keep the house clean and she can cook."

Darcy saw the color rise under Bingley's collar. His younger sister was one of the most spoiled, privileged girls of his acquaintance. Prior to her leaving for the school in Boston, she had made it as clear as glass that she was destined to be Mrs. Will Darcy, whereupon she would elevate Pemberley to the showcase of Clackamas county where only the most important individuals would cross the threshold.

His vivid imagination could never stretch far enough to see Caroline Bingley volunteering to cook for anyone, especially not her brother and his wife.

He looked at Jane Bingley closer and tried to hide his disappointment. Then he looked at Elizabeth. Was he ever happy that he'd chosen the right Bennet girl after all!

Chapter 9

Charles Bingley stayed behind when the women left Darcy's room. They didn't speak until they heard the screen door close behind their wives. He easily pictured Elizabeth sitting in her chair—rocking with Mrs. Bingley alongside her.

"How are you, Charles?"

"Do you mean to ask, 'How is your marriage'?" He grinned at his friend. "I'll tell you without you having to inquire. I am married to the finest woman this side of the Mississippi—actually, both sides of the Mississippi. Jane is everything I could have hoped for and more. There isn't a speck of dust to be found in the place, and she brings me a whiskey and my slippers every evening before we turn in for the night. She is the kindest, most cooperative woman I've been around, and I'm sure she will be a positive influence for Caroline when we bring her home."

"You are sure about that, are you?" Somehow, unless a miracle happened, Darcy thought it was a tad far-fetched to believe Caroline Bingley would take well to having another woman run her home. Caroline had been demanding and commanding and was constantly reprimanding her brother when he did not give in to her every desire. Darcy shuddered at the memory of Bingley's sister. She would be the last person he'd ever want permanently in his house. There would be no peace.

"Well, of course," his friend was quick to reassure him. "Jane has done everything she could think of to make the ranch house as comfortable as possible for my sister. She says it will be like having Elizabeth with her from sunup to sundown each and every day." Bingley smiled even bigger, and his chest puffed out with pride. "We need to get Caroline home to take charge of the kitchen before winter, as I doubt the roads will hold for us to get to town to the hotel each day and back. I'd hate to starve to death because of the weather. Of course, if I died in my wife's arms, I'd die a happy man."

"Hmmm…yes, well." How Darcy restrained himself from rolling his eyes, he wasn't sure.

"Besides," Bingley continued, "I can't see any single woman staying that way for long. My sister is returning home all refined and spit-shined to perfection. As soon as word gets out that she's here, some gentleman will latch onto her, and I'll be losing another cook. Hey, maybe Richard would be interested in her as a wife. Now that he's a hotshot Portland lawyer, he's probably thinking it's time to start setting up his own household."

In his memory, the only woman Richard had ever expressed interest in was Elizabeth—who was as opposite to Caroline Bingley as the East was to the West. No, he couldn't see Richard pairing off with Miss Bingley. At the thought of his cousin's interest in his wife, a nervous feeling started in the pit of his stomach as he felt his breathing getting faster. *I wonder why?* Rather than think on it further, he replied. "Well, it's good to know you are getting your own house in order, and that you are happy in your marriage."

"What about you and Elizabeth? How are you two getting along?"

"We are doing just fine." Darcy suspected Elizabeth was being asked the same by her sister, and he wondered how she would answer. Would she tell Jane how she wished she'd never come west and attached herself to him? Would she relate to her the demeaning tasks she'd had to care for since his accident? Would she speak disparagingly of him to another? She had told him she wouldn't be like her parents by speaking against her husband, but would that still apply to the one person she had shared confidences with her whole lifetime?

He had no answers, though he wished to be a mouse in the corner as the two sisters visited out on the porch. Darcy sucked in a breath when he discerned the task was entirely possible.

"Bingley, would you mind opening the window to let some fresh air in?" His friend never batted an eyelash at his request, though the afternoon breeze was stiff and the curtains immediately floated away from the casing as soon as Bingley raised the glass.

He heard her.

When Bingley started to speak, Darcy shook his head and put his finger to his lips. He whispered, "I don't want to disturb them. If you don't mind sitting here for a bit, I'll probably doze off for a while."

He felt like the worst sort of man, but his brain screamed at him to eavesdrop on his wife, to see if he could determine a means to begin to make things right with her. The first words out of her mouth sent chills down his spine.

"No, Jane, we aren't trying for a baby."

Good Lord in heaven! Do women talk about these things?

"I understand, Lizzy. With Will's accident, it has to be hard for you both."

"Our circumstances are challenging, but you know how my courage rises at any attempt to intimidate me. This has been difficult and threatened to overwhelm me at first, yet each day I find something more to love about my new home."

"This house is beautiful and solid. I see why you love it here."

"Jane, it's not so much the building itself, though it is a beautiful residence. The river and the forests draw me and, no matter the problems I face inside our home, I feel a calmness set in each time I sit here and rock. I adore both Mr. and Mrs. Reynolds. They are a fine couple with a solid marriage."

"Quite unlike our own parents, right?"

"Yes, Jane, quite unlike them. But it's even more than the sum of all these parts as to why I am pleased to be in Oregon." She paused. "I sense the pioneer spirit here—that desire to take the raw materials and make something that will grow from them; to build my own heritage."

"I don't understand, Lizzy."

"Sister, it hasn't been thirty years since the first wagon trains arrived and early settlers started building this area into a permanent settlement. Sure, people lived here before that time, but those travelers had a vision of what the Willamette Valley could be for the future, and they worked diligently so their dream would become a reality. I often sit here and ponder what the next thirty years will bring for Will and me, and I dream of working together to build something even more permanent than this big log house."

"I guess Charles and I have much simpler dreams. We are perfectly contented with things the way they are. Well, except for the food situation."

The ladies both chuckled.

"I am very pleased for you both, Jane. He appears to be a fine man. Are you and Charles planning to stay at Netherfield Ranch?"

"Well, of course we are. There is plenty of room for children and plenty of land to support a large, growing family. I can't even begin to imagine us having the worries we had in Baltimore."

"And aren't we happy that is so."

Darcy could hear the smile in her voice.

"Do you worry about our sisters much?" Jane seemed hesitant to ask.

"Absolutely!" Elizabeth's response was immediate. "Every single day I worry about whether or not our sisters have enough to eat and whether or not our parents are giving Lydia and Kitty proper oversight."

"I worry as well, but I am certain our parents are caring for them as best they can." Jane's voice was wistful. "I wish they lived closer."

"What will you do if you find them to be in dire straits?"

"I am sure they won't be, Lizzy, as they have fewer mouths to feed. Father will seek more students to tutor, I am sure. And Uncle Gardiner will be there to offer assistance if needed."

"I hope you are right." Elizabeth paused. "Come, Jane, and I will show you my favorite part of the garden out back. Will's mom must have loved roses because the flower garden has a bloom in just about every color of the rainbow."

"You know I adore roses."

"Let's go."

Darcy had learned much from the conversation. He opened his eyes to see Bingley's knee bouncing and his hands wringing.

"What's the matter with you?" He hadn't mean his voice to sound so gruff.

"What's the matter? I'll tell you what the matter is." Bingley jumped from his seat and walked to the opened window and back. "I don't have a rose garden at my home. According to the conversation I had no right to be listening to, my bride *adores* roses. That's a fine how-do-you-do, Will. What am I supposed to do now?"

"I hope that's a rhetorical question, my friend, because I haven't a clue what to tell you."

"Well, I can't come over here in the middle of the night and steal yours because we are leaving in two days to head back east and they would die of neglect in the meantime." Bingley ran his hand through his already tousled hair.

"In the spring, Charles. My mom only transplanted roses in the spring after the first frost. That will give you plenty of time when you return to select a plot, dig it up, and shower your wife with rose petals."

The image of him showering Elizabeth with flowers flashed across his mind and he smiled at the thought of doing so.

"Bingley, enjoy the peace and quiet of your travels to Boston, and I wish you well on your return journey."

"Thanks, I think."

Darcy thought long and hard about his wife's comments to her sister and wondered at how foolish he had been in wasting his emotions on regret.

After the Bingleys had left, he was almost overwhelmed when he reflected on all Elizabeth had accomplished in the week she had been at Pemberley. Daily, there were heavenly smells coming from the kitchen as she and Mrs. Reynolds filled dozens of canning jars with the garden's bounty. Unlike Bingley, his household wouldn't suffer from a lack of food during the winter months when the rain and ice made it a challenge to get to town.

His next visitor was Dr. Henderson, who was exceedingly displeased though unsurprised to find him sitting up in bed. Less than a half hour after his departure, he heard sounds of banging moving from the back door to outside his rooms. His wife swept in with Dan and Melvin following close behind. The mystery intensified as he spied a brand new galvanized iron horse trough being carried into his room by the two men. Elizabeth slid the small table from beside his bed until it sat under the opened window, which she closed.

Behind them came the foreman with the painted wooden chairs from the porch under each arm. As soon as the trough was set next to his bed, the chairs were place inside, one facing the long end of the large, oval container and the other sitting sideways. Without a word, the men left and returned with one more chair and three buckets filled with hot, steaming water. Again, they left. More water was brought in, and Darcy figured they'd used every pail to be found on the ranch. Whatever was going on would need to be finished before it was time to feed the horses.

"Are you ready for a bath?" She waited until they were alone in the bedroom.

He was so ready that he wanted to squeal like a girl. Elizabeth threw back his blankets and started carefully removing the pillows which kept his leg propped up. Dr. Henderson had already taken off his splint, explaining that Elizabeth would replace it later, and Darcy was pleased to feel the air against his skin. Comprehending her plan, he bent his left leg and his right elbow until he could prop and scoot himself over to the chair. His wife held the weight of his right leg—placing it carefully on the two chairs facing the side of the trough.

"Lean forward."

149

As soon as he did, Elizabeth poured several mugs of warm water over the top of his head. When she lathered her hands and started rubbing the soap into his scalp, he may have moaned. The process was slow: water, soap, and rinse, but he felt better than he had since before the accident.

Elizabeth was thorough, washing every inch he was unable to access. He didn't know if her face was red from the exertion or from the intimacy of her touch, though modestly, she kindly offered him the wet rag to take care of what he was able to easily reach. Once he was clean, he looked over to the seven buckets lined up in a row behind her. Elizabeth had wisely taken water from each bucket so she was able to lift what was remaining and pour it over him for a good rinse. He had to smile at her efficiency.

"Better now?"

He felt like a man renewed. "Thank you."

She looked at him in shock, and he felt immediate shame that he had not used those words before. Or, he had used them in her hearing, but it was not her who was receiving his gratitude.

"You are welcome." That was it, the sum total of her words. After drying off his hair, back, and lower legs, she handed him a fresh towel and then started stripping the blankets and sheets from his bed. Apparently Maggie had carried up a pile of new bedding as Elizabeth opened the door and brought the fresh linens inside.

What did he expect? That their conversation would suddenly become as easy between them as it had been for her and Jane? He was a dunce!

"Elizabeth," he swallowed hard. "I have to admit...it shames me...." He cleared his throat.

"Yes?" The last of the blankets was on the bed, and she was stuffing the pillows into their cases with no small amount of force. *Was she imagining that was my head she was shoving out of sight?* He wanted to smile at the thought. His wife's emotions were strong, and he was glad she wasn't as wishy-washy as her sister appeared.

"I appreciate all you have done and are doing for me and the ranch. This is not how I imagined my life would be when I finally brought a woman home as my wife. I imagine it wasn't your vision of wedded bliss either."

She laughed—and his heart melted a little.

"No, I'd hoped we would be married at least fifty years before I had to clean up after you and wipe up your messes. Of course, then your hair would have thinned and you would most likely have less teeth to brush as well."

"And your hair would be streaked with gray and white and your figure rounded while you shoo-ed our great-grandchildren from their grumpy grandfather." The picture was inviting.

"I don't believe that for a minute."

151

"What? That I'm a grumpy grandfather?" The sparkle in her eyes was an invitation to set aside the weight of his injury. His heart hadn't felt so light since…well, he couldn't remember when.

"Not at all. I have no trouble seeing you as surly." Her smile reached from ear-to-ear.

He chuckled at the probable truth of her opinion. "Then, what?"

"My mother, at forty-five, has retained her figure after having birthed five children. I will *never* be rounded, sir." She dropped the last pillow to the top of the bed. "Do you like to play with matches around gun powder?"

Darcy was afraid to look close to see whether or not she was upset or if she was just teasing. In retrospect, mentioning a woman's shape was undoubtedly not the wisest course, especially a lady he would be spending the rest of his life with. He wanted to kick himself. *How had he said something with the potential to offend when he'd wanted to have an enjoyable conversation?*

He looked down at the towel draped across his lap so He didn't see the pillow until it flashed before his face, hitting him on the chest with a resounding smack. He grabbed it before it could fall into the water below.

"Keep this clearly in mind, Mr. Darcy." She giggled. "You have married a woman with unusual skills. With four sisters, two of them particularly mischievous, I am ever ready to defend my honor against disreputable pirates, shady gunfighters, and errant husbands."

"Pirates?"

"Of course." Her laughter rang from wall to wall. He couldn't keep from smiling. "Little did you know that you married Captain Lizzy Bennet, scourge of the pirates of the Caribbean and sworn enemy of Blackbeard himself."

"Captain Bennet?"

"For a certainty, though I have not taken on the role for years." Elizabeth plucked the pillow from his hands and put it back on the bed. Then she pulled the blankets back, ready for him to return to the same position he'd held for the past week. "We had little when we were growing up except marvelous stories from my father's library. Those books fueled our imaginations which provided hours and hours of play-acting entertainment. Jane was always the princess or the damsel in distress. I," she rubbed the back of her fingers on her chest, "was the hero."

"You?"

"Sure. Somebody had to be. Why not me?"

As he scooted back to the softness of the bed, he wondered at this woman in front of him as she immediately bent to the task of repositioning the splint on his leg.

"Didn't you ever want to be the princess or the damsel who needed rescued?" Darcy had no clue why her answer suddenly seemed so important, but it did.

"Me? Never." He felt her gaze. "You seem disappointed. Why?"

He should have given his reply more thought because as soon as the words came out, even though they sounded good in his mind, he knew he had given her grounds for misunderstanding, which she did. "Because men want a woman who relies on his strength."

"You wanted a weak woman as your wife?" Her hands instinctively went to her hips and then she started stuffing the pillows under his leg with vigor. "Well, I'm sorry you didn't get what you wanted and that you are stuck with me."

Before he could say a word, she was out the door. Moments later, the sound of footsteps outside his bedroom gave him hope she had returned and he could attempt to explain what he'd meant. However, it was Dan and Melvin coming to retrieve the bath and the chairs. Later, Maggie brought him his food tray. He didn't see Elizabeth the rest of the night.

Chapter 10

A typical summer day in Oregon City could start with a morning sky so clear and blue it would hurt a person's eyes to look at it for long. Minutes later it could rain. Since Elizabeth had been on the ranch, there hadn't been one day without the chill of falling rain rotating with the heat of the July sun. When daylight broke on her twelfth morning at Pemberley, the temperature hovered between hot and hotter with no hint of precipitation. The weather seemed to settle into July, as if it would be taking up permanent lodging.

Roses stood tall as they raised their glorious heads to the heavens and bumblebees flitted from one blossom to another. The fruit trees and the garden woke up and busied themselves in producing a bounty which would need harvesting before the rains fell again.

In spite of it being just after breakfast, Elizabeth's arms ached as she picked one ripe peach after another, placing them carefully into the bushel basket. Most of the orchard contained apple and pear trees, but the abundance of pale orange globes from the few peach trees had already filled three baskets. A slight breeze carried the scent of sweetness and she knew her kitchen would smell like heaven when she started making pies and cobblers.

The foreman and his wife had taken the wagon to town the day before to attend services and load up on supplies at the mercantile so there was enough flour and sugar to make even the sourest person sweet. She hoped it helped Will Darcy.

Smiling at the remembrance of the sounds of pure joy he had emitted when she dug her hands into his scalp and scrubbed his back around the purplish-yellow bruises a few days prior let her know more than anything that he was a man who could be pleased.

Setting aside the last of the peaches, she selected one so ripe that beads of juice gathered on the outside. Raising it to her nose, she smelled the intense perfume, closing her eyes so she could remember the fragrance during the cold winter months. Elizabeth felt the need to share. Despite provocation, there was no sense in her being mean-spirited, and it might please him enough to make him smile.

Returning to the house, she peeked her face around her husband's bedroom door, holding the fruit behind her back. "I brought you something."

"You have a look of mischief about you, Elizabeth. What are you hiding?"

She was pleased he wasn't grumpy. Surely, he liked peaches. Who didn't like peaches? Well, actually a friend from Baltimore, a Miss Weekly, broke out with red bumps each time she ate one. Hopefully, this wasn't a bad idea.

"Close your eyes," she said softly.

"I'd rather not." He crossed his arms over his chest and his face took on his typical grouchy look.

"I won't share if you don't. You will love it, I promise."

"You promise?" His surliness evolved into uncertainty.

"Why don't you trust me, Will?" Suddenly, it was about much more than the peach, and he seemed to recognize the import of his reply as well.

"Richard and his brother, both of them being older than me, used to torment me with the same request—only it usually was a trick. I most often ended up with snakes, dead mice, rotten potatoes, and once, a picture of a scantily clad lady in my hands because I had closed my eyes when they'd asked."

"Surely, you didn't mind the picture, did you?" she had to tease.

"I was only eight years old and my father caught me, so, yes, I minded."

Shared laughter was a rarity for them, but it went a long way towards Elizabeth not thinking so poorly of Darcy.

"I understand your trust issues, Will. However, you will learn that I would *never* torment...well, actually, I can't honestly say what I had intended because I have been known to tease a time or two myself." Their merriment filled the room. "I will promise you that *this time* I will play no tricks. In fact, if you watch me closely, I will turn my back to you and raise both my hands so what they contain is under my own nose before I attempt to put it under yours. You will see that I have nothing nefarious in mind."

Turning her back to him, she did as she had said she would, inhaling deeply and sighing.

"I'll do it." Before she could turn back around he replied, and she was grateful he was willing to trust her in this.

"Then close your eyes and breathe in deeply so you can smell summer."

His eyelids dropped and his long black lashes lay heavily on his cheeks. As soon as she moved the fruit closer, those same cheeks lifted into a smile.

Elizabeth wanted to suck in a breath. He really was the handsomest man she had ever known.

"Mm mm...peaches." With his eyes still closed, he moved his hands up to gently clasp hers. Opening his mouth, he took a large bite. Juice shot everywhere—down his chin, on her hands

158

and his...—so he had to flick his tongue out to lick the peach where he had bitten. She freed one hand and grabbed a towel from the stack she kept on hand, tucking it under his chin to catch the dribbles.

He opened his eyes and suddenly she was having a hard time breathing. She wondered if the sweetness of the fruit was too cloying. Darcy seemed to be suffering the same affliction.

Keeping his eyes on hers and her hand in his, he took another, much smaller bite. This time he was prepared for the mess. He didn't even blink until the only thing remaining in the hand being cupped by his was the pit.

She cleared her throat. "Good, huh?"

"Oh, yes." Before she realized his intentions, he drew her hand closer and licked the juice from her palm. Then it was Elizabeth who closed her eyes.

"A-hem." From the doorway, Maggie cleared her throat in the same manner Elizabeth had just done. "A wagon has pulled up with some sort of contraption in the back. Richard is driving and Georgiana is here."

"She's here?" Immediately Elizabeth's focus turned to their guests. She had no curiosity about the piece of equipment in the back of the wagon as Dr. Henderson had explained its purpose and that he would be sending it today. What held her attention was the young lady Darcy's cousin was handing down from the seat. From the small glimpse through Will's bedroom window, she could see that Miss Darcy was an elegant young lady who looked strikingly similar in appearance to Jane.

Without looking back at her husband, she threw the peach pit in the garbage can and ran downstairs.

Darcy was stunned. To say the tender moment hadn't affected him would have been a blatant lie. As his wife had teased him and asked for his trust, he'd impulsively decided to do exactly that. He doubted she had any idea how hard that had been for him. He'd had a lifetime of putting himself forward, trying to glean a smidgeon of attention from his father, only to be shoved back so Wickham could be praised and petted. While his tale of the Fitzwilliam boys had been true, those had been the actions of cousins who would never do him real harm. He could not say the same for his parent.

Footsteps far too heavy to be his wife's or Georgiana's approached his door. He was unsurprised when his cousin entered the room. What did momentarily unsettle him was the presence of his foreman and the White brothers carrying one of the heavy dining room chairs.

"Rise and shine, Darcy. You are about to taste freedom." Richard had his ever-present grin as he threw back the covers from his cousin's injured leg and carefully started removing the pillows.

The men sat the chair next to his bed after moving the small table like they had done for his bath. At the same time, he noted muffled noises from downstairs, like chairs being slid under a dining table.

"What's going on?" His wife had said nothing about Georgiana's appearance, and he worried suddenly that something was keeping her from climbing the stairs. Had she broken her leg too and nobody told him? Was that what the contraption was for, to help her walk? Panic filled his chest until he noted Richard's smile. No, whatever it was would be for him. Undoubtedly, Elizabeth had known and chosen not to share it with him. *Wouldn't that be just like her, to surprise him like she had done with the peach?*

He couldn't contain his smile as he donned a shirt his cousin tossed at him, the top half of a nightwear set his wife had stitched for him in the evenings. The bottom half, which he would particularly need for modesty, took considerable effort to pull over the splint. Having a panel in front and in back attached by three buttons each made them practical for a man in his position to wear. He secretly praised his bride for her thoughtfulness.

Covering his new clothing with an old robe, he pulled himself to the chair as Richard held his right leg. Without a word, the four men grabbed the two chair legs on the side facing

161

them—two hands on the bottom of the rung and two on the top, and slid the chair on the wooden floor until they could move to all four corners of the seat. When they started to pick him up, they found they needed one more person to hold his leg.

"Elizabeth!" Richard bellowed from right next to Darcy's ear. Within seconds, they heard her light footsteps on the stairs. Once she was in place, they lifted him and moved him, feet first, out the door, down the hallway and down the stairs. It was his first time out of his room since the accident and he gloried in seeing walls that were not the same ones he'd been staring at for what felt like forever.

"Brother." No, there was nothing broken with Georgiana. She was taller than he'd remembered and far more hale and hearty than the last time he had seen her—though she was still painfully reticent. Her heart had been broken and crushed by George Wickham, and Darcy hadn't known how to handle a fifteen-year-old who erupted into tears from only a look.

Had it really been a year already? Shame filled him from head to toe that he'd neglected his closest living relative for so long. The running of the ranch had been his only excuse and, looking at her hesitancy, he only now realized it was not a valid enough reason.

He had expected her to at least embrace him, though carefully. Instead, she stood as still as a statue and stared at him.

"Georgie, it is good to have you home." He held out his hand as the men sat the chair on the floor. The crack in his heart,

162

broke a little more as his sister's eyes dropped to the floor. "Georgie?"

"Hey, let's get you settled in your new wheeled chair, cousin." Richard slapped him on his uninjured shoulder. Darcy looked up at him in time to see his shrug. Apparently twelve months hadn't made being around his sister any more comfortable for either man.

Darcy finally looked to where his wife had moved. Next to her was a straight-backed chair sitting on two large wheels in the back and two smaller ones in the front. Crudely attached to the front was a shelf extending on the right side of the chair for him to rest his broken leg. There were handles on the back for someone to push him around, but he quickly realized he would be able to use his left leg to propel himself as well.

Excitement at being able to control his movements somewhat had the palms of his hands sweating and his breathing shallow. Dan pushed the chair over to him and with an ease that surprised them all, he was situated. Elated, he smiled at everyone in the room. His sister still hadn't looked back up at him. His victory felt hollow, leaving his insides quivering.

"Thank you to those who brought this contraption from town and to those who hefted my carcass down those stairs." He waited for the men to stop guffawing. "I believe the tides, which have always flowed steadily at Pemberley, will move even stronger with my ability to roam throughout the house. With that

163

said, my greatest gift this day is to have my sister home where she belongs."

Maggie Reynolds, possibly carried away at the emotions emanating from her employer, applauded. The men and Elizabeth joined her. His sister turned tear-stained eyes to him, sobbed, and ran upstairs to her old room. The door slammed behind her.

Darcy rubbed his hands over his face. *What had caused Georgiana to react in that way? Was she unhappy to be home? Was she unhappy to be with her brother? Didn't she like Elizabeth? Was she still upset over Wickham?* He wondered if he would ever know.

To his relief, Elizabeth's voice broke into the tension of the room. "I've left a basket of fresh-picked peaches on the porch along with a pale of water and some towels for washing up. Please eat your fill, gentlemen, and I'll see to fixing something to eat."

Elizabeth herded Dan, Melvin, and the foreman out the door and returned to grab Richard by his shirtsleeves to get him outside the house as well.

"Me too?"

Darcy wanted to laugh at the expression of disbelief on his cousin's face, but the pain of rejection by his sister was too deep. Instead, he nodded his head to Richard, and the man, for once, complied with no argument.

"Maggie, will you see to adding the vegetables to the stew?"

At the woman's nod, Elizabeth walked towards him until she stood directly in front of him. "I'll make sure she is settled in." She kept her voice soft.

Gratitude filled his heart towards her. He nodded, no longer able to lift his head to look at Elizabeth. He felt like a sissy, like he was less than a man should be in not facing the hurt, in not demanding his sister be happy at coming back to Pemberley, in not asserting his authority in making her love and respect him.

Lord, but he was a mess! Why would it be any different for his sister than it was his own wife? What had he done to earn her love and respect? Absolutely nothing. His own foolish belief that William Darcy, by the simple fact that he was a Darcy, deserved admiration was ridiculous. *Hah!* His pride, tasting like bile, rose inside him until it threatened to choke the life from him.

"William, are you well?" Elizabeth put her hand on his shoulder.

"I hardly know." He was ashamed to admit it. He was the head of his household, yet he was powerless to take the lead with these two females. Huffing and puffing did nothing but make his wife respond like he was talking to a tree stump. Giving her the silent treatment did the same. He didn't know what to do anymore, and it frightened him.

"I'll see what I can do." She was too quick to reassure him as she turned to go upstairs.

165

"Of course you will." The bitterness of his words tasted like metal in his mouth.

"Well, I am sorry!" Elizabeth stepped further away from him as he watched her guard go up—a tall wall to keep out unwanted intruders.

"No, please, I don't want to fight." As soon as he spoke the words, he comprehended the absolute truth of each syllable. He felt the need to purge his soul. "I'm sorry, Elizabeth. I'm sorry you are having to carry so many burdens on your own. I'm sorry I waited so long to bring my sister home. I'm sorry that when I get upset I act like a…"

"Donkey's hind end?" she suggested with a small smile.

He chortled. "Yes, a donkey's hind end."

Her righteous indignation made her eyes shine and she was, to him, the most beautiful woman he'd ever seen. Rather than rushing to change into her best clothing to greet her sister-in-law for the first time, she'd spent precious minutes with him feeding him that luscious peach. The memory stirred him, and he fought to regain control of his thinking.

She inhaled slowly. "You will find that we set up a bed in your study last night. You will be able to eat, sleep, and bathe downstairs. While the men were helping you into the chair, Maggie and I moved the two small bookcases in the hallway so your path is cleared."

166

He saw her tilt her head to look closer at him, and he barely heard her words. Darcy watched her mouth move and thought he heard her add something about Georgiana. He nodded as she expected him to and then she left him on his own.

Turning, he watched the sway of her hips as she climbed the stairs. When she drew closer to the top, he spied her trim ankles where she lifted her skirt to clear each step. She was the best of women, and he could pound his head against the solid log wall that he hadn't figured this out until now.

He knew what would happen. His wife would kindly and tenderly tend to his sister until she became confident that this was where she was supposed to be. Looking around the living area, he saw evidences of small changes Elizabeth had made since her arrival: bright, patch-worked quilts padded the hard chairs, tables covered in yellows, whites, blues, and reds with matching curtains lightened the room where the sun shone through the butter-yellow fabric, and decorative pillows in the same palette strewn around the furniture. Vases of roses were on every table surface and white, crocheted 'things" were underneath each vessel.

The living area had a relaxed feel, and he rejoiced in her taking the initiative to become the true Mrs. of the house. A home. That's what it was. His house was now their home.

His breath caught as he found he suddenly wanted her back alongside him. He wanted her slim fingers to entangle with his own. He wanted her to tease him and laugh with him... and feed him another peach. He wanted her to tell him all she had accomplished for his household during the day and what she was reading at night. He wanted to gaze into her eyes and have her full focus on him. He wanted to hold her and caress her until she placed her head against his chest and sighed with the comfort of being in his arms. He wanted all of this and more. He wanted her to feel for him what he was feeling for her. He, Fitzwilliam Alexander Darcy, was falling in love with his wife.

Chapter 11

"Georgiana, might I come in?" Elizabeth had tapped lightly on the door frame. She heard no sounds of activity from within the bedroom, and she wondered if her newest sister might have fled to an unknown location instead of the safety of her old bed chamber.

"Come in." Her voice was so soft, Elizabeth barely heard.

Elizabeth opened the door to a pitiful sight. Georgiana had pulled her chair to the window. She was leaning against the glass, her hand pressed to the pane as if seeking help from outside.

Moving into the room to sit on the bed, Elizabeth quietly inquired, "Are you mad, sad, or hurt?"

Georgiana slowly turned towards her, though her eyes appeared to flit to and from every object in the room except for Elizabeth.

"Why do you ask?"

There were no tears, and Elizabeth thought she had never observed a person so alone.

"I have four sisters, three of them younger, two of them close to your age, and only one of us close to perfection, my eldest sister, Jane Bingley. If you were to ask any of them, including Jane, they would tell you that I am the nosiest, the busiest, and the bossiest of all five Bennet girls. I've learned there are only those three emotions which will cause a young lady of sense and good health to become despondent, so I will ask again. Are you mad, sad, or hurt?"

"All of them." The words were blurted out as if they were vomit she had been unable to hold in. Georgiana immediately slapped her hand over her mouth, trying to keep from saying more.

"I imagined this to be so." Elizabeth carefully rested her hands on the top of her legs with her palms up and her fingers extended. Modulating her breathing and smiling slightly, she sought to consider how she might have felt at sixteen to be in Georgiana's tightly-laced boots. "If I'd had a brother who was severely injured, my heart would have broken into a million tiny pieces when he told me not to come to him. Even though almost two weeks have passed, my heart would still ache." Georgiana's eyes never wavered from focusing on the floor. "I'd be livid at the thought that it might have been his new wife who had encouraged me to stay away, a woman so unknown to you that you'd not even known of her existence prior to the horrible note telling of the accident. I would be despondent at wondering if I

170

would ever have a place at Pemberley, the place I had just as much right to as this new person who had planted herself in my home."

Without reply, Georgiana turned her head back to the window, a sigh weighing down her shoulders.

"Do you love my brother?"

"No."

Another sigh.

"So you married him for Pemberley." Rather than an accusation, it was a cold statement of fact—one that was highly offensive to Elizabeth. With each passing second, she realized how alike the siblings were—neither having boundaries for polite conversation.

"No. I knew nothing of this property or this home before we wed." Taking a slow breath, she considered how much to reveal to this young girl. "There were many reasons I agreed to marry Will, and I'm fairly certain you will learn them all before too long. What I will tell you is that the process of learning about each other after such a terrifying accident has been slow and, to be honest, just as painful as his injury. At times, your brother can be quite challenging to be around. Other times, there is a pleasantness about his mouth when he smiles, and I'm drawn to know him better. But for the most part, he's an irritable, old man."

Georgiana looked at her, her face devoid of expression.

"Oh, it's not like I lie awake at night dreaming of ways I can inflict torture on him for being so bad-tempered...well, actually," Elizabeth smiled, her eyes finally moving away from her sister to the ceiling, "the truth is that I've done just that more than once since I said, 'I do.'"

Elizabeth witnessed a slight movement in Georgiana's shoulders.

"Does it surprise you to hear of the imperfections of your brother?"

"But he has no flaws!"

Georgiana's quick reply shocked Elizabeth to the core.

"You truly believe that to be true?"

"Absolutely. Will has been a perfect brother who has never complained about the difficulties in having me as his sister. There is not a better man in Oregon than he."

Surprised at the firmness of her response, Elizabeth noted the erectness of Georgiana's spine, the lift of her chin, and the squared shoulders. She was nonplussed that this young woman apparently believed her opinion was the truth.

"If you think you are a difficult sister, which I cannot begin to imagine to be so, you should meet my youngest sibling, Lydia. Never have I known another who was born knowing more than everyone else, including her parents. She is brash, bold, and so much fun to be around when she's not complaining of not having enough attention."

172

"Oh." For the first time, Georgiana looked directly at Elizabeth, only to glance quickly away.

"Please, do not get me wrong. Should you ever need someone to take your side when you feel you have been wronged, you would want Lydia there. She is fiercely protective should someone speak or act against someone she loves." Elizabeth scooted to the edge of the bed. "Would you want someone like her in your home?"

"I do not know." Georgiana pressed her head back to the glass, her voice a whisper. "She would…well, I would think she is…actually, I'm sure you would prefer her to me."

Twice her new sister had indicated she was either unworthy or unwanted in the less than five minutes Elizabeth had spent in her company. Her look of dejection made Elizabeth examine her even closer. *Did she truly feel undeserving of being at Pemberley?* In spite of all the challenges Mary, Kitty, and Lydia brought to the Bennet household, each was confident of their place in the family.

"Are you happy to be back home, Georgiana?" she hesitated to ask, but needed to know.

"I suppose so."

Elizabeth wanted to shake her, to stir her to express herself or get involved. Or course, she had also wanted to do the same to the girl's brother a time or two—or three or four.

"Please accept that I am overjoyed to have you live here."

173

"Oh, I believe you are incorrect." Finally, Georgiana looked at her directly. "I doubt I will stay any longer than it takes for Will to heal from his injury. He will then want me to return to Portland to my aunt."

"No, you are wrong. Unless it is *you* who wants to live with the Fitzwilliams, you will remain here as long as *you* want. This is your home."

Georgiana merely shook her head slowly and turned back to the window. Not knowing what else to do, Elizabeth stood and walked from the room.

For the rest of the day, Darcy had taken to showing up everywhere Elizabeth happened to be in the house. He'd even started coming out to the porch to sit alongside her as she watched over the traffic on the river.

Georgiana had not joined them for their meal and had chosen not to extend the courtesy of a goodbye to Richard when he left. Her presence seemed to put a sopping wet blanket atop the minute flames of family life at Pemberley. Like the initial and present difficulties with her brother, Elizabeth refused to allow reticence or rudeness, no matter the cause, to rob her of finding joy with the beauty surrounding her.

174

She turned her eyes towards the trees to see a large bird soaring above. *Was it an eagle?* She had yet to ask anyone if moose were to be found in this portion of Oregon. She had so much to learn about this new place where she would spend the rest of her life.

"Why is she staying in her room? Didn't you have a talk with her?" John and Maggie had left for their cabin and Will was again sitting by her on the veranda. His tone was abrasive and insulting.

So rapidly it surprised her, cold fury rose in her chest until she thought it would explode. How dare he assume it was her responsibility or fault that Georgiana had stayed in her room. *As if she had the power and skill to easily influence someone who was a new acquaintance!* She was not going to fight! Breathing deeply, she said nothing.

"I'm sorry." He was quick to apologize. "That didn't come out like I'd wanted."

"Then what was it you intended to say, and how did you intend it to sound, Will?" She watched as he ran his hands through his hair.

"I am worried about my sister." He moved his chair closer and flinched from his muscles being overused for the first time in more than a week. "Richard told me she only comes out of her room when Aunt Helen demands it. I don't understand her. She used to love being here. She would run down the stairs and jump when she got to the third step from the bottom so I'd catch her.

175

I'd swing her around, and she would laugh until I'd laugh with her. We had some of the best times of my childhood together before Father sent her away."

Elizabeth didn't know what to say. "Were you expecting me to spend a few minutes in her company so she would return to that joyful little girl? If you were, you are doomed to disappointment."

"No. Yes. I don't know."

"Well, that's plain." She chuckled softly. "You will have to give us time, Will. I don't know her, and she doesn't know me. She doesn't know you either. How many years has she actually lived with the Fitzwilliams?"

"Since before I left for school. I guess she would have been about six."

"Did you see her often?"

"Not really, though I wanted to. We became so busy trying to increase the ranch, and then I went to university where I wrote her daily."

"I remember your telling me you did so, and I'm glad of it." Elizabeth reflected on her first impression of Georgiana Darcy. Fragile as thin glass. "Can you imagine her sense of abandonment by you and your father?"

"Good Lord! I have done so much wrong." She saw the movement in his throat as he swallowed hard. "Is she okay? Will she be okay?"

176

"I don't know. I don't know at all. Apparently there is much we don't understand." Looking directly at him, she waited until she had his attention. "You were not solely to blame, Will. Correct me if I'm wrong, but wasn't it your father who removed her to Portland? Wasn't it he who insisted you attend school in the East and then in England? Could you have supported her and cared for her during those years you were gone?"

He huffed. "No, you are right. I could have done nothing *then.*" Again, he looked away. "But I have no excuse for the past five years. The first thing I should have done after father died was to get Georgie back here. I failed."

"We all fail, Will. We all stumble, do we not?"

He nodded, though he did not look at her.

"Can we catch the river to regain the water that has already flowed by us? No. Can we turn back the clock to be able to make different choices and enjoy different results? Not at all. We can only make better choices in the future."

"Yes. There are many reasons I do not want to go back and relive that time. Becoming manager of this property and the business investments my grandfather and father were involved in was a heavy weight for me. And who's to say that I would have done better for my sister than my aunt did? Who knows?"

He paused, as if to gather his thoughts. "Are we okay?" He hesitated over the question.

Now it was she who would not meet his gaze. "I don't know." Elizabeth started her chair rocking, finding the steady rhythm comforting. "With my family, I always knew clearly where I stood, who was upset and the reasons for it, and why things were done as they were. I knew how each individual would react under a variety of circumstances because I knew them intimately."

She looked away from him. "I can't read your mind, Will, so when you react in a way very unexpected or you speak in a manner that's exceedingly blunt, it catches me by surprise and I respond with anger and frustration." She blew the air from her cheeks. "Apparently your sister has the same difficulty with speaking up as you do. It must be an inherited Darcy trait."

"I'm sorry."

"And I am pleased that you are." Elizabeth rocked a little faster. "I imagine you have said those two words more in the past twenty-four hours than you have in the past twenty-seven years, and I appreciate your effort. Nonetheless, saying the words is much easier than doing something about them."

She could see Darcy's struggle as he tamped down his ire. He had been on his own long enough that he hadn't had to take someone else's opinion or needs into consideration.

"I've never been married before, and I've not been around many married folks other than Maggie and John. I'm trying, Elizabeth."

She heard the petition in his tone and thought to meet him halfway.

"I'm trying as well, and I fail many times," she easily admitted. "My propensity to jump to the wrong conclusion is legendary; not an accomplishment I'm proud of." Elizabeth stilled her chair and reached over to rest her hand on his arm. "What we both are is determined, I believe. We both have strong opinions and both believe we are in the right when those opinions clash against each other. But know this, Husband, I am fiercely determined to not be the only one in this marriage to make sacrifices and adjustments."

"I was there too, Elizabeth. I said my vows just as you did." His eyes strayed to a distant location apparently only he could see. "We promised to become husband and wife, binding ourselves together for the rest of our lives. I am no longer unwed, free to go my own way without consideration to you. I am bound to you are you are to me. We are united both by law and by God. My injury has tipped the balance where my burdens have fallen to you. As a man…having you bear the weight of such tasks is unpalatable. As your husband, it is my responsibility to care for you physically and in every other way. I mean to do so as soon as I am able."

"I am glad to hear this."

"You told me I lacked integrity and honor when I spoke your sister's name while I was having laudanum-laced dreams."

"I did."

"I will tell you now that those words were some of the most painful I've ever heard uttered in my presence. Having you call into question the most fundamental aspects of my being was an affront I've had to set aside with much effort. With that said…," he raised his hand when she started to speak. "With that said, Elizabeth, you were correct and, though it was equally as painful—if not more so—than my leg to hear it, your words and actions helped me understand how pleased I am that you are my wife."

She tilted her head and looked at him carefully.

"You told me what you expected from a marriage, from your husband. And I heard each and every word. As I lay in my bed day after day, I pondered what my expectations were in offering you my hand and my name." He no longer looked away from her. "I want a partner, for better and for worse. I want a woman who isn't afraid to meet in the middle nor afraid to go against me privately when I've not been clear or I've been impulsive with my words. I want your visions of building a heritage, a home filled with future generations of Darcys to settle and grow on this land."

She inhaled quickly. "You heard Jane and me talking." Elizabeth chortled.

"I will not keep anything from you, Elizabeth, ever again. We have a task ahead of us to see to the future happiness of my sister and to start working on our own."

His words were exactly what her soul lacked—that dark void in her marriage which needed filled. She was grateful he'd been unexpectedly open with her. Returning to a slow-moving pace of rocking, she felt a small smile grace her face. *It was about time!*

The day had been long, filled with both intense joys and disappointments. By the time Will was settled for the night in his new room, Elizabeth decided to take advantage of the cooler temperatures so she walked to the orchard for a fresh peach. They would finally start cutting and slicing the peaches for pies and filling the canning jars on the morrow. She was pleased with the harvest and wished her sisters were here to enjoy the long summer days in the outdoors. She wondered if Georgiana had ever helped in the kitchen. Her sisters had all avoided the duty like the plague.

She needed time alone with her thoughts to process her reactions to each of the Darcys. It had been almost too much to take in.

She wasn't alone for long.

"Elizabeth," a man whispered into the twilight, his voice slightly familiar.

"Who's there?" She shifted her weight to her toes, poised to leave.

"George Wickham."

Wickham! "You shouldn't be here. My husband will be upset." Elizabeth's curiosity was piqued. She had no doubt that Richard Fitzwilliam had let the man know he was unwelcome on Darcy's property.

"I'm not here to see Darcy." Wickham stepped out from the shadows of the trees until he stood before her. "I only need a few minutes with Georgiana, that's all. Once I see her, I will leave for good. You have my word."

Elizabeth was torn. Unrequited love would explain the young girl's forlorn attitude and the overly protective attitude of both Richard and her husband. *How harmless could it be? Or, how harmful?* Pondering her actions, she decided what to do. Her husband had shown a willingness and determination to change his attitude. If she could help him see the need to soften his bitter resentment of the man in front of her, she would do all she could to help.

"I shall not arrange for you to meet her, but I will deliver a note to her. She may read it and respond in private. Once, Mr. Wickham. Only once will I do so."

He nodded his head in acceptance. "Promise you will meet me here tomorrow evening at this time, and I'll have all I need to say written down." He reached for her hands, stepping closer. Instinctively, Elizabeth stepped back. "Know that I love Georgiana with all my heart and soul. I will do anything for her. Anything within my power and ability. Just one word from her saying she does not return my feelings, and I will be gone from your lives forever. However, if she says she will be my bride, I will wait 'til the day she is ready to start my life with her."

"I do this because my sister has the right to know how you feel. But once she decides, her decision is final. If she doesn't feel the same, you will not be welcomed at Pemberley in the future unless you are here at my husband's invitation."

The man sauntered off, and Elizabeth left the peaches behind to return to the house.

Chapter 12

Darcy greeted the morning with resolution. He would have patted himself on the back had his shoulder not been so tender. His talk with Elizabeth the day before had given him a goal, and he would start that very day by not shying away from his sister or from his wife. He would help Georgiana to see that her place was in his home. He knew he had much to prove to both her and Elizabeth. He'd give his life for either of them, if necessary, but even more so, he'd be willing to do whatever he needed to do to live with them in harmony.

His resolve lasted until just after breakfast.

The men had left and Maggie had cleared the empty dishes, leaving Elizabeth and himself alone at the table. Georgiana was not yet out of bed, a matter he planned to change by the following day. Elizabeth had cooked smoked ham and eggs for breakfast and followed it with hot biscuits covered with sliced peaches and cream. Peace had settled into his bones, and he felt contentment for the first time in years. His path was clear and he was on his way. Then she shared with him the details of her evening stroll.

"What?!" He was instantly livid. Scalding hot coffee spewed from his lips and his fists pounded the table. "You did what?"

"Before you completely lose your temper, recall that I did not invite the man to Pemberley nor did I welcome him once I realized he was here." She stood to get a cloth to wipe up the spilled liquid.

He opened his mouth to stop her, and she put her hand up. "Allow me to complete this task. I need to cool down and so do you." She scrubbed at the spots with vigor. "I gave no consideration to keeping this to myself, Will Darcy. Had you been awake when I returned, I would have told you then."

"I could have…"

"What? How? For another two and a half months you are stuck in the house so you would have done exactly what?" She plopped into the seat alongside him. "Not telling you about Wickham's presence in the orchard would have shown a lack of trust on my part. I knew you would be upset, and you have not failed to react in the manner I'd expected." She paused. "I told him to bring a note to me tonight so your sister would know he still loved her."

"Loved her?" Darcy was incredulous. "He has no clue how to love anyone other than himself. George Wickham has enough charm to fill the ocean, Elizabeth. He uses it for his advantage

186

only. Love Georgiana?" He scoffed. "He wouldn't begin to know the meaning of the word?"

"How do you know? He sounded sincere."

"Of course he would. It's the only way he knows how to act, but believe me, it is an act." He leaned towards her. "Wickham doesn't know the first thing about the close bonds between family. His sole interest is whatever benefits him the most. I love Georgiana. I love her with my whole heart and soul. He would never understand those types of feelings."

Her tone was cautious. "He used almost those exact same words, Will. When he spoke of your sister, it was with tenderness and concern. Are you certain you are not overreacting?"

He dropped his face in his hands. "Why are you defending him?" he yelled through his fingers. "Why?"

"Because the only thing I know about him is that he was raised at Pemberley and spoiled by your father. I know he is now unwelcome here and, from what he shared yesterday evening, he wants to marry your sister. *That* is what I know about George Wickham." She gulped in air. "What I know about *you,* is that you have been equally as critical of me as you are of Mr. Wickham and, until yesterday, you acted like I was not welcome at Pemberley as well.

In the melee, Georgiana's appearance surprised him. She stood inches inside the dining room doorway with her hands clasped tightly together in front of her. Her neck was bowed.

"I do not want to marry George Wickham."

Darcy cursed under his breath in frustration. Elizabeth easily discerned he was upset at being overheard discussing a man he despised, as well as being disappointed in his physical limitations which kept him from going to his sister.

Elizabeth stood and went to her, taking her elbow and drawing her closer to Darcy's side of the table. Georgiana followed like a lamb.

"Thank you, Georgiana, for expressing yourself clearly. When I meet him, I will be sure to tell him your exact words. We will be done with him. He promised never to bother us again."

Darcy growled. "You will not be going alone, Elizabeth. Reynolds will accompany you. Your directions are to invite him to the porch where I will be seated so I can watch out for you. I'll have my rifle handy in case he attempts to bring you harm."

"I'm sure that won't be necessary, but I will do as you say." It horrified her that he would speak about shooting a man in the same tone he would have invited his foreman or his cousin to shoot rats in the barn."

She sought a means to draw Georgiana out. "Are you hungry, Sister?"

Georgiana looked between them both and shook her head in the negative.

"You need to eat." Darcy tried his best to keep it from being a command. "Sit, and Elizabeth will serve you."

Georgiana sat complacently, and Elizabeth watched her start picking at the fabric on her skirt, her head still bent. Her hair had been pulled back into a braid and her face had been washed. The blouse and skirt she wore were wrinkled, and Elizabeth sighed at the remembrance of the huge pile of laundry she needed to do before the next day was done.

Maggie had helped her with the task at the end of her first week at Pemberley, and she greatly appreciated the woman's strong back and arm muscles. It was a thankless job which would be made easier with the hot sunshine. Elizabeth did enjoy burying her face in clean laundry. Having the smell of fresh bed sheets and towels was a worthy reward for their hard work. Bending over a scalding iron heated on the kitchen stove, on the other hand, was not her favorite task.

As she placed a small portion of food on a plate, a thought occurred to her.

"Georgiana, other than not wanting to marry Wickham, I'm wondering what it is you do want in life? I know so little about you."

"I don't know."

"You've not thought of it then?"

She shrugged her shoulders. When the girl shook her head without replying, Elizabeth decided to change tactics.

"Then I will tell you what we want instead." Elizabeth swiped at a few crumbs left on the table. "We want you." Finally, Georgiana looked up and focused on her face. "We want you to wake up each day happy you are here because you know your presence is desired and that your happiness is fundamental to our own happiness. Above all else, Georgiana Darcy, we want you."

"You want me?" The unexpected joy in her voice ripped a small tear in Elizabeth's heart, and she could only imagine what it was doing to her husband's.

"More than my next breath." Darcy was floored that his sister assumed he wouldn't want her. Then he thought of how the past years would have looked from her perspective and knew for a certainty that she'd felt unwanted and possibly, unlovable. He couldn't blame her at all.

In spite of Elizabeth's bad judgment in having contact with Wickham, Darcy was eternally grateful she was his wife. His sister was not the little girl he'd remembered from year's past and, in truth, this sixteen-year-old seated across from his wife scared him. She was like a stranger tucked into the features of his sibling.

He looked to Elizabeth, his eyes pleading for her assistance to smooth their way.

"You want *me?* You really want me?" Georgiana repeated in hushed tones.

"I do. We do." He hurried to correct himself. "I'm sorry, Georgie. I assumed you were happier to be in the city with our aunt for female company, or I'd have come and gotten you years ago. I love you dearly."

"But I *love* Pemberley. I love you as well. I have all your letters and would read them over and over and over until they are almost falling apart at every fold."

Darcy hesitated. "Yet, when I saw you last summer, I asked you if you wanted to come home and you didn't want to return here. Was I wrong to not push harder?"

"I thought you really wouldn't want me at Pemberley. I thought you wouldn't want *me.*"

"Never!" Darcy desperately needed better words or actions to express himself. *How could he convince her that he'd been so, so wrong in not bringing her home?* Reaching his hand out for hers, he squeezed gently when she put her small hand in his. Blowing out a breath from his nostrils he kept his eyes on hers—unwavering. "Had I known this was how you truly felt, Georgie, I would have picked you up, tossed you into the wagon, and raced those horses back to Pemberley to keep you here under lock and key. Now that I have you here, I don't...I won't ever let you go."

191

The movement of her lips was the first sign of a smile Elizabeth witnessed from the young girl.

"Since your brother has firmly stated in his boss man's voice that he'll never let you go, I have to ask, do you want to marry?"

"I do not know." Georgiana cleared her throat. "Truly I do not, Elizabeth. In spite of the fact that I had thought I was ready for marriage a year ago, I quickly became aware that I was not at all prepared to manage a home or a husband. I lack confidence in determining whether or not a man is interested in me or my half of Pemberley."

"Your half?" Elizabeth looked between brother and sister. "Half of Pemberley is yours? That is the best of news."

"I'm glad you are pleased, but why?" Her husband had a curious look on his face.

"It means Georgiana will always have a home here. Oh, I'm so happy!" Elizabeth squealed in delight. "As you are aware, females—unattached females—are a rare commodity here, and there will be many boys your age who will seek your attention. Should you find one you love and who loves you, a home would be built and we would be neighbors, just like the Bingleys. What a perfect situation."

"They would want Pemberley." Georgiana flatly stated.

"No, it would not be solely Pemberley they would want." Elizabeth reached her hand across the table, her hand covering the joined hands of the siblings. "One day, a fine young man will see your beauty, your sweet nature, and your quiet dignity and he will want you for his wife. He will be appreciative to be able to build on such fine property, but it will be you he will want in his home."

She wanted to hug the girl, but inherently knew it would not be appreciated. "Oh, Georgiana, I am delighted. Girls are marrying at your age and having the weight of caring for a household and a passel of children. We are grateful you have no definite plans to look for a husband now that we finally have you here."

Seeing, for the first time in a decade, the light in his sister's eyes, Darcy's mind became mired in the past. "You look much like Mother."

For the first time since her arrival, the girl's face lit up like a lantern.

"I do?"

193

"Very much so." Darcy had missed his mom over the years—someone he could talk to and who would listen to him. Now he had an intelligent, caring wife and he felt the blessing even more so. "She had an elegant grace about her, Georgie, and you walk in the same manner she did. Your hair and eyes are so like hers that it's like I'm looking at a younger version of her."

"I wish I had known her," Elizabeth whispered.

"I do as well," Georgiana added. "I desire to be like her in every way."

Into the silence, Elizabeth spoke. "Part of being in charge of a household, which I understand your mother was, are the summer chores. We have a busy day ahead of us, and I would appreciate your help today as we tend to our tasks. We have pies to bake and fruit to process to fill the larder for the winter. Would you be willing?"

"Yes. I do not know how to do what you are asking me, but I'm willing to try."

Darcy had a glimmer of hope for the first time since Elizabeth told him of Wickham. It was a start.

"Georgiana, can you cook?" The dirty clothes could wait, but the peaches would not.

"No, I've never made the attempt."

Well, neither could Jane nor any of her other sisters so it wasn't too much of a disappointment.

"How about laundry?"

"I've not done laundry. In fact, I've never done any housework at all."

"None?" Now it was Elizabeth's turn to be incredulous. "Who performed the tasks at your aunt's home?"

"There was an Oriental woman named Mrs. Chung. She did all the daily chores while her husband worked in the gardens and the yard. I did what my aunt assigned me to do."

"And what was that, might I ask?" Elizabeth knew from the young girl's attitude that her life would probably not be getting any easier with Darcy's sister home.

"I would accompany her on visits to her neighbors and friends and help her choose fabrics for new dresses, as well as ribbons and trim for our bonnets." By the time she finished her sentence, her voice was so soft that both Darcy and Elizabeth leaned towards her.

"Well, that's a fine sort of accomplishment, I imagine." Gesturing towards the plate in front of the girl, Elizabeth got up to refill Darcy's coffee cup. Seating herself alongside her husband, she closed her eyes briefly as she thought about how the morning had unfolded so far. Though it was as she'd expected, she felt they had taken two steps forward and two steps back. She was hoping the steps forward had been giant leaps so there was at least some small progress to show.

Sweat dripped off Elizabeth's brow and the wet patches under her arms had grown until they almost reached her waist. Georgiana and Maggie looked the same. Darcy had tried to help the women by peeling peaches, but the fragile fruit didn't survive the calluses on his fingers.

He was amazed to see the many rows of jars on the drain boards and four warm pies in the window cooling.

The outside temperature had risen to record highs while the inside temperature was sweltering due to the constant feeding of the kitchen stove. It took a lot of wood and heat to keep the pots of water boiling so the jars would be safe to eat from during the cold. When the last kettle was empty and the hot water poured into the sink to drain, Darcy felt the heat was so intense that what moisture was left in the pot would evaporate on its own.

"Who wants first turn at the bathing room?" Elizabeth looked over the jars with pride. "Maggie?"

"Not tonight. I'll clean up at the cabin. If you ladies are finished, I'll head on home now."

"Please, go." Elizabeth went to throw her arms around the older woman, but changed her mind at the last minute. It was just plain too hot. Once Maggie was gone, she touched Georgiana's arm.

"Ack! You are as sticky as I am. Do you want to bathe first to get rid of the peach juice we are wearing?"

"And the smell?" Georgiana replied.

Darcy's hearing picked up the sound of his sister's whisper-soft giggle, and he was amazed at how quickly it went from his ears to his heart. His wife had, indeed, worked her magic on his Georgiana, chatting to her about ugly bonnets and the antics of the two sets of twins who had been on the train, and then the boat to Oregon City with Jane and her.

Darcy had listened with pleasure as the three females bickered back and forth. Together, they accomplished a phenomenal task. His chest filled with pride and contentment.

Then he remembered Wickham.

"Mr. Wickham." Elizabeth called into the grove on the evening of the next day. "Mr. Wickham, I have a message for you."

When he didn't show himself right away, she was concerned he had changed his mind about showing up at Pemberley and relieved at the same time.

Finally, he stepped out from behind a tree. His hat was tilted to the side, and he was chewing on a stalk of grass. His clothes were neat and pressed, and his smile was as friendly as it had been the day they met.

"You didn't bring Georgie with you."

"That was not what we agreed upon, sir. You were to give me a note for her. However, that will not be necessary. She stated clearly in front of her brother and me that she has no intention or desire to marry you. Whatever relationship you had prior to this time is ended." She took in a quick breath. "My husband is seated on the porch with his rifle to his shoulder. He tells me you would know whether or not his aim was reliable."

Wickham's face took on a pale hue.

"He asked that you walk directly to him should you have a question or any confusion as to the stance of the Darcys. If not, you are to leave."

"You can't want this, Elizabeth." He whispered so his voice would not travel in the stillness of the air. "Surely your woman's heart screams at the unfairness shown to me by your husband."

"Mr. Wickham," she was now exasperated and wanted the interview to end. "My greatest desire is to have peace in my household and right now you are disturbing it. I ask that you follow Will's directive. It was not a suggestion."

"I'll go, Mrs. Darcy, only because you asked me so nicely. But tell Darcy that I will not forget the way I've been treated."

She nodded, turned, and marched briskly back to the porch. She felt the discomfort of his eyes piercing between her

198

shoulders, and she wished she had not refused the foreman's presence as she wished George Wickham far away from Pemberley. The instant she put her foot on the first step, Will's gun discharged. The barrel was aimed at the peach trees. The bullet spun its deadly path towards Wickham. Spinning around, she looked to where they had been standing. He was gone.

Chapter 13

"You shot him?" Horror filled her chest and Elizabeth feared her brain would explode.

"No. I did not." Calmly Darcy leaned the barrel of the rifle against the door frame, then pointed to where Wickham had been. "Although I do believe that big, fat peach about six feet above his head might not have survived. Of course, I was hoping to break the stem so it would drop and make a mess all over him before he fled."

"Fitzwilliam Darcy!" She couldn't believe he'd actually pulled the trigger. "Well, I am certain he messed himself, but I doubt it's his head he'll need to wash when he gets back to town." Elizabeth was so relieved, she dropped into the chair next to him and smacked him on his arm. "I can't believe you did that."

Darcy giggled—like a girl. Then he burst into laughter, and she knew his mirth was because of her.

"Oh, Lord, that was good." Using the collar of his robe, he wiped the tears from his eyes and reached over to take her hand in his. He ran his thumb back and forth over hers as if the gentle movements were instinctual. "Of all the things I thought would come out of your mouth, Mrs. Darcy, that absolutely was not it."

His smile was so beautiful that her heart flip-flopped right in her chest. Her fingers tingled where her skin touched his and she worried sweat would gather in her palm, making the position of their joined hands less than pleasant.

Out of necessity, her hands had traversed every square inch of his body from his toes to the tips of his hair, but this was the first time since he had handed her out of the wagon her first day at Pemberley that he initiated contact with her. She liked the feelings his touch inspired far more than she'd anticipated and wondered at this new aspect of being so close to him.

"Will?" While she hated to disturb his pleasant countenance, Elizabeth needed information to explain what had just happened.

"Yes?"

"While Thomas Gray said that ignorance is bliss, I choose to disagree wholeheartedly with him. Ignorance of a man's character can lead a woman or a girl to become entangled in something disastrous, and she can be endangered while being completely unaware of the risk. Often it only takes a few facts to help her clearly see her course." He closed his eyes and she knew he was aware she was speaking of Wickham. "What has happened to cause dissention between you two?"

When he started to pull his hand away, she tightened her grip. Once she felt him relax again, she understood he would finally provide the answers to this conundrum.

"If you asked him, he would tell you I was jealous of the attention my father paid to him—and in many ways, he would not be wrong."

"Husband, if your father was here, I'd give him a piece of my mind." She was angry.

He smiled, then his thumb stroked faster on hers.

"Thank you for that." Taking a deep breath, he continued. "About a year and a half ago, Wickham ran into Georgiana while she was shopping in Portland with Aunt. I don't know…," he brushed his free hand through his hair, "it seems like he, at that time, hadn't sought her out. The meeting was quite by accident as I understand it. By then, Georgie had shot up and was starting to get her womanly form. She was painfully shy and uncertain with all the changes she was going through. She wasn't yet fifteen."

He tightened his grip. "Over the next few months, George made sure he would walk by the Fitzwilliam's house when my sister was sitting on the porch enjoying the spring. Then he would follow her into the bookstore and seek her out. My aunt is not a great reader, so she typically left her there alone until her own purchases were completed elsewhere." He paused. "Apparently, Wickham decided the best way to get ownership of

Pemberley was to marry my sister. He pursued her secretly until she believed herself in love."

"Where was your aunt? Your cousins? How could they have allowed their unprotected family member to venture alone in a city? Fitzwilliam! Responsible parents don't do that."

"I was unaware of this at the time."

"Did it not bother Georgiana that Wickham was older than you, and you are far older than she is?"

"You think I'm old?"

She heard his hesitancy. "Does it matter? Will!" She squeezed his hand hard. "Listen to me, please." Elizabeth was surprised a man Wickham's age had pursued someone of such tender years.

"Portland is a busy place and my aunt is constantly flitting here and there. I now know that she wasn't paying that close of attention to my sister, so, no, she was completely unaware."

"Oh, no." Now it was her turn to stroke his thumb with her own. "But she was too young to marry."

"Not by law."

"I understand they could have married with permission from family, but who would have given their approval? Certainly you would not, and I can't imagine Richard would accept their plans either."

"No, we would not have voluntarily done so."

"Then they could not have married. While she is a lovely girl who is truly sweet, her features still have the fresh bloom of youth. She looks her age. No Justice of the Peace with eyesight would have thought her old enough."

Darcy's grip became firm and his body tense. "Elizabeth, had they…had Wickham…oh, Lord." He rubbed his whiskers with his right hand. "Had he convinced her to be intimate and there were consequences, there would have been nothing else we could have done except allow a wedding."

Elizabeth's inhale pressed her against the back of the chair. "Oh, no. Oh, No! Oh, NO!"

"I happened to travel to Portland on business and desired nothing more than to see Georgie. You can imagine my surprise when she shared the joy of her heart's attachment to George Wickham. He had convinced her that, as a longtime family friend, I would be pleased with their courtship and happy when they wed. Especially since, according to him and apparently her as well, I didn't truly want her at Pemberley."

"Oh, my!" She could think of nothing else to say. Her pulse pounded to the point it was all she could hear, and a sick feeling churned in her stomach. "Oh, no! Did he?"

"No, thank God!"

"I can't imagine. Poor girl."

"Since they hadn't expected my arrival, she was prepared to meet him at the back of the bookstore for a picnic he had planned in a secluded spot by the river. Even though she didn't realize what was bound to happen, I knew." Darcy shuddered and Elizabeth tightened her grip.

"Did you tell her? Will, please tell me you told her the truth about his nefarious plans."

"I did not." Darcy sighed. "I told Richard and my aunt so they could keep Wickham from her. Then I met him behind the store. I thought I'd made my displeasure known, and told him never to attempt to see Georgiana or come to Pemberley at the risk of his own safety."

Elizabeth released his hand and threw both of hers into the air.

"Do you see what I mean? Ignorance is not bliss." She stood and marched down the porch steps, turned and marched back up. Sitting back in the chair, she pondered what she'd learned. It distressed her that she had inadvertently invited such a vile man to their home, putting Georgiana at risk. "I wish I had known."

She could see his frustration and knew it was with himself. "How could you? There was no priority to share that particular information with you while I laid in bed that first week. Trust me, I had plenty of other things on my mind when I was even able to think clearly."

"But you said nothing since. Will, I can't help but wonder if there's anything else you haven't shared that I ought to know."

He reached back over and took her hand. This time she felt solidarity.

"I'm not sure, to be honest. I'll try not to keep anything from you if you ask. I can see how my keeping this to myself was misplaced protection."

"So you weren't just trying to be bossy and in control?"

He chuckled. "No, I wasn't."

She rocked back in the chair, his hand sliding back and forth with hers.

"I appreciate your reassurance," she chuckled softly. "Since you are being so verbose, I'm wondering why you have not hired help for Maggie before now? The thought of her cooking and cleaning for you four men boggles my mind."

He appeared relieved at the sudden change of topic. "Simply, there was no one to hire. Each time a woman came into town, she was quickly snapped up by someone who had their own property. And it hasn't been terribly hard for Maggie. We tended to wear the same clothing for a period of time as there wasn't a woman here to complain about our smell. I purchased canned goods in bulk at the mercantile. Our fruit and vegetables in the orchard and garden tended to fall to waste. Obviously, it wasn't an ideal situation, but it was what worked. Melvin loves to garden. He uses his evenings and free day to plow and nurture, while Dan loves to hunt and fish." Darcy moved their joined hands to the arm of his wheelchair. "There is more ready work and housing in Portland so few want to move upriver to the Willamette now. While there is still land available, most can't afford the filing fee or the expense of setting up housing on acreage this far from town where there are no roads and no help to build."

"Is that why John and Maggie didn't build on their property?"

"No. Their circumstances were different." Darcy's brow furrowed. "They had 640 acres of prime forestland with an adequate water supply and plenty of level ground. They had built a small rough cottage so they could stay the years needed to satisfy the government that they were homesteading the land grant. Their plans were to expand and build onto their home when babies came. That first year, the weather was fierce. Too much rain and snow in the winter and no rain and soaring temperatures in the summer. For Maggie's protection from the elements they accepted an offer of temporary housing in the cabin here. They never left."

"No children."

"No, there were none."

"I see." She looked down at her lap, sadness for the Reynolds' filling her soul. "Do you want a large family, Will?"

Speaking of something so personal while seated next to him, her hand in his, flushed her cheeks and caused her heart to pound. She was afraid to look at him to see his reaction.

"I want a happy home."

"Then we are finding something to agree upon." It was the perfect answer.

"Are you happy, Elizabeth? I mean, do you see the potential for happiness between you and me in the future?" He waved at his leg and she watched the movement of his hand.

Pausing to consider her reply, she realized that everything about her marriage other than her husband was pleasing to her. She didn't mind hard work, especially when she saw the immediate benefit to others. But she missed the freedoms of having time to herself to read, take long walks, and enjoy being alone. The few minutes she was able to spend on the porch were not enough.

A thought occurred which immediately excited her.

"Will, do you remember the family with the two sets of twins who disembarked at the same time I did?" She blushed again at the remembrance of the first impression she made, her clothes sopping wet and her hat and hair askew.

"I recall very little about that day."

The redness in his cheeks belied his claim, though she was pleased he was being cautious with his speech.

"We traveled from the East Coast with them and found them to be exceedingly pleasant. They had saved to purchase some acreage, but if the only property available is distant, they might need a place to live. I'm concerned about them." And she was. They had not been able to afford accommodations at the Occidental in San Francisco and watched every penny as they shopped in China Town. They had packed a large hamper of food for the travels so little money was spent at the train stops.

He answered. "The bunkhouse is divided into two parts. If you would like to have John invite the family here until they settle, you are more than welcome… if you do not think all those children wouldn't get in your way. If they would be willing to help on the ranch, I'd pay them a wage and provide their lodgings."

"Would you?" *Who was this man?* She had expected him to be belligerent when she'd asked to go see Wickham alone. Instead, even though he'd had to practically swallow his tongue, he'd acceded to her desire after she explained that she doubted Wickham would show himself with the foreman visible. Her willingness to have John, Dan, and Melvin hidden in the area before Wickham's arrival had seemed to make it easier for him to agree.

During the whole of their acquaintance, from the first moment she'd set eyes on his disapproving, disdainful countenance at the docks, she could never have imagined the freeness of speech they were sharing on the porch. She liked it. A lot.

"If it would please you and provide assistance during the ranch's busiest time of the year, then, yes, I'd agree to host them here. However, do not get your hopes up, Elizabeth. We are not the only family who could use hired hands. They may already have found a situation that works for them."

"I thank you."

He cleared his throat. "I had asked you if you were happy here, and you did not respond."

"I didn't, did I?" She sighed. "You've asked a question that is not easy to answer. Even though I was busy in Baltimore helping my family with the same tasks I'm doing here, I certainly was not as busy. I've had so little time that I feel I've lost myself."

"I'm sorry."

She smiled at him. "There you go again—apologizing." She untangled her fingers from his and patted the top of his hand. "I've a reputation in my family for being stubbornly independent, quick to display my temper, and quick to judge. I fear I still have those tendencies, and you, sir, have been my target of choice. Nonetheless, my worry about your health, my future, learning what I need to manage your home properly, and the shear abundance of tasks that greet me each day, has allowed tiredness to creep in and soften my worst characteristics. I fear that an improvement in your situation, a reduction in needing to perform these tasks, and more time to think and ponder, will return me to unrestrained fits of anger and belligerence that you will not welcome."

Elizabeth bravely looked to see his disgust. No wonder he'd been so attracted to her sister. She had none of those flaws, and apparently Georgiana had none of them either. Except it wasn't abhorrence she was seeing. Rather, he was grinning from ear to ear.

"What is the matter with you?" she quizzed him, her brow raised. "You shouldn't be so pleased."

Again he laughed, and she wanted to keep him doing so for the rest of their lives.

"You amaze me, Elizabeth Darcy. There's not a woman I know, not that I know many, who would be so honest about herself. Every day that passes, I am more and more pleased you are the woman who stood beside me at the Justice of the Peace. Do not think I've failed to notice your hard work and your tender care of me and my sister. I've come to value your opinions and hope I don't fall back into selfishly disregarding them in the days ahead."

"Thank you, Will. That's good to hear." She again clasped his hand. "I look forward to when you are able to stand on both legs and walk through the trees with me. I miss taking long walks. I don't even mind doing so in the rain."

"I ask you not to go alone." He shook his head when she started to speak. "If you do, take a pistol. We have bears aplenty in these woods and other varmints who could bring you harm."

212

His request was reasonable. "Very well. I will have you know that had I tried to dislodge that peach with your rifle, I would have hit it bullseye and Wickham would have worn the fruit in his hair all the way back to town."

Surprised, he asked. "You know how to fire a gun?"

She again patted the back of his hand and rose to reenter the house.

"Not at all." Smiling, she whisked her skirt to the side and walked through the door, his laughter following her all the way to her room.

Later, when the house was settled, Elizabeth sat in front of the vanity to brush out her hair. One of her favorite things about Pemberley was the showering room. Having sun-warmed water stream over her, washing the perspiration and dust of the day from her head to her toes, was refreshing. Remembering sharing bath water with her sisters made her enjoyment all the more pleasurable.

It had been quite a day. Drawing closer to both Georgiana and Will had been a challenge, and she felt like she had only taken baby steps towards her goal of a happy home life. Hearing her husband laugh and seeing him being comfortable in her presence was more than she could have hoped for on their wedding day. Hearing his words of appreciation nourished her starving heart. And, his hands…his touch…she sighed, looking at her image in the mirror. The dreamy look in his eyes was a perfect reflection of the small seed of affection growing in her heart. *Would it continue to flourish or would his unthinking words and her quick temper lop it off at the roots?* She knew what she wanted, but she also knew herself—and Will.

His expression of being happier each day they were married excited her to her bones. *What woman didn't want to hear this from her mate?* She had no clue he felt that way. No clue at all. She snorted! *Who was she to know his mind?* They truly knew so little about each other.

Yet this was the fate of all mail-order couples, this coming together, taking vows before man and God to live together until death parted them. Over the years, both she and her sister had heard rumors and reports of occasions where the woman had been put in peril, where one or the other of the couple—or sometimes both of them—had been less than honest about their looks, circumstances, or character. Will had promised her nothing before she'd accepted him. She had allowed herself to be romanced by Bingley's letters into accepting a situation unknown to her. Hoping Bingley's friend was much like the man who authored the missives, Elizabeth had tied her name to Darcy's before she'd ever seen him. Finding out he'd written the letters had been a shock. Remembering that he'd been responsible for each winsome word was a challenge.

She sighed again. Placing the brush back on the table, she considered her husband's easy acceptance of having the Pedersen family join them at Pemberley. Tomorrow, she would travel to town with John and Maggie for services and to gather supplies while the White brothers stayed with Will. While she hoped the family had found a good situation for themselves, she also, in the most secret place of her heart, wished they had not. It would be a wonder to have another female set of helping hands, another married woman to talk to, and children to fill the place with noise.

Children. For the first time since the accident, Elizabeth thought of what would have to happen before there would be a pregnancy and a baby. Before, it had been something she was resigned to do, knowing it was a fundamental part of married life. Now? She blushed even though there was no one else in the room to see. The possibility of finding enjoyment, as Jane had whispered was achievable for newlyweds, was disconcerting, but not unwanted.

Picking up the brush, she pulled at her hair with vigor. Lord, she was a wreck at the thought of it. Imagine when it came time to actually…well, she would think on it no more.

215

Chapter 14

The next morning, before she left for services in town, Darcy spilled the whole pitcher of pancake syrup down the front of himself and his robe. It hadn't been entirely his doing. His sister had accidentally bumped his elbow when he'd lifted the container to pour the sticky sweetness on the tall stack of cakes. Fortunately, the brown sugar and water had cooled, leaving no burns to treat.

The stored rainwater would have been too cold to use the shower room. Instead, water was boiled and the horse trough retrieved. The downstairs make-shift bedroom had no room for the desk, which had been pushed against the back wall, the narrow bed Darcy was sleeping in, and the galvanized container, so they put it in the middle of the living room. Georgiana quickly finished breakfast, as did the others, while the men filled the buckets and put the chairs from the porch inside the large oval vessel.

This would be only the second time she had bathed him. Since the first time, he'd been able to roll himself into the bathing room and scoot himself over to a chair in the shower. Elizabeth had been required to reposition his leg both before and after he finished. They had both seemed relieved it was a task made much easier with the wheelchair and his position on the first floor.

Her introspection of the previous night was still embedded in her mind, and she wondered at the task before her. Gathering towels, wash clothes, and a clean robe, she set them on a small table next to the large sofa where there was enough space for him to maneuver into position.

She had to marvel at the skill he had developed. His mobility came at a price. The bruise on his back was ringed with purple and filled with mottled yellows and green, though they were not nearly as bright and deep as they had been.

When he lowered his robe to his waist, muscled cords rippled down his upper arms, and his forearms flexed as he wiped the initial mess from his chest with the damp cloth she'd handed him. Dark curly hairs sprung back from his scrubbing and Elizabeth was amazed at not paying attention to them before.

She moved her eyes before he could catch her gazing at him. It would only embarrass him and humiliate her.

He untied the belt and scooted to the front of the chair, again using his powerful arms. They had developed a routine of her bending so he could put his arms around her neck while he

218

lifted with his good leg and she steadied him with her hands while he stood. He would then twist on his good foot until he dropped down onto his bed or the chair in the bath. They never made eye contact. This time was different.

She was powerless to look anywhere else and, in retrospect, she was aware that the glimmer in his eyes was attraction. She had no desire to look away. Her mother had openly discussed the impact of desire on a man to both her and Jane before leaving Baltimore, but Elizabeth had no appetite for finding out how accurate her brief descriptions had been.

Some strange emotion traveled through her, and even though she'd been in his close proximity before, it was as if it was the first time. He had to be feeling the same as she watched him look from her eyes to her mouth and back.

Was he going to kiss her? Instead of being appalled, which she felt she should have been, she was curious. Would his lips taste of the slice of bacon he'd already consumed before the spill? Would they be firm or soft? Would they be a good fit? It was all so disconcerting. She turned her head towards the makeshift bath.

"Can you make it?"

"I can." The timber of his voice seemed deeper, but she wasn't going to look back at him now. The hairs on the back of her arms still stood tall and the weakness at her knees threatened to topple them both. *Get ahold of yourself, Lizzy!* Her admonition worked, and she settled him on the chair and hefted his leg so it

219

rested properly. Completely disconcerted, she hurried from the room.

The sun was peeking over the horizon when the happy group piled into the buggy to head to town. Dan drove the wagon behind them for ease in picking up the supplies, and Elizabeth was grateful Darcy had insisted in case the Pedersen family required transportation to Pemberley. Melvin would keep an eye on her husband in case any needs arose.

When they stopped for a break, Georgiana stepped next to Elizabeth and whispered into her ear.

"Lizzy, I hope Wickham hasn't *messed* around and delayed his departure from Oregon City."

Elizabeth had been surprised to learn that the young girl had a sense of humor that easily matched her own. A picture flashed in her mind of Wickham standing below the peach tree, juice dripping from his hair down his face. "Oh, I'm fairly certain he didn't *mess* around."

"What I would have given to have seen the expression on his face when Will fired the rifle."

"I do believe you have recovered from his treachery, Georgie dear." Maggie had been charged with keeping Georgiana in the house while Elizabeth had walked to the orchard grove. When the events had been repeated to the ladies, Georgiana had laughed until she'd cried. Her brother had delighted to see her mood lifted, and it made for a happy atmosphere in the house.

When they arrived at the small church, Elizabeth was pleased to see Cynthia Pedersen with her husband Harald. Their children were clean, with large smiles on their faces. The parents' faces, upon closer inspection, were lined with stress.

Elizabeth got straight to the point. "Have you found property yet?

"We have not, Elizabeth. Harald has searched for good land, but he has had to take on work at the lumber mill so we can afford the cramped rooms behind the hotel. He is a farmer, not a laborer. He knows cows and crops." Tears showed at the corners of her eyes. "The pot of gold was not located in Oregon for the Pedersen family."

"I am sorry to hear of your distress, Cynthia. However, my husband has offered you housing and work at Pemberley. We have a large garden tended by one of our workers, but have need of someone who understands when to move the cattle from the bottomland to the fields hidden in the timber. Each year, the beef is sold at auction, so he's hoping to find someone knowledgeable to cull out the herds."

"Please let me speak to my husband." Cynthia placed her arm on Elizabeth's. "It sounds like you know much about cows yourself, my friend."

Elizabeth laughed. "Heavens, no. I'm only repeating what Will told me. I wouldn't know a boy cow from a girl."

After the service, the women met again with a hearty, unhesitating agreement from Harald Pedersen. Arrangements were made to pick them up from their rooms as soon as the supplies were loaded. It promised to be a pleasant return trip.

With the family settled at Pemberley, the conversation between the four females during chores made the tasks seem to go much faster. Harald, a quiet man just like the others, settled in to his new responsibilities with gusto, and the children all took turns entertaining Darcy as he watched them from the porch.

"Your man, he's a good man, Lizzy." Cynthia noted as the women each held the end of a bedsheet and twisted it until the water poured out onto the ground. "He will make a good father. My children already adore him."

"They like him because he knows how to tease them, Cynthia." Georgiana added with a smile as she fastened the clothespin on the corner of the towel where it hung over the line.

"I knew from the way he used to carry you around on his hip when he was a lad that one day he should have a houseful of his own." Maggie Reynolds had to add her opinion, which made Georgiana's smile grow from one ear to the other.

"Ladies!" Each time the women gathered, the topic vacillated between their families and food, such is the nature of females. Elizabeth watched over her sister as she was unmarried and innocent. She had to laugh at herself. She was married and innocent—a circumstance she was thinking more about as each day passed. She wondered if Will spent so much time thinking of the same or if men were different from their counterparts.

"Oh, do not worry, Sister." Georgiana immediately jumped in. "Living with men like Richard and his brother, Simon, I found out where babies come from a long time ago."

"Georgiana Darcy!" Elizabeth burst into giggles. "I didn't learn that until just before I left to head west. You are a daring young lady, and I believe we need to lock you in your room when a single boy is around."

The other females joined in the merriment, including her sister.

"Of course, my two might be a bit young yet at eight-years old. But they grow up quickly—too quickly." Cynthia added, her voice filled with curiosity. "I am wondering, Georgie, what exactly did you learn from your cousins?"

The question was bold, and Georgiana's face flared a vibrant red. She swallowed before she blandly stated, "They said that when a man and woman get married and they decide to have a child, the woman gets fat around the middle. When the baby's room is decorated, it is ready to come out."

Elizabeth looked at the shock on Maggie and Cynthia's faces and knew it mirrored her own. That was certainly not what her mother had explained.

Maggie softly inquired. "And how does the baby get in her tummy and come back out?"

If anything, Georgiana's discomfort increased, though it seemed it was humanly impossible.

"Oh, I don't know *that* part."

"And I hope you don't need to know for many years yet." Elizabeth added as they all laughed so hard they had to wipe their tears on the washed clothes only to have to wash them again. None of the women minded.

The hot weather continued, and the ground was starting to show the absence of rain. Harald, Cynthia, and their four children had been at Pemberley for almost a month and the ranch was running smoothly. A full moon promised to light the sky that night as Darcy and Elizabeth sought what little coolness could be found on the front porch after Georgiana had stepped into the bathing room to cool off.

"We've not had much rain, Will. Is this typical for this time of year?"

"Yes, and no." It had become automatic for him to reach for her hand as they sat alongside each other, and she accepted it willingly. "Some summers it rains more days than it does not. Other years, we've had fierce sun through the whole of the month."

"In Baltimore, I'd read news reports of dust storms in the middle of the country from lack of rain and of families having to vacate their homes because they didn't have enough water for basic necessities. I'm afraid I'm not familiar enough with Oregon to know its habits. Do we need to conserve water in the bathing room? How about the wells? Will we be able to pump water if this continues?"

"I thank you for worrying, Elizabeth, but I wished you wouldn't. Pemberley, and any of the other farms and ranches in the area, has never suffered from drought. The rain will come."

Only it didn't. Day after day and night after night the temperatures soared. By the end of August, the water in the reservoir above the bathing room had long run out so that buckets had to be filled from the pump and carried up the ladder to fill it up enough for a quick wash. The men and boys, with the obvious exception of Will, bathed in one of the many creeks found fairly close to the buildings which lightened the demand on the wells. Will worried about his neighbors as Elizabeth repeated the talk from both before and after services on Sunday. It was all about the lack of water.

Elizabeth sat on the porch and watched the river traffic. The Willamette flowed at the same speed and level it had done since her arrival and she wished for the millionth time that they could pump the water to the house—an impossible dream.

She listened as the foreman leaned against one of the posts holding up the roof over the porch as he spoke with Will about the situation.

"I'm concerned about Bingley's place, Will. His property sits on higher ground, and his well wasn't dug as deep as ours."

"I'm glad you brought that up. There are no streams close to his house, and I've no clue if he cleared the trees and underbrush from around his buildings. I've been after him about it since he built there, but being from the east, he's uncommonly attached to the timber."

"Well, I can't imagine him taking the time to log it off once he married. He hadn't done it when I took Maggie over to get the house ready for the new missus." He shook his head at the young man's foolishness.

"No, I think you are right." Darcy considered. "He has a good foreman to care for the place, and I'd hate to step on his toes by sending you over to check on them."

Elizabeth chimed in. "Will, the letter I received from Jane two days ago said they would be traveling from Boston to Baltimore to see my family and expected their stay to be brief. They could be home in about three weeks to see for themselves what needs to be done. I'd wish to have Jane come to a home ready to be lived in, especially with her bringing Miss Bingley back to a place she hasn't seen in over a year. Jane would be mortified if she couldn't make her comfortable."

Both men nodded. Will squeezed her fingers gently. "We will see what we can do."

"Thank you."

Each day that had passed had revealed another layer of her husband's character, and she was growing fonder of him as time sped by. He treated his sister with open love and tenderness and had never once been impatient with the twins, though he hadn't failed to be firm, but kind, when needed.

Thinking back to the first week after his accident, his growly demeanor and grumpy responses, it seemed like he was now a completely different man. Maggie had assured her that Will was unchanged. Elizabeth was left to wonder what it had been about her that had made him incredibly mulish.

227

She wondered if she had changed as much as he had. Oh, she still had her little teases and rebellions, but he met each one with a smile and a quick reply. Sitting out on the porch each night had become their special time. It was then that she finally was introduced to the man behind the letters. Each night, as she followed him to his room to see him tucked in, he quoted William Shakespeare.

Good night, good night! Parting is such sweet sorrow, that I shall say good night till it be morrow.

On this night, as they sat beneath the moon and stars, his rich baritone spoke into the night sky.

The heavens declare the glory of God; and the firmament sheweth his handywork.

Day unto day uttereth speech, and night unto night sheweth knowledge.

"The 19th Psalm; one of my favorites," Elizabeth whispered. "Did you miss the night sky when you were at university?"

"I mourned the loss of sitting under the heavens where nothing impeded my vision of the night sky. When I sailed to England, it was during the summer months and for a week there was no breeze to move the ship. The sailors all complained, but I found such beauty in the stars twinkling from overhead while being reflected on the dark waters of the sea. It was like we were surrounded; encapsulated by pinpoints of light. In my lifetime, I've not seen anything as grand."

She sighed at the vision his words created. His ability to look at nature and appreciate its wonders filled her heart with rejoicing and appreciation for the man she married. He was an intellectual man who she often wished could meet her father. She imagined them having conversations rich in meaning and wisdom. But it was not to be. Darcy had no desire to travel east and her father certainly would never leave his bookroom.

"What are you thinking of so seriously?" he inquired. "You are too silent."

"My father. My family." She placed her free hand over where theirs were already intertwined. "He would like you, I believe."

"That's good to know, Elizabeth."

"Will?"

"Yes."

"Why do you still call me by my full name? Everyone else calls me Lizzy."

He chuckled softly. "I will one day, I promise."

She speculated what might occasion his doing so and wondered if she would be ready when he did.

Chapter 15

"Why did you break your leg, Mr. Darcy?"

"It was an accident, Whitney." The little Pedersen girl stood with her face resting in her cupped hand, her elbow firmly planted on the arm of his wheelchair. Her nose was close to his left arm. Her soft blue eyes were staring directly at his.

"Why did that tree fall on you?"

"The tree didn't fall on me. Only a branch fell on me."

"Why didn't you move the branch? My Daddy moves branches all day long. My mama has to pick slivers from his fingers every night. Does Mrs. Darcy pick slivers from your fingers?"

He thought of all his wife had done for him and realized he'd not had the pleasure. "No, Whitney. I don't have any slivers. Do you?"

Her sweet voice giggled at the question. "No, silly. I don't move branches."

"Then what do you do?"

"I play with my dolly like a good little girl."

Darcy could hear Cynthia Pedersen's tone in her reply.

"And where is your doll?"

"She broke her leg and is in bed."

"She broke her leg? How did she break it?"

Six-year-old Whitney, the precocious half of the girl twins, tilted her head sideways as if wondering at his intelligence.

"A branch fell on it."

He wanted to laugh out loud, but he didn't want to hurt her feelings.

"Well, how about that. What a coincidence."

"What's a coincidence? I kiss my dolly's leg to make it better. Does Mrs. Darcy kiss your leg? It will make it better."

What a thought!

"No, she hasn't yet done so."

"Then you better tell her to try it. Or, probably the doctor should tell her. He would know a kiss is always the best medicine. My daddy says so."

"Your daddy is a smart man."

"I know." She took in a deep breath. "He told me that you have a first name last name like me."

"A first name last name?" He wondered if the little girl had understood and repeated her father correctly.

"Sure, Mr. Darcy." She rolled her eyes like he was a bonehead. "My first name, you know, Whitney? It used to be Mommy's last name. Now it's my first name last name like yours."

It made perfect sense. His mother had chosen his Christian name. When he was little and spent time in his cousin's company, having the Fitzwilliam's being called by their full names when they were into mischief, which was often, had been confusing.

"Do you like your first name last name?"

The little girl shrugged her shoulders. "Not so much."

"Then what would you prefer me to call you?"

She didn't even hesitate. "You can call me Princess Cinderella Whitney Pedersen."

"I can? That sure is a mouthful. Are you sure Whitney isn't good enough?"

She huffed out her little breath and dropped her chin. The resemblance to Elizabeth when she was frustrated with him was uncanny.

"Why do you growl like a bear?" she demanded.

"Why did you change the subject?"

"I didn't change the subject, silly. You did." With that, her eyes moved past him.

He shook his head in confusion. However, Princess Cinderella Whitney Pedersen was distracted by a butterfly who

233

apparently needed chasing as she flew down the stairs and around the corner of the house.

When Elizabeth joined him, he was still shaking his head. Her smile indicated she had possibly been attending to the conversation before coming out onto the porch.

"Why *do* you growl like a bear, Mr. Darcy?" She laughed, and he didn't mind at all.

"I've never been asked 'why' so many times in one conversation since the last time she visited me. That little girl is quite unlike Georgie when she was that age."

"Oh, dear. I hope you do not mind. She is, according to what my mother has long said about me, very much like I was, or am."

He automatically reached for her hand when she sat.

"I don't mind at all."

Over the weeks, a blissful relationship had developed in his household and he was grateful. Georgiana delighted in her interactions with the Pedersen children and Elizabeth was finally able to relax some with the additional help. Harald Pedersen was as knowledgeable as any man about the workings of a cattle ranch and tree farm. John and Maggie were spending less time at the main house and more time together in the evenings. Each building at Pemberley seemed to be filled with contentment.

Life seemed good. Then, he smelled smoke.

The regular discussions between Darcy and Elizabeth about the weather were no longer conversations of the mundane. The water levels in the creeks had fallen to a trickle and the banks of the river below them could be seen where the water line had fallen, turning the muddy soil into parched earth. Even the trees were weeping and drooping from the lack of water. The earth had gone from green to brown and the air popped with static from the dryness. Darcy was worried. Because of him, Elizabeth worried as well.

September weather had been even harsher than July and August, with temperatures remaining hot throughout the night. Dr. Henderson had told Darcy on the day before that he was approximately two weeks from being able to start putting weight on his leg and her husband rejoiced at the news. But his constant fretting over the lack of rain placed a damper on their relief.

The Bingleys were expected within the week… if their arrangements had turned out as planned. They'd had no news since the couple left Boston with Caroline to travel to Baltimore.

Elizabeth could not imagine Jane not corresponding with their latest plans, but suspected the letter had been lost in the long distance it needed to travel. She was excited and anxious to hear about the rest of her family and whether or not the Gardiners would be joining them soon in the Willamette Valley.

Caroline Bingley was a mystery. Each time Elizabeth had asked Will about the younger woman, he merely shrugged and replied, "You'll see." Georgiana had never met Charles' sister, so she was no help at all. It was Maggie who finally shed light on the soon-to-be newest addition to their neighborhood.

"She's a sharply dressed gal with a regal bearing, elegant manners, and the personality of a possum."

Elizabeth had been quite taken aback at the description. Her first contact with the small marsupial, she more commonly knew as an opossum, had been less than pleasant. One had wandered onto the back porch in the early evening when she had surprised it. The teeth-baring, long-nosed critter growled, snarled, and hissed—a frothy foam coming from the sides of its mouth. Scared to her core, she grabbed the broom to swat at it only to have it fall over as if it were dead. Nasty creature! And Maggie had compared Caroline to *that* animal? Unless the school Miss Bingley had attended for the past year had not done their job, it would be a horrible return trip and home life for Jane. Elizabeth was grateful to be at Pemberley and not at Netherfield Ranch.

Looking over the trees off of the back porch, a thin column of dust-colored cloud drifted towards them on the slight breeze. It was the worst of signs. What started as a trickle of smoke and a waft of the smell soon turned into a pillar making their eyes water.

Netherfield!

No orders had to be given. Will was proud of his crew as they grabbed axes and saws, throwing them into the back of the wagon along with blankets the women hauled from the house. Georgiana took the kids to the front porch to get them as far from the putrid air as possible while Elizabeth, Maggie, and Cynthia filled every canteen and covered container possible from the pump. The men were off in minutes.

Darcy yearned to be next door more than he longed for his next breath. Charles Bingley was a good friend who had already suffered devastation from the loss of his parents. Losing his home…well, Will couldn't think of it. He'd hoped the younger man had gone ahead and instructed his foreman to clear the land around his house. At this point in time, that's all that would save his property.

"Will," Elizabeth moved next to him and rested her hand on his shoulder. It was a comforting touch. "Whatever happens, we will help out how we can."

Though it was a statement, it was cloaked in question and concern. Surely she knew him well enough by now to know he would do anything for someone he cared for. Surely.

"Yes." He nodded, looking to the sky.

Fire has a funny way of telling its own story. Whatever is burning can change the color of the smoke from pale to black. Dry Douglas fir, hemlock, spruce, and pine would snap and spark, sending up smoke that was fairly pleasing to the nostrils—a woody smell common in campfires and fireplaces. Adding in foreign substances found on a home site would alter the sight and fragrance until you didn't have to be close to know what was burning.

By the afternoon, Darcy knew the fire had reached the house or the barn. A summer's worth of stored hay would disintegrate in seconds, fueling the flames and intensifying the heat. All the memories Bingley had treasured of his parents were possibly gone, as were the items the new Mrs. Bingley had packed and brought west from Baltimore. He suffered for their loss.

"Will, the children need you." Elizabeth roused him from his negative thoughts. "They are fearful the fire will reach Pemberley and want to run home and grab their things. I don't believe they will be able to settle down unless you talk to them."

Again, he nodded his head. Grabbing the crutches from where he had earlier rested them next to his chair, he hobbled into the house. He had barely sat down when Whitney took up her post.

"Are you afraid of the fire, Mr. Darcy?"

"Yes and no, Whitney."

"Why is there a fire?"

"Because we have had no rain."

"Why hasn't it rained?"

"Because there are no rain clouds."

"Why aren't there any rain clouds? Don't they like it here anymore?"

Although he sighed, he smiled at her questions.

"My Pa says the rain will come." Markus, or maybe it was Timothy, spoke up. He had yet to be able to tell them apart, though Elizabeth and Georgiana seemed able to do so.

"He's right. The rain will come."

"When?" All four little voices chimed in at once.

"That, I don't know." Darcy sat straighter in his chair. "But what I do know for a fact is that a fire at the Bingley place will not make it as far as Pemberley. My father took on the task of cutting the timber back from the creeks between us to clear the way for the water to run freer and to keep a fire from having anything to burn. Once it gets to the water, there will be no place for the fire to go but out."

"Pemberley won't catch on fire?" the other boy twin asked.

"Son, listen closely. Pemberley will not catch on fire. We are safe here."

"Is my dolly safe in the bunkhouse?" Whitney's eyes appeared bigger and brighter than he'd ever noticed before.

"Yes, missy. Your dolly is safe and snug, which is where you should be right now, in your beds snuggled down for the night."

Whitney's twin, Christine, was the shyest of all the Pedersen children. She'd never approached him and, as far as he could remember, she'd never said a word to him. Before he could guess what the little girl was up to, she'd carefully climbed onto his lap and tucked herself under his left arm. The wispy softness of her hair tickled his chest where his top shirt button was opened. Christine laid the side of her face against him and started worrying the second button on his shirt with her little fingers.

He hadn't held a child of six since the day he left for university. Georgiana had been exactly the same size and shape. Her hair even held the same smell of sunshine he'd remembered all those years.

Searing pain ripped through his middle at the amount of time he'd lost with his sister. Instinctively, his long arms captured Christine to him and he began to whisper comforting nothings only she could hear. He was so grateful his family was close— pleased Georgiana enjoyed her place on the ranch and that Elizabeth was his wife. So pleased.

At that particular infinitesimal second in time, Elizabeth Darcy fell heart-stoppingly, overwhelmingly, head-over-heels in love with her husband. *How could this tender man be the same person who, almost three months ago, had used such harsh words against her?* The memory seemed so long ago, and she vowed right then that she would bury it as deeply as possible so it would no longer affect her view of this man.

The door to the back door slammed, causing them all to jump. The men must be back.

Darcy looked in the direction of the noise, but Elizabeth knew he couldn't get up with his leg and the little one on his lap. However, when she went to investigate, she found the hallway empty. Before she could turn around, the front door shut with a resounding bang.

"Elizabeth!" Darcy yelled. "A storm is coming. The wind closed the doors. Everyone to the porch."

Cynthia hurried to remove Christine from Darcy where he pulled himself up to walk to the front porch. Blessedly, in the setting sun the approaching dark clouds were a welcome sight.

Lifting his nose, beyond the acrid smell of the neighbor's turmoil, he smelled the dampness signaling incoming rain.

"Come!" he yelled back into the house. They were about to witness a marvel not often seen this close to the Oregon coast. Thunderstorms and lightening were not exceptionally rare. Nevertheless, the typical rainstorm was one heavy cloud attempting to lighten its load after another with very little reprieve, noise, or flash.

Once the children were gathered on the porch, he instructed, "Look for the first strike of lightning and then count as far as you can until you hear the thunder. In this way, we can find out how close the storm is."

As soon as he sat in his chair, the twins surrounded him, the boys at his back and the girls at his side.

"I'm afraid of the noise," Christine whispered as close to his ear as she could get.

"It's a smart girl you are, Christine," Darcy reassured her. "What we will witness is power unlike anything man can perform. It is fear-inspiring. But think of what it will do for the earth, little one. What will it bring?"

"Rain."

"Yes, Christine, it will. And what will the rain do for Pemberley and Netherfield Ranch? And the rivers and the trees?"

"They will fill up."

"Absolutely." He leaned over and buried his nose in her hair. "So we need to look at the thunder and lightning as God's way of announcing good news to us. Rain is coming."

Timothy—or was it Markus—spoke up. "I imagine God would have to make such a big noise cause he's so big."

"I imagine so." Darcy's explanation and agreement seemed to ease the concerns so when the first flash hit, the children started counting in unison.

Elizabeth wanted to throw her arms around her husband and hug him tight or, better yet, bump little Christine off his lap and take her place. Bright red flushed her cheeks as Cynthia cleared her throat, a knowing smile on her lips.

When the thunder clapped, they all jumped. None of the children heard the wagon approach, so intent were they on watching the sky.

Elizabeth noticed first and immediately stepped from the porch to welcome the weary, soot-covered men. Earlier, the women had taken turns hauling bucket after bucket into the reservoir for cleaning the men when they returned. Cooler water had been set aside to tend any burns the men might have sustained.

With intense satisfaction, only minor wounds dotted the arms and hands of the tired firefighters, though their shirts and pants had small pinholes where the fabric had been scorched. Behind the men came another wagon, this time with Bingley's ranch hands in the back. Exhausted and discouraged, they accepted Darcy's hospitality, quickly eating the meal Elizabeth provided, and then settling in the end of the bunkhouse where the Whites lived to sleep the night away.

The children followed their parents to their home, while John Reynolds sat on the porch in Elizabeth's rocking chair.

"It's not good news, Will." Weariness sat on the foreman like a heavy blanket. "Bingley hadn't cleared the land so the barn went up first. Damage to the house is fairly minimal, but the smoke will take some time to clear and things are mighty charred." He wiped his hand over his face, smearing the ash from cheek to cheek. "I hate to say it, but it could have been much easier contained had he done so."

"I know."

"And there's something else you need to know." John swallowed, as if biting back bitter words.

"Go ahead."

244

Shaking his head, the foreman drained the cup of cool water Elizabeth had set on the small table next to him.

"Bingley's foreman, old Hank, is a good man. He knows his job and he knew what should have been done." He waited for Darcy's nod. "Before the couple left for the east, Bingley hired a couple of extra men to help out."

Darcy started to get a bad feeling in the pit of his stomach.

"Yep!" The foreman nodded his head. "I believe you guessed it. Bert Denny and George Wickham." Leaning forward, he huffed out a breath, his hands hanging uselessly in front of him. "According to Hank, Wickham had used his tale of being raised here and being trained by your Pa to convince Bingley that he needed to have as much authority as his most trusted employee. It became a constant battle to get the work done. The rest of the men chose sides. Those who supported the foreman were few. The others lazed the days away, smoking, drinking, and playing cards."

Darcy's instinct to strike at something was strong. Anger boiled and his rage became a living, breathing thing. Instantly regretting that he hadn't aimed lower when he shot the peach above Wickham's head, he vowed to bring the miscreant to justice. *Why had he never told Bingley about Wickham?* The guilt he felt was intense.

"As soon as the fire got out of control, those men high-tailed it off the ranch." The foreman sat back and rubbed his face again.

"I hope they run until they hit Portland or beyond, because if I ever see either of those two again, I'll shoot 'em."

"You will have to get in line." Bitter remorse at not having taken a more direct course against his old friend filled him.

"We'll ride out tomorrow to roundup the cattle and bring them over to Pemberley. Harald says we can put them in the lower pastures now the rain's here."

Fat drops of rain hit the dirt, bouncing off the hardened ground as if unwelcomed.

John Reynolds stood and stepped to the porch railing. "I suppose the women should take a gander at the house. They'll know what can and cannot be saved, I imagine."

Not waiting for Darcy's reply, he walked out into the rain and around the house to the cabin. Comfort awaited him in Maggie's arms.

Darcy rose and moved carefully to the same post the foreman had leaned on. Looking over the river below, he wondered if he and Elizabeth would be able to find such peace. Certainly, with Wickham in the area, he needed to be even more vigilant.

Breath rushed from his chest at all the Bingleys lost on that day. They would be excited to be home where they had plans to settle in for the winter and possibly start their family, plans that would be changed without them even being aware.

He leaned his head against the hard wooden beam. Darcy felt as weary as the men.

He didn't hear her come up behind him. When her arms slowly snaked around his waist from behind, he felt the first threads of release from the pressures in his soul. When Elizabeth turned the side of her face and laid it between his shoulder blades, tightening her arms in the process, he wanted to weep, losing almost all the strength he possessed in the one leg holding him up.

He wrapped his arm over the top of hers and pressed it into his gut. Their first time being so close. Their first time they spoke with no words. Their first embrace.

Chapter 16

The rain starting that day failed to stop until after they received word of the Bingleys' arrival in Portland. They would reach the docks at Oregon City in two days, taking opportunity to have their clothing laundered and enjoy the amenities of the city. Their party would be staying with Mr. and Mrs. Hurst.

The note had been poorly written with smudges and drops of ink. Darcy had immediately recognized its author as Bingley. Overall, it contained the minimal amount of information possible—only their arrival. He had immediately written back with news of the fire and the current situation at Netherfield ranch.

"Well, Son." Dr. Henderson finished bending Darcy's foot, flexing the calf muscles unused for the past ninety days. "I'll tell you to take it easy the first week or so. Your leg isn't used to your weight, and you will feel the loss of muscle as soon as you stand and lean upon it."

"I thank you, Doc. This has been a trial."

"What? To have your wife waiting on you hand and foot?" The physician, a man married for over thirty years, snorted. "If only most marriages had that kind of a start, I believe fewer men would ever turn their eyes away to other women. They would appreciate what they have at home."

"Trust me. I appreciate Elizabeth more than I could ever say." Darcy was quick with his comment. "She continues to take on adversity and challenge with a dignity that bears credit to the Darcy name. I'm fortunate in my choice of wife and I know it."

"Have you heard from the Bingleys then?" The doctor rolled down his sleeves after washing his hands.

"We expect them day after tomorrow. The house was merely charred from the fire, and the women have spent days scrubbing while the men repainted to get rid of as much of the smoke smell as possible. All the hardwood furniture was able to be salvaged, but the mattresses and the stuffed pieces had to go."

The doctor shook his head in disappointment for his young friend.

"They will stay at Pemberley?" The doctor raised his brow, as if his question had a particular purpose.

"Of course, they will."

"Now, Will. In case you have already thought this through and reached the same conclusion I have, you need to know that you are approved for all sorts of activity."

"Well, I should hope so. There's so much to do on the ranch. With company coming, especially Elizabeth's sister, who she has missed terribly, she has already started baking. I hope to help Bingley get settled and my own men to finish the final touches on the new cabin for the Pedersens."

Dr. Henderson cleared his throat.

"How many bedrooms does Pemberley have, son?"

"Four." He raised his shoulders at the odd question.

"One for you. One for Georgiana. One for the Bingleys and one for Miss Bingley." The doctor smiled. "And where will Elizabeth be sleeping?"

Realization dawned and Darcy wanted to slap himself on the forehead and grin like a fool at the same time. He imagined his face was beet red. "So we?"

"Yes."

"Thank God!" He stood and slapped the doctor on the back, possibly a mite harder than he should have, and then shook his hand, pumping it up and down like he was trying to draw water from a dry well. *Probably the man was the wisest physician known to mankind.*

Elizabeth looked out of the kitchen window. What she saw on the front porch warmed her heart until it melted. Her husband, that bigger-than-life man, was holding Christine's tiny doll in his arms like a baby. He was attempting to tie the strings of the miniature bonnet under the toy's chin and his large fingers were meeting with little success. By the time he'd knotted something which finally garnered the little girl's approval, she had gone on to another activity. Darcy gently placed the doll on the table beside him, though he carefully smoothed down the dress and pushed back a lock of hair after doing so.

"I know you weren't aware of it when you married him, but he's a good man." Maggie Reynolds had stepped alongside her.

Elizabeth looked at the housekeeper. "Yes, he is." They both smiled and then went back to work.

Fluffing the last pillow in the last of the bedrooms, Elizabeth surveyed each corner until she was confident nothing was out of place and everything was as it should be. She would put Bingley and Jane in this room, as the bed was almost as large as Darcy's. The light blue coverlet and curtains happened to be her sister's favorite color. Only one more day until they arrived.

Elizabeth had counted guest rooms as well and comprehended she would need to give hers up the next day for Charles' sister. In her heart of hearts, she hoped Maggie was not correct in reading the young woman's character, or that Miss Bingley was a much kinder version of what she had been. Jane would never be able to stand up to a forceful sister, as had been proven year after year with Jane taking neutral ground with each of Lydia's tantrums. Their youngest sister had a wicked temper and no amount of calm from the eldest had helped.

Elizabeth was desperate to see Jane—to see what three months of marriage and a trip across the country and back had done to her most tender sibling. *Was Jane as happy in her marriage as she was?*

Since the day of the fire, Darcy had taken every opportunity to touch Elizabeth—his fingers stroking her arm, leaning his shoulder into hers as they sat next to each other, or resting his hand on the small of her back as she stood alongside him. Each time it happened, a chill went from her heart to her toes, making them wiggle in delicious delight. Surprised at her own response, she finally admitted to herself her longing for more from the man she married.

And she had touched as well. Their hands now came together so easily it was as if they had been born joined, palm to palm, their fingers entwined. She would step up behind her husband as he stood at the same post looking out over the river, placing her hand on his shoulder blade, slowly sliding it back and forth to the middle of his spine as she spoke to him, feeling the strong muscles and the cotton of his shirt under her fingers.

Sighing deeply, Elizabeth was pleased with her life. Construction was far enough along that the Pedersen family now lived in a three-room cabin with an attached shower room. Neighbors had come to help and the continual rain failed to slow them in their efforts. This left the other half of the bunkhouse empty in case there was needed overflow from the main house. However, she could not put her sister or Jane's family so far from her.

The pantry was filled with canned fruits and vegetables. Every hole was darned and tear was stitched until she was satisfied with the contents of the house.

And she loved Will Darcy. Smiling to herself, she admitted that her favorite part of him was his response to her teasing.

"Will Darcy! Are you encouraging those boys to jump in that puddle? Cynthia will have your hide when she goes to do the wash."

"Who me?" He completely failed to hide his mirth in his efforts to look innocent.

"She will have you scrubbing those pants and wringing them out to dry. You will be the tallest washerwoman in all of Clackamas County."

The baritone of his laugh rumbled from his chest. "That I will."

Though it had happened yesterday, she easily remembered the look he gave Timothy and Markus as they challenged each other to see who could make the water fly the highest. Darcy's desire to join their antics was a pleasant surprise, one of many to add to her list of favorite memories of their first months married.

Gazing out the upstairs window, she watched Darcy's tentative steps away from the porch. As soon as she saw him

254

stumble, Elizabeth flew down the stairs into the yard, completely unconcerned that by the time she arrived at his side and wrapped her arms firmly around his waist, he might be stable.

"Will, are you okay?" Anxiety riddled her voice. Since Dr. Henderson had given him freedom to move the day prior, she existed in dread of Darcy reinjuring himself and found herself watching him like a hawk.

For the first time in their marriage they stood face-to-face, chest-to-chest. He wrapped his arms tightly around her and pulled her even closer. When she looked up, he leaned forward, his mouth stopping only an inch from their first kiss. He whispered, "Oh, yes, Lizzy. I'm perfectly okay."

The last thought before his lips met hers? *He called me Lizzy.*

Fitzwilliam Darcy was in no hurry to disturb the woman tucked under the covers beside him. They'd slept little, taking advantage of their newfound closeness to whisper hopes and dreams of their future as well as become man and wife. She was a wonder, and his heart filled to the brim with affection for her.

At one point, when the night was at its darkest, she had whispered her worries about the Bingleys' disappointments.

"My love," Her endearment made him smile. "Had it been you and I, and even Georgiana, who had suffered a fire and the damage to our home, I believe we are stalwart enough to withstand both the shock and any efforts we would need to take to help our situation along. But I worry about Jane. While not weak, she would rely solely on the decisions and actions of her husband to care for them. On her own she would be lost."

"And you would not rely on me if it was us?" His question was not borne of anger, but curiosity.

"Why would I do that?" She sounded adorably confused, making him chuckle. She continued, "One benefit of having you so close every day for the past three months is I feel confident in knowing how you would go about a multitude of matters. Therefore, I would not hesitate, if a situation came up and you were not available, to do exactly as I would imagine you would do in my place. I know you, Will, and you know me as well as I believe most couples who have been married for years."

"You do, huh?"

"I do."

He easily saw in his mind the set of her jaw as he felt her chin lift from his chest.

"I am happy you do, Lizzy." He hugged her closer, wrapping his arm around her waist. "And I would expect no less from you." He kissed her forehead, her nose, and her chin. "So why are you talking of Bingley on your wedding night?"

256

He kissed her mouth right after she murmured, "Who's Bingley?"

By the time the first buggy pulled into Pemberley, Jane Bingley had had to stop twice to empty her stomach on the way from Oregon City. Elizabeth was frantic when she observed how pale and thin her sister was upon her arrival.

Once Bingley helped her from the transport, Elizabeth hugged her briefly, smelling the remains of the dried vomit in her hair. Ignoring the others present, she rushed her sister into the showering room and tended to her until she was scrubbed and wrapped in one of Darcy's robes. In the background, she heard Maggie setting out food and drink while Darcy directed Dan and Melvin where to put the multitude of trunks and cases.

"I thank you, Lizzy." Even Jane's voice was weak. "You can't know how good it feels to be on solid ground."

They heard the demanding female voice of the other female Elizabeth had briefly noticed was in the carriage. Surprisingly, Jane stood from the bench in the bath and walked out the door, Elizabeth following closely behind.

Caroline Bingley was everything—and more—that Maggie had described. As tall as Jane and Georgiana, her flaming red hair topped a face pinched by disdain, her lips pressed together tightly.

"I insist on having the largest room in the house. I do not want my dresses wrinkled nor my precious possessions crowded together."

Elizabeth knew Jane would try to make peace, so she stepped ahead of her to address the young lady. However, Jane bumped Elizabeth out of the way.

Icy disapproval filled her voice. "Caroline, this is not our home. Your demands are not proper. We are guests of the Darcys."

"Then I want a room of my own. I am not willing to share with…"

They heard another buggy pull up to the noise of Lydia and Kitty Bennet's screeching laughter and Mary's unsuccessful attempts to calm them down.

"…them." Miss Bingley finished, turning and pointing her finger out the still opened door.

Elizabeth was stunned. Not a word had been mentioned by her sister or Bingley about having all three of her sisters accompany them to Oregon. She looked at her husband and noted his surprise as well.

Without waiting to be helped, the two youngest girls jumped down, landing on the gravel pathway, and walked into the house as if they owned it. Mary and another woman who, hopefully, was

Bingley's new cook, stayed until Bingley quickly went outside to assist them to the ground.

She turned to her sister. "You didn't think to let me know?"

Jane blew the fringe on her forehead from her eyes. "We weren't aware of their plans until our last morning when we stopped to say our goodbyes. There they were, all lined up like ducks, sitting on their luggage. Mama kept hugging each of them and Papa never came out of the house."

"Oh, Jane." Elizabeth could imagine how her eldest sister felt. She knew how she was feeling now, and she was both blisteringly angry with her father and deeply disappointed. But she was happy they were here in a puzzled sort of way.

"You have a lovely home, sir," Mary politely mentioned, though her words were drowned out by the cat fight occurring only a foot from where she stood.

Caroline Bingley was nose-to-nose with Lydia Bennet, and Darcy feared fists would soon start flying.

"If you had been trained at Mrs. Fletcher's School for the Betterment of Young Ladies, you would know how crass you are, Lydia Bennet." The red face of Caroline's abhorrence clashed violently with her hair.

"With your turned up nose and freckles, you are the last female I would call a lady, Carrie Bingley. You will never get a husband looking like you do, all pinched and puckered."

"And you will never get a husband acting like a floosy willing to accept the attention of any man, no matter how pretty you believe yourself to be."

"Ladies!" Darcy had had enough. At any moment, he expected hair to fly and talons to be extended. He had yet to be introduced to whom he assumed were younger Bennets, but he knew Caroline and he vowed then and there that any daughter he and Elizabeth would be blessed with would not be attending Mrs. Fletcher's School for the Betterment of Young Ladies.

While his deep voice was still reverberating back and forth from one end of the living room to the other, sweet, humble Jane Bennet stepped between the two females and grabbed each one by their ears. Ignoring their yelps of pain, Jane looked to her hostess.

"Where do you want them, Lizzy?"

In the three months of their marriage, he had rarely seen his wife's smile so big. The chaos hadn't bothered her at all.

"Follow me." Elizabeth marched up the stairs, her shoulders lifted, though Darcy spied a quiver she quickly forced herself to contain. She was waiting to burst out in laughter and he wondered how long she could master her glee.

Jane never loosened her grip as she pulled the two combatants behind Elizabeth. The two other Bennet girls followed.

He couldn't help but shake his head. Georgiana, Maggie, and the unknown woman had moved into the dining room to get out of the way and he didn't blame them at all.

"You should have been with us on the train." Bingley spoke up, Darcy having forgotten he was in the room.

"I imagine." Again, his head went back and forth as he looked to where the females had gone. He heard his wife direct the two youngest Bennets into the room intended for Caroline. Miss Bingley and the other of Elizabeth's sisters would go in the blue room she had planned to give Charles and Jane.

"This has been hard on Jane. She is with child." Pride surged in his friend's chest, and Darcy saw it literally puff out. Then it collapsed. "Between her daily bouts of sickness and trying to keep peace between the sisters, she's exhausted."

"And what have you done to corral the girls?"

"Me? What do you mean, me? Jane is doing fine on her own." Bingley hitched his thumbs into his belt. "In fact, about two days into our journey, my Janey took on Caroline and Lydia until they both sat silent and still for hours. I couldn't have been more proud."

"Bingley, if it's as you say and your wife is carrying your babe, it should be you taking care of matters to protect her."

261

"Protect, Jane?" Bingley was incredulous. "Are you kidding me? I thought I'd married a mild-mannered wife brimming with kind submission. As soon as she turned up pregnant, she made a mountain lion look friendly. I have no idea how your marriage is going, Darcy, but when she's in a mood, I've learned to wisely raise my hands in surrender and back off."

The mental picture of Bingley doing so made him want to chuckle, though he did not. Immediately, he wondered how Elizabeth would react when she was with child. She was fierce enough without being pregnant. *How he admired his wife.*

Soon, Elizabeth returned downstairs to see to the woman who, indeed, was the new cook and housekeeper for Netherfield Ranch. Eventually, she turned her attention to the men.

Darcy knew what was coming and he had no regrets. As soon as the door slammed behind the single women, he had heard the familiar creak of his bedroom door. The Bingleys would have their bed, while he and Elizabeth would be across the yard in the bunkhouse. *Thank the Lord!*

Chapter 17

Elizabeth greeted the morning sun with a smile. The second night she had spent in her husband's arms left her feeling cherished and admired. His tender caresses and winsome words made all the worries seem to disappear.

They were still several steps from the main house when their worries returned with a vengeance.

"I always have one piece of toast, lightly buttered with my tea. I will accept nothing less."

"You cow!" Lydia screamed with vigor. "The war between the States ended years ago. I am nobody's slave. Fix it yourself."

Elizabeth turned to Darcy, a wry look on her face. "Who knew she was aware the war was over? I'm stunned at Lydia's knowledge of current events."

"I am assuming the two have not yet learned to get along?"

"You think?" She reached up and kissed his cheek, looking back to the house with a heavy sigh. "'Such a smart man I married."

"Perceptive too." He quickly added, kissing her back.

Elizabeth snorted. "And humble." She hugged him to her, laying her head on his chest for a second, then stiffened her shoulders and marched into the house.

Bingley was descending the stairs so she first inquired of Jane.

"Mornings are the hardest for her. I begged her to sleep as long as she might." He glared at his sister. "Though how she could do so with the bellowing from these two heifers would be a miracle."

"Charles," Caroline interrupted and Lizzy, again, had to wonder what she had been taught. "I have been sitting here for almost a half an hour and no one has seen to my meal. I cannot imagine being so poorly treated."

Lydia began to reply when Elizabeth raised her palm for silence.

"Allow me to explain the rules of our household, Miss Bingley." When Lydia started to gloat at not being addressed, Elizabeth included her as well.

"This is *my* home. In my home everyone pulls their weight."

This time it was Lydia who interrupted. "Where are your servants, Lizzy? Mr. Darcy is a rich man. Surely you don't have to do housework anymore? I can't imagine."

Elizabeth took in a shuddering breath as she felt her husband move alongside her.

"I will state this only one more time. In this home, everyone pulls their weight. Everyone cares for their own needs and helps others." She looked between the two miscreants. "Maggie and Mrs. Nichols have already left for Netherfield to see to the delivery of your luggage. You will be leaving to stay with your brother and sister-in-law, Caroline, as soon as a room can be prepared for you there.

"I prepared food for ourselves and for the men at the bunkhouse so you lovely, accomplished ladies are on your own. If you want bread, you make it. If you want to turn it into lightly buttered toast, you make it. If you want tea, you make it. If you want your clothing cleaned or pressed, you do it. You will clean up after yourself and make sure your room is tidy before you leave it in the morning. Am I clear?"

Caroline Bingley either had no sense or she had an overly-inflated grasp of her own importance. A look of sadness covered her face as a lone tear pooled at the corner of her right eye.

"But, Charles, I was not born for this, you know I was not." The young woman walked to her brother as if her body was wracked with pain so that each step jarred the sorest of muscles.

Elizabeth was duly impressed. Miss Bingley should be on the stage. She whispered to Darcy. "Is there a theater in Oregon City, by chance?"

The low rumble of his chuckle was answer enough.

Bingley finally spoke up. "Might I ask, Caroline, what was it you learned at Mrs. Fletcher's School? Did you not learn how to manage a household? How to care for a husband, family, and a home?"

Instantly gone was the puppy-dog attitude. It was replaced with a smirk.

"I will have you know that I can draw, paint, embroider pillows, and converse in both French and Italian. I have been taught every aspect of what a man desires most in a wife."

At that the eyebrows of both men threatened to reach their hairline.

"Is that so?" Elizabeth folded her arms across her chest, her shoulders back, and chin lifted. "What most men desire from a woman this early in the morning is breakfast. Therefore, it is your task to prepare a meal for all those not yet down to the table. That would be Jane, Kitty, Mary, Lydia, Georgiana, and yourself. The ingredients are in the pantry." At Caroline's frustrated huff, she added. "Of course, you will need to light the stove first."

Lydia, never one to find the course of wisdom and follow it, pointed her finger at her nemesis and laughed uproariously. "That will show you, Miss High and Mighty."

"Lydia?" Though she had been gone from Baltimore for the past four months, she well remembered her youngest sister's

266

most hated task. "While Caroline is preparing your meal, you can start washing the men's socks and shirts. I suspect you will have plenty of time to finish before it's time to meet at the table."

"Lizzy!"

"No, don't 'Lizzy' me, Lydia May Bennet. Had either you or Caroline acted like the ladies you insist you are, your time would be spent this morning in activities you desired—after you cared for your own clothing and room."

Both Caroline and Lydia plopped their fists on their hips and wore a similar look of displeasure and rebellion.

"I believe they look close enough to be twins." Darcy injected, though neither of the young ladies thought him funny.

Charles jogged to the bunkhouse for the remainder of the coffee left on the edge of the stove. At Elizabeth's request, he returned with some biscuits Elizabeth had left covered in the oven so Jane would have something to nibble on. The men left for Netherfield soon after.

"Jane," she knocked softly on the door. Not only did she not want to wake her sister if she slept, she didn't want to wake any of the other girls as well. The two downstairs didn't need any assistance, though they would have commanded obedience from any of the three remaining upstairs.

"Come in, Lizzy." Jane's soft voice drifted through the barely opened door.

Jane Bingley looked miserable. Her complexion was an odd sort of green around her mouth and the rest of her face was pallid.

"Is it like this every day?" Elizabeth couldn't help but inquire. Her sister nodded. "I brought you bread. I hope it helps."

"Thank you. It usually does once my stomach empties." Jane reached behind her to the wooden slats of the headboard and gripped it tightly. "I heard Caroline and Lydia."

"I imagine you did. I'm hoping our other sisters either slept through it or are fearing to go downstairs in case I put them to work as well."

They both chuckled.

"Oh, Lizzy. I am so happy."

It was the last thing Elizabeth had expected to hear.

"How is that, Sister?"

"Charles is just what a young man ought to be—tender and caring. And so attentive to me in every way." She sighed, her eyes softening with devotion. "To know I am carrying his child makes the misery of each morning worth the discomfort. He will be an excellent father."

"I am exceedingly pleased for you." And she was. "So what does your good husband think of the forceful woman he discovered in my home yesterday?"

Jane giggled. "I was a bit like one of those Amazon women you used to read to me about, wasn't I?"

Shared laughter felt normal between them. They had missed each other dearly.

"You were definitely pretty mighty." Elizabeth was delighted to see her sister's color change to a soft pink.

"Lizzy, I am finding that if I don't take charge of my happiness, then I will not be happy."

"What about Charles?" Elizabeth had not been surprised when Bingley had not stepped in to control his sister, and she had been slightly appalled that he had let Jane take the lead the night before. It was a definite unbalance of power.

"I know what you are thinking and he's not like that at all." Jane smiled slightly and her eyes lit with fire. "My husband knows how much I value peace, therefore he does whatever he can to remove conflict."

Elizabeth shook her head back and forth, in complete disagreement with her sister.

"Oh, yes, Sister dear." Jane was insistent. "When Caroline decided to travel with us to Pemberley instead of stay in Portland with the Hursts, she made certain promises which she broke within seconds of entering your home. And so you know, Lydia made promises as well."

"That she broke." It was not a question.

"Yes." Jane looked her straight in the eye and Elizabeth was pleased at her determination. Things might work out well for the Bingleys after all. "Charles will return after looking at the ranch. If you noticed, Caroline's belongings were not taken to Netherfield this morning. They should still be stacked in the back of your parlor. They will be loaded up and he will take her to Oregon City and stay with her until they board the stagecoach for Portland. Whether she wants it or not, she will not be living with us."

"Jane!" Elizabeth was impressed.

"Charles is a gentle man. He does not raise his voice and he does not demand. He quietly, and with a smile, goes about his tasks. But when he's crossed by someone who threatens my peace and contentment, he acts without delay."

"I…I am happy to hear it."

Jane giggled. "I love it when he's manly."

Elizabeth rolled her eyes, then realized she loved it when Darcy was manly as well.

By the time the men returned from the ranch, all the females were sitting around the dining table except Caroline and Lydia. Miss Bingley was leaning back against the drain board, her arms stiffly at her sides and a scowl on her face. On the back porch, Lydia's stance was the same. None of the work had been done as required.

Elizabeth was more than joyous to have Caroline Bingley removed from her home. Lydia, she could handle.

Earlier she had taken the other girls to the bunkhouse for breakfast and a chat. It warmed her heart to see how quickly Georgiana and Mary started speaking exclusively to one another. Kitty followed Georgiana like a shadow.

Elizabeth asked, "What are your hopes and dreams, Kitty?"

"I want a home of my own and a handsome husband who loves me as much as Charles loves Jane."

"That's an admirable goal, sister."

"Mama said there is more chance we can find mates in Oregon than in Baltimore. I hope she's right."

Elizabeth chuckled, until she considered how bad things must be for her parents to give up all three daughters at once.

"Tell me, Kitty. How are things at home?"

"I'll be honest, Lizzy, it's been rough." Kitty's whole countenance looked weighed down by a millstone. "Papa did even less after you left, claiming you abandoned him. Mama frets more and more each day because of the lack of money. What you left Uncle Gardiner was spent foolishly on pretty ribbons for Lydia. Mother has no sense of money at all. When men came demanding payment for taxes on the house, there was no money to pay. By the time Jane arrived, we had loaded up all of Papa's books and the furnishings to move in with the Gardiners."

"But their house isn't large enough!"

"And that's why we are here. Papa let Mama pack us off without even a goodbye. The only daughter she wanted to keep was Lydia. Had Lydia not insisted she also wanted a husband of her own, it would be only Mary and me here. We lost our home in more ways than one, Lizzy."

Elizabeth was so stunned she could think of nothing to say. Placing her arm across Kitty's shoulders, she pulled her close as the girl wept. At almost seventeen years of age, it had to feel like she had been abandoned. Looking to Mary, Elizabeth observed the same pain as her sibling and that which Georgiana had worn when she'd first arrived at Pemberley. It was horrid to think the people who should love you more than all others, loved their own selfish desires more. *She would gladly knock her father over the head with his heaviest book if she thought it would do any good.*

"I am so sorry. I'm so, so sorry," she whispered into her sister's hair until Kitty finally calmed. "If you only knew how pleased I am that you made the trip. We welcome all of you to our family."

By evening, it was just as Jane had said it would be. Caroline Bingley was gone. Although Elizabeth had packed a small picnic for the two travelers, she stood firm in not providing a meal or even a cup of tea before she left. If she gave in, Lydia would know it, and that would have been intolerable.

The socks and shirts had been given a cursory rinse. None of the stains had been scrubbed clean and Elizabeth knew if she dared to put one of the stockings close to her nose, it would still bear the fragrance of the wearer.

Just before retiring to the privacy of the bunkhouse, she told Lydia she would have to try again in the morning after the clothing worn on that day had been added to the pile.

"You have Maggie here to see to the clothes. You are mean, Lizzy Darcy. You want to ruin my hands so they are as unattractive as yours. You aren't being fair." Her voice rose with each word. "Kitty and Mary haven't done a thing all day. Only I have been made to work like a servant and it's not fair!" The last word was accompanied by a stomp of her foot, not yet done with her tirade.

"I'll show you. I'll show you all." Lydia bent forward and Elizabeth almost expected her to stick out her tongue, so childish was her behavior. "I'll leave here and marry the first handsome man I find. Then I'll have a house bigger than this and more money than I can shake a stick at. You just wait and see."

"Go to your room, now." Darcy's voice brooked no argument. Lydia glared at him before she spun on her heels and obeyed. "In fact, I think it's time we all retire. We can hope for a better tomorrow."

Darcy had placed Dan at the front door and Melvin at the back. Leaving a volatile female like Lydia in the house, he worried she might try to burn it down before morning. It had been a long day of hard work and he doubted the men would be able to stay awake. Yet, once Wickham and Denny had run off, there was no threat except from wild animals. They were protected as long as they stayed in the house.

There had been a heated discussion between Mary, Kitty, and Lydia over who would get the lone spare room. Darcy had given it to Mary as the eldest single girl. Lydia had flounced off in a fit. He was happy Elizabeth was his wife and no other Bennet sister. His appreciation and admiration grew second by second.

Arriving at the bunkhouse, he stopped his wife before she could walk through the door. Bending down, he scooped her up, kissing her in surprise, hopeful his leg would hold. It did. They were due some time alone, and he vowed to himself not to think of what might be going on in the main house. He had more important matters to care for.

Neither Dan nor Melvin heard the young lady creeping down the stairs and approaching each door to see who snored the loudest. The sun had just started its early morning rise and silence still reigned over Pemberley and the surrounding land. Not even the forest creatures had begun to stir.

Lydia Bennet had gathered together her most precious items, and a few of Kitty's, as well as the last of the coins she had talked Bingley out of while they were in Portland. Stuffing everything into a carpetbag, she kept her walking boots and stockings off until she was far enough away from the house that she could make noise with impunity.

How dare Lizzy act like the queen of the house towards her! Their mother had long proclaimed Lydia as the liveliest of all the Bennet girls. She would show them! She was not made to serve.

The dim light from the early October sun made it easy to see the road. She would rather ride a horse, but she hadn't yet been to the barn. She was angry enough she was willing to walk the whole way to Oregon City, even if it rained. Once there, she would either find a husband or obtain transport to Portland where there would be more men to choose from.

The dampness of the early mist muffled her footsteps until she was beyond the first curve in the road. Placing her bag on the ground, she quickly donned her footwear and set out walking. Her ire kept her focused on the end destination.

"Drat!" she spoke to the autumn air. "I forgot to grab something to eat."

Instead of blaming herself for her own foolishness, she wished Elizabeth was there to lash out at.

Kicking a rock out of the ruts from the heavy wagons which had brought their luggage to the Darcy home, she reflected on how jealous Kitty would be when she married ahead of her. At just sixteen, her mother would be beyond joyful at having another daughter, most particularly her youngest, well settled. She could imagine the glee on her mama's face and that kept her mind occupied for almost a half of a mile.

Her husband would be taller than Bingley, but not as tall as Lizzy's mate. He would be fair haired with lovely blue eyes that only ever looked…no gazed. He would only ever gaze at her with love in his eyes as he bought her everything she wanted. She would have servants so her greatest responsibility would be to see and be seen by only important people.

She'd walked another half a mile when her feet started hurting from where her old boots rubbed. They hadn't had time to replace them before they had left Baltimore.

Lydia was somewhat embarrassed for her feet as they were long and narrow, with equally long, well-knuckled digits at the ends. Kitty used to tease her about having eagle's claws instead of toes. *Well, she would show Kitty. She would marry a man who liked a woman with hawkish feet.*

By the time she'd walked another quarter of a mile, she was equal parts sweaty from the exertion and cold from the outside air. Her feet hurt even worse, and she was hungry and thirsty. Stopping in the middle of the road, she listened to see if anyone had discovered her missing yet. Kitty slept like the dead and hated to wake early, so unless someone else looked into their room, she would have a few hours to make it to town.

The forest was no longer silent. A breeze moved the tree branches against each other, making a whispering sound, though Lydia had no clue the cause of the noise was so innocent. A herd of elk crossed the road in front of her and, while she marveled at their majesty, she didn't particularly like the size of the horns on the last one to cross. Fortunately, the animal paid her no attention at all.

While she stood there, she heard a grunting right before a crashing sound came from the woods beside her. Imagining all sorts of man-eating critters she'd never find on the streets of Baltimore motivated her to set aside the pain in her feet and run as fast as her legs could carry her.

It was when she came to the crossroad to the Bingley property that she finally paused, dropping the carpetbag and bending to grab her knees and catch her breath.

"Well, hello there."

"Who's there?" She straightened immediately, fear filling her chest and making her voice sound weak.

"Do not fear. I'm a friend of Darcy's."

One of the handsomest men she had ever set eyes on stepped away from the trees bordering the road to Netherfield Ranch. His smile of appreciation was a welcome sight to her.

"I am pleased to meet you. My name is Lydia Bennet and I am traveling to Oregon City. By chance, are you headed that direction as well?"

The gentleman doffed his hat and moved to within only a few feet of her. Upon closer inspection, he was even more handsome.

"As a matter of fact, that's exactly where I'm headed." The man's voice was smooth as glass. "My horse went lame not too far back so, like you, I decided the easier choice was to go to town where I could get another mount rather than bother Bingley for aid."

"You poor man." Lydia handed over her bag, certain he was on the brink of offering for it. "I am pleased to have your escort." She wrapped her hand around his bent elbow. "You don't happen to be married already, do you?"

He chuckled. "No, I'm unattached."

"Then it is my pleasure to meet you, Mr...."

"Wickham, ma'am. George Wickham."

Chapter 18

"You are enjoying having all of your sisters here." Darcy's deep voice rumbled in his chest. With the side of her face pressed into his shoulder, she could feel him speak.

"I am." Within minutes of Bingley and Caroline leaving the prior afternoon, the bickering had started between Kitty and Lydia over some trivial matter. Mary unwisely entered the fray in a fruitless attempt to calm them. Jane had pressed her fingers to her temples and retreated to her room upstairs, while Georgiana's head bobbed between the two combatants in puzzlement.

Elizabeth should have been frustrated with the sheer volume of female voices, yet she had rejoiced instead. Years of memories poured into her mind as she found solace in what had been normal for so long.

Nonetheless, the sound was not normal for the Darcys. Soon, Georgiana had sought refuge in her room while Will left the house for a task only he knew needed done at that particular second in time.

Elizabeth slid her foot up his calf, scratching an itch on the bottom of her foot with his hair-covered skin, grateful she didn't have to bend like a contortionist to use her fingers to find the exact spot on her sole. Satisfied, she stretched her toes as far as possible to the end of the bed and arched her back as she groaned at the thought of getting out of their warm cocoon to begin their day. People needed to be fed.

"Elizabeth Darcy! You are worse than a housecat rubbing against a post." Darcy chuckled softly in her ear.

"Who knew having a husband in my bed would be so convenient? Had I known, I would have married you the night we arrived instead of waiting until the next morning."

He snorted. "I do believe, my dear, that you would not have had me should I have made that suggestion." Wrapping a long strand of her hair between his fingers, he tugged gently. "Actually, I'm still surprised you married me the next morning after the start we had."

She heard the disappointment in his voice and knew it was regret at his own behavior. She had let go of her anger months ago. He needed to do the same.

"I'm happy I became a mail-order bride. Very happy." She sighed into his neck. "There are so many risks to both the man and the woman in attaching oneself permanently to a stranger. I knew nothing about you except how you helped Charles establish himself on his property and that he considered you a friend.

However, when I realized on that first night that you authored those four beautiful letters, I felt a glimmer of hope that we just might do well together—eventually."

Stroking his fingers down her jaw, he whispered, "Elizabeth, you outshine every woman I know, and I'm proud you are my wife. I have no regrets."

She giggled as she snuggled closer, and he wrapped his arms tight around her torso. "Can I quote you on that the next time you wish the letter you mailed asking me to be your bride had gotten lost between here and Baltimore?"

He kissed the smile on her face. Elizabeth kissed him back. Breakfast could wait.

Mary and Georgiana set the table while Maggie and Elizabeth cooked the meal. Jane was indisposed. From past experience, Elizabeth knew her two youngest sisters liked to sleep in and she allowed it this morning, relishing the peace their absence brought to the kitchen.

Over an hour later, Kitty descended the stairs complaining about her youngest sister at the same time a rider was heard. Pounding hoof beats approaching the house was never a good sign. Wiping her hands on a towel, both Elizabeth and Maggie went to the door, Mary and Georgiana following close behind. Kitty brought up the rear.

Darcy and the men evidently had heard and were hurrying to the front porch.

"Hello, Jim, what's your hurry?" Darcy came right to the point.

"I've a message from Mr. Bingley." Jim Thornton, though nondescript in looks, was a constant and steady young man. Elizabeth had noticed him working at the docks when they had arrived in Oregon City. His skill in handling the heavy ropes in tying up the craft quickly had caught her attention. She was amazed at how rapidly he could wrap the heavy line around the pilings at the pier. Mr. Thornton looked about Bingley's age and most likely he was single.

"Are he and Miss Bingley well?" Darcy asked, though anxiety filled her. Only an emergency would have caused Charles to send someone so far away from town.

"They are. Have no worries there." Jim dismounted and draped the reins over the hitching post, stepping in front of Darcy. "They arrived at the station this morning to an unexpected surprise."

"Yes?" Darcy briskly inquired.

Elizabeth could hear the frustration in her husband's voice.

"His wife's youngest sister was at the station waiting to board."

"What?" a chorus of voices asked at the same time.

"Lydia?" Elizabeth turned to Kitty.

"That's what I was trying to tell you." Kitty whined. "When I got up, I stepped on my purse which had somehow moved from the drawer at the top of the bureau to the floor at the end of the bed. I opened it and found all my money gone. When I checked the closet to see what else was missing, Lydia's carpetbag was gone along with my favorite green dress. You know, the one with the lace around the collar and the cuffs? I can't believe she would steal my best clothes. When I see her I'll..."

"She's gone?" Elizabeth was incredulous. She leaned against the post on the front porch next to where Kitty had moved, bereft at how this could be. "Of all the foolish things to do."

"Not only that," Jim continued. "Mr. Bingley wanted you to know that she got married as soon as she got into Oregon City."

"Married!" "Who?" "How?"

"That no-good George Wickham is who," Jim almost spat out the words. "I don't know anything else other than Miss Bingley was apparently not willing to travel with the new Mr. and Mrs. Wickham on the stagecoach. Therefore, the Bingleys were headed to the docks. That's when he asked me to ride to you as fast as possible so you would know where the young miss was. He thought it would ease your worry. They will have gone by the time you could ride back to town, Mr. Darcy."

"Oh, good grief!" Elizabeth was appalled at her sister's actions.

"What a mess." Maggie uttered from behind her.

"Are you single?"

Elizabeth swiveled her head to look at Kitty. *What an unbelievable question under the circumstances!* Kitty had a small smile on her face that Elizabeth knew she had practiced for hours in front of the mirror over the fireplace in Baltimore. Both of her youngest sisters had done so in hopes of portraying a simpering miss with a hint of flirtation. They assumed they were made more attractive because of the expression. Elizabeth had thought they looked silly.

Kitty may have been looking at Jim Thornton, but it was Mary he had his eyes focused on when he answered. "I am."

Darcy threw his hands up in the air and growled. "Of all the stupid, idiotic, hair-brained schemes. Running off in the middle of the night and attaching herself to the lowest scum on the planet." He turned to look at Mary, Kitty, and Georgiana. "That's it! From now on, you will all stay in the house and you will remain there until you are thirty. Am I clear?"

Their day had started so well. Elizabeth wanted to crawl into a hole and drag her youngest sister with her. She was deeply ashamed, though not surprised. Her parents' lack of involvement in the lives of their children was legendary, and now she and Will would have to tend to the results of their indifferent parenting.

Elizabeth felt like she had taken a blow to her gut and was just starting to recover her breath.

"Come into the house, Mr. Thornton, and I'll provide you something to eat. There's no need to punish the messenger by sending you back to Oregon City hungry. We appreciate your taking the time to let us know Lydia's fate." Elizabeth opened the screen door and let Maggie step in ahead of her.

As he followed her into the dining room, the girls turned to walk behind him. Darcy cleared his throat and the young females froze in place. "Thirty, I said."

Charles Bingley had arrived at the hotel the evening before with Caroline too late to catch the stagecoach. His mind still reverberated from almost three hours of listening to his sister's constant ranting about her situation. *She was unappreciated. She was not born to cook. The roads were too muddy. The wagon moved too slowly. She despised the Bennets—each and every one of them. She hated the rain.* He could not wait to get her delivered to his brother-in-law and sister in Portland, then return to his peaceful, contented wife.

Rising early, he had roused Caroline to be downstairs and fed within the hour. His plan was to deliver her to the Hursts and hurry back to Jane. His relief at having his wife stay with the

Darcys until his return was the only thing allowing him to leave her.

"Lydia Bennet! What in the world are you doing here?" He was incredulous. Bingley looked back up the hill, trying to figure out how a child—for that is what she was—could possibly be in two places at the same time.

She stood outside the station with her carpetbag on the ground next to her. For the millionth time since he'd met her in Baltimore, the look of stubborn rebellion flashed from her eyes.

"What am I doing here? What are you doing here? You left yesterday for Portland. Why aren't you there?"

Bingley's mouth hung open at her effrontery. His sister had no such loss of speech.

"Why if it isn't little Lydia Bennet. Did you run away from home like a bad girl?" Caroline gloated in her own superiority. "What will your brother-in-law say when he finds you? Oh, you will be in so much trouble!"

"You know nothing, Caroline," Lydia snorted. "I am no longer Miss Bennet. As a married woman, I am able to come and go as I please."

"What?" Bingley was finally able to recover his speech. "Married?"

"Yes, I married the most handsome man in Oregon only a few minutes ago. He has gone to purchase our tickets to Portland." Lydia's chin lifted as her face filled with pride.

"If you are married, Lydia *Bennet*, where is your ring?" Caroline smirked, assuming the younger girl was lying— something she had caught her doing several times on their travels west.

Lydia held up her left hand, her palm to them. From the look in her eye, she was picturing just how the ring of her dreams would look.

"My dear George said there was not a diamond large enough to be found in Oregon City. We will wait until we arrive in Portland to purchase the perfect jewels for my finger."

Just then, a man came from the station.

"Wickham!" Bingley's horror at the realization of who his newest brother-in-law was could not be contained. "How is this possible?"

"Hello, Brother." George Wickham oozed confidence. "I met my bride coming into town this morning and it was love at first sight. Why, I do believe our marriage was quite similar to Darcy's and your own."

"That's *Mr.* Bingley to you," Caroline interrupted.

Charles sputtered. *Brother-in-law!* He was becoming angrier by the minute. "Darcy said you fled the area before the fire at my place could be put out."

"Well, that just goes to show you that Will Darcy doesn't know everything, doesn't it? I'd already left Netherfield before the fire started."

"That wasn't what I heard."

"Well, Bingley. Whoever told you has their facts wrong." Wickham's arrogance was equally matched by his young bride.

"Say, Charles," Lydia simpered, in what she had to assume was an attractive purr. "We are a bit short in the pocket with the cost of the wedding and all. Might you be able to advance us a sum until we get settled in Portland?"

"Of all the unbelievable things to do, Lydia Bennet. Begging for money before you've been married an hour. I do believe that's some sort of a record, even for you," Caroline sneered.

"You are jealous because I married before you, you old hag." Lydia showed her maturity by sticking out her tongue. "I'm Mrs. Wickham!"

"So you say." Caroline mirrored her actions, and Bingley wanted done with this ugly business.

Bingley knew he shouldn't accede to their request, but he saw no other option for keeping peace. Walking past the couple, he went to the counter and purchased the tickets. The horses were already harnessed. The stagecoach was soon to be on its way.

"Here they are." He handed them to the couple. Without a 'thank you' they took their place in line to board the passenger area. Neither of them looked back.

"Oh, Charles. To be attached to such a family." Caroline shook her head wearily. For the first time since his marriage, Bingley felt exactly the same way.

Kissing his wife goodbye, Darcy left her and the womenfolk to the care of his foreman. Elizabeth had packed his saddlebags with clean changes of clothing and a few snacks to see him on his way. There was no hurry, as he would have to wait until the next day to catch the stage himself. Both the boat and stagecoach were already gone by the time he made it to Oregon City.

Taking a room at the hotel, he walked across the road to the Justice of the Peace.

"Were you aware the new Mrs. Wickham was barely sixteen?" Even though, in reality, there was nothing that could be done, Darcy needed answers. He had three more girls in his household who longed to be married. Well, maybe only two. He wasn't sure about Georgiana. Darcy couldn't recall ever seeing her as livid as she was when she figured out she was now related by marriage to Wickham.

"No, I was given a date of birth where she was eighteen." The older man rubbed his chin whiskers as he looked over his records.

"Can the marriage be dissolved if the information was false?"

The older man looked directly at him with piercing blue eyes.

"Would you really want to see that happen? It was clear to me that the little lady was far more determined to become a bride than the gentleman was to be a groom, if you take my meaning. But he was eager for one thing, so I doubt that, by the time you find them, she will not have consequences to consider."

Darcy was sick at the thought. George Wickham intimately touching any woman of his acquaintance was deplorable. "Was there anything else out of the usual?"

The man rubbed his chin some more.

"Now that you mention it—when it came time to pay the fee, I saw her slip him the funds from her purse. He turned back to me and paid like it was his money he was using. I felt sorry for the lady as I'm sure she's going to have a hard time of it once the money runs out."

Darcy stood and shook his hand.

"I thank you, sir, for the information and hold no resentment against you for performing the wedding. I understand how those two fools could hoodwink an honorable man."

He went back to his room and stood at the window, watching the activity below. Jim Thornton was leaving the dock, walking back into town. Darcy was unsurprised at the knock on his door a few short minutes later.

292

"Mr. Darcy, sir."

"Yes, Jim." He invited him into the room.

Thornton cleared his throat several times before he started to speak.

"I have a steady job and have had it since I left school. My place in town is my own. There's a small yard and room in the back for a garden. I owe no one. I'm a good Christian, and I would never mistreat a woman or child. I wouldn't even kick a mad dog, sir."

Darcy heard his intent with every word.

"Miss Mary?" he asked, in an effort to put the other man at ease, then wondered why he was making it easier for someone else.

"Yes, sir." Jim Thornton finally took a breath. "She seems a fine woman. Seeing she's Mrs. Darcy's sister, I imagine she would make a capable wife and I would be happy if you would allow me to come courting before the other men in town spot her."

Wiping his hands over his face, Darcy remembered his earlier words. "I told the girls they could not look for a husband until they are at least thirty."

"Then I'm hoping Miss Mary is far older than she looks."

Darcy had no other option, and he knew it.

"You can come to call."

"Thank you, sir." Thornton put his hat back on his head. "I'll be heading up to Pemberley then."

"I imagine you will," Darcy muttered to the closed door, unsurprised at the man's haste.

He walked back to the window and watched Thornton run to the stables. Short minutes passed before he whooped and hollered until his horse was running through the streets of town. Shaking his head slowly, he closed his eyes. *When had his life become so difficult? How had they gone from the joy of the morning to where he was chasing his nemesis west to Portland? How in the world had Lydia Bennet come from the same parents as Elizabeth and Jane?*

Moving to the bed, he sat and flopped back on the quilt. He wanted Elizabeth. He needed her.

Weary to his bones, he sighed.

Chapter 19

Early morning sunlight danced across the glistening water as it flowed steadily towards the sea. Where the road followed the river on its right side, the view across the Columbia to the high bluffs of the Washington territory was a sight Darcy normally enjoyed when he traveled to Portland. Not today.

The pained expression on Elizabeth's face when Jim told them the news was what drove him on his journey. On his own, he could care less what happened to either Wickham or Lydia. He despised his former friend and confidently discerned that without the youngest Bennet in the home, they would have peace. But Elizabeth loved her sister—for better or for worse. And this was definitely worse.

He would attempt to move mountains for his wife, so deep was his love for her. The ache he felt in his chest hadn't left since he rode away from Pemberley, and he sincerely doubted he would find relief until he was back in the arms of Elizabeth.

Portland was a bustling city with a population of almost ten thousand permanent residents with hundreds arriving to work in the sawmills and the construction trade from every steam and sailing ship coming into port. Though more than twenty churches dotted the streets in both the residential and business sections, it was the wharves where the gamblers and the lowest of humanity gathered together into a cesspool of immorality that contained the majority of the new arrivals. The demand for housing kept the boarding houses and hotels bursting, so Darcy was unsure where the Wickhams would have ended up staying. He was glad he would bunk with the Fitzwilliams.

"Bingley, what are you doing here?" Darcy was surprised to see him with his cousin.

"I knew you would come and knew where you would be staying when you got here."

"Does Jane know where you are?"

"She does. I sent a note as soon as I got to Portland last night." Bingley explained. "I figured with Richard being a criminal attorney, he would know more about the seedier side of life in the city than you and I would ever know."

Richard Fitzwilliam nodded his head. "You two have taken on a difficult task. It's almost impossible to find someone who didn't want to be found."

"But that's where you are wrong, Rich." Darcy took a sip of the coffee he had been provided once they were settled in his cousin's office. "Any money Bingley gave them will be gone in no time. It would not surprise me at all to find out Wickham attached himself to Lydia because of her connection to all three of us. We will hear from him either when he's broke or when he's tired of his new wife's complaining when she can't have whatever she desires in the shops."

Richard looked to Charles. "What can you tell us about the new Mrs. Wickham?"

Bingley shook his head slowly. "She is as unalike her two eldest sisters as night is to day. I've never met a woman with the sweetness of my wife and the sense of Elizabeth. Lydia possesses neither quality, I'm afraid. She has been indulged by her mother and ignored by her father her whole life, and I found her to be demanding and selfish."

"Lord, she sounds like Wickham," Richard said, rubbing his hand over his face. "A match made in heaven."

"Or hell," Darcy muttered.

"What's your plan?" Richard looked to his cousin. "There are about thirty hotels and rooming houses we can search, and who knows how many saloons rent rooms to paying customers."

Darcy nodded. "I can't see Wickham wasting his money on a fancy hotel nor can I see him staying any distance from the waterfront. With the bit of money Charles gave them in his pocket, he'll want to be where he can attempt to pad his stash."

"I think you're right." Richard rolled his eyes. "I loathe George Wickham. Seeing firsthand how he preys on innocent young ladies, makes me sick." Richard looked between the two men. "My last question is: What are you going to do when you find them? By now, they have spent the night together so the marriage can't be annulled. Divorce is possible, though it would take legislation from the state to get it done."

Bingley shrugged his shoulders. "I hadn't thought that far. All I know is that my wife has to be heartsick with her sister running off like that. Jane's being with child has tested her physical stamina, and I will not have her upset. I'd love to take that young girl by the ear and knock some sense into her. I'll do whatever it takes or pay however much it costs to see that girl settled."

Darcy chuckled. He'd never seen Charles so worked up— not even when Caroline was at her rudest.

Both men turned in his direction.

"Lydia is now Mrs. Wickham. There's nothing that can be done about their marriage, and I suspect she would fight any attempt to separate her from him." He breathed in deeply and exhaled slowly. "Where they go and whatever they do will be together. However, it will not be within an easy journey to Oregon City. Having them stay in Portland is not an option."

"What do you have in mind?" Richard asked.

"They will be offered a one-way ticket back to Baltimore. I will pay for their transportation and give them enough for costs on the way. My bank can wire a lump sum by Western Union to a bank in Baltimore. The only way they can access the account will be to present themselves in person."

"They can stay with the Bennets in the small rooming house I rented for them," Charles volunteered. "And help them out at the same time. Their circumstances were quite dire."

"That's mighty positive of you, Bingley. To be honest, I can't see them helping anyone but themselves." Even though Richard said it, Darcy agreed.

Darcy continued. "I'll put the money in the name of their uncle, Mr. Gardiner, and Lydia so they both need to sign to remove the funds."

Bingley nodded, his head bobbing up and down like a cork on water. "Good idea, Darcy. He's a trustworthy man."

Richard, ever the skeptic, commented, "You always think the best of everyone, Bingley."

"This time, he's correct." Darcy gave his immediate support. "Everything he said about his nieces proved true. His purchase of the Goulding place was handled honestly with little haggling on his part as he was not trying to get something for nothing. Nor was he attempting to gain advantage from the unfavorable circumstances the Gouldings faced with the death of their only child."

"He said my Jane was beautiful and kind, and he's right. My wife is an angel."

"We know." Both Darcy and Richard spoke at the same time.

"Then let's do what we need to do to find them."

All three stood, gathered their hats, and walked out the front door.

Their husbands being gone from Pemberley brought a tension to both Jane and Elizabeth that weighed them down like an anchor. Pears they had harvested and set in the cold to mature were ready to process, as were the last of the apples that had been waiting for the first frost. Game meat and salmon needed cut up and dried. Their day was filled, but the night… That period when it was time to retire to their beds was by far the hardest.

Receiving Bingley's note had comforted them in that their husbands were not alone in their search.

Obstinate, headstrong Lydia!

"Why are Will and Charles trying to find Lydia? She's a married woman now. She can make her own way in the world."

Kitty continued to fail to comprehend the seriousness of her sister's situation.

Before Elizabeth could speak, Jane did.

"When we arrived in Baltimore, it was to find there was no food in the house and Mama and Papa were being forced to leave because they had not paid their expenses. How do you think it made me feel to know you were having to do without the basics of life because Mama would rather have a new ribbon for Lydia and Papa chose not to work?"

"I have never seen you as angry before." Mary spoke up. "Never. In fact, I didn't know you could get that angry."

"I was livid, Mary, I will not lie." Jane laid her hand atop Kitty's. Her tone was kindly. "Kitty, you need to answer my question."

"It was not so bad." She pulled her hand out from under her sister's and folded her arms across her chest. "Besides, we aren't talking about our parents. Lydia wed at sixteen. It's so romantic!"

"You liked eating oats fed to horses twice a day? You liked wearing our shoes until there was more holes than soles? You liked your belly rumbling night and day because you were hungry all the time?" Mary's indignation rose with each question. "Well, I did not. I prayed and prayed for help. Daily, I beseeched God for deliverance. He provided it when Jane and Charles arrived to save us."

301

To Elizabeth, each one of Mary's questions felt like a blow—one after the other. She was weary and pained to the core. Because of the decisions of her family, the Bingleys were not settling in their home, their husbands were on a mission of mercy where the one they sought to help would treat them with disdain, and with a house full of females, she felt alone.

"Kitty," Elizabeth decided it was her turn to try. "What would have happened had Jane not stopped by? What if Mr. Bingley was like Wickham—with no money and no inclination to work?"

"We would have been tossed to the streets."

"Are the winters friendly to the homeless in Baltimore?"

"No," Kitty whispered.

"Why? Why were you in that situation?" Elizabeth's voice was firm and her eyes never left her sister. Mary kept quiet and even Georgiana, who was also sitting at the table, was still.

"Because Papa wouldn't work."

"And neither will George Wickham. He is lazy and negligent. He will take Lydia's innocence and throw her away when he's through with her or leave her in a room somewhere—alone."

"But they have to be in love or they never would have married," Kitty insisted.

Jane started laughing. The bitter sound filled the room. "How can you believe that to be true?"

Finally, help came from an unexpected source. Georgiana touched Kitty's arm and kept her hand there until Kitty looked up.

"From experience, I can tell you that neither Jane or Elizabeth are expressing clear enough how vile Mr. Wickham is. He preys on innocent girls and will continue to do so until he attaches himself to someone with money. He lies. He cheats. He steals the hearts of girls and then abandons them so they feel less about themselves, as if they have no value." She sucked in a breath. "He is evil."

From the look on her face it was obvious Kitty was horrified. Tears pooled at the corners of her eyes and traced a path to her chin, where they dropped to her lap. "Oh, poor Lydia."

"Yes, poor stupid, stupid Lydia," Elizabeth embellished.

"What will happen to her?" Kitty gazed directly at her.

"I do not know, Kitty. With both men looking for her, they are sure to find her. I suppose it will depend on Lydia, won't it?"

"But they can give them money to live on. Will and Charles have plenty."

"No!" Both Jane and Elizabeth declared.

"That will not happen, Kitty," Elizabeth explained. "Neither Wickham or Lydia understand the value of money. It would flow through their fingers like water. I do not know what Will intends, but I am absolutely certain they will not be returning to

Pemberley or Netherfield as a couple, and they will not be supported by us either."

"She won't be coming back? At all?" Kitty's tears fell faster.

"I cannot begin to imagine Will allowing it. You see, he wants you, Mary, and Georgiana to have wonderful lives. Happy futures. To bring her back would bring turmoil. Plus, Lydia is unrestrained. How do you think she would speak of her adventure if she was to make her home here again?"

"She would brag that she's a married woman and that none of us would ever find a husband as handsome." Bitterness filled Kitty's voice.

"Is that true?" Elizabeth pointedly asked. "Could you ever consider a man attractive who callously fails to care for his wife and family? Would he be handsome when his smiles turn into sneers and his tender words to unfair demands and expectations?"

Elizabeth was pleased to see all three of her single sisters shaking their head 'no'. "Then we will accept that whatever our husbands decide will be what is best for all of us. Lydia included."

It was a sorry end to an even sorrier day. Before retiring, Jane stayed behind when the other girls went upstairs.

"I feel bad that we had to be harsh with Kitty. And I feel bad that she was so clueless about the consequences Lydia faces." She raised her hand when Elizabeth started to speak. "However, I do not feel bad enough to want Lydia back. After the trouble she and Caroline caused all of us, I want neither of them within fifty miles of Oregon City."

"Why, Jane," Elizabeth smiled. "How very Lizzy of you."

Her sister snorted into the silence. "I have learned much since leaving our home. We were fairly powerless while on the train and ship. However, I've seen the extent my husband is willing to go to so we have a good home for our family. He is a good man, Lizzy. Like me, harsh realities have hit us in the face, and we've had to open our eyes so we see how to protect ourselves. Lydia will be faced with a much firmer man than she probably ever could have imagined when next she sees Charles."

"And you love him for standing firm, don't you?" Elizabeth chuckled. For the first time since Jim rode in with the news, the frown was off her face.

"I do." Jane sighed, a dreamy look filling her eyes. "I love Charles with my whole heart."

Elizabeth felt the same about Will. Yet, she was hesitant to share it with even her most beloved sister. Her feelings felt precious, like she needed to hold them close to her for safe keeping.

"Oh, poor Mary!" Jane blurted. "All of this discussion about marrying the wrong sort of man has to have unsettled her. I hope she doesn't allow it to keep her from Mr. Thornton."

"Well, maybe it's not such a bad thing. Will said he's a fine young man, and I have no reason to disbelieve him. However,

305

there's no need to rush, is there?" Elizabeth patted Jane's hand. "We have too much to do to plan a wedding, don't we?"

"We do."

With much lighter hearts, they went upstairs. As soon as the candles were out and night crept in, the fears returned. It would be another long, lonely night.

Four days of diligence produced nothing. Darcy had been in more bars than he had in his lifetime and he had no desire to enter another. Bingley had the same result. On the fifth morning, they woke to a pounding on the door. Lydia Wickham had arrived.

Throwing on his clothing, Darcy arrived downstairs at the same time as Richard and Charles. Lydia had been seated in the parlor, and she lifted her nose in a very Caroline Bingley-like manner.

"I cannot imagine how you can have a large house like this when Wickham and I can't seem to find a clean room to rent. Might one of your spare rooms be available?"

The audacity! The men were struck dumb with her inquiry.

"Poor Wickham. Had he been given what he deserved, we would already have a house larger than Pemberley to live in with

306

servants to cook and clean for us. As it is, I have had to take on tasks below a woman of my stature." Lydia rolled her eyes to the ceiling and sighed. "How droll."

Richard found his voice first.

"Mrs. Wickham, your husband will never be welcomed to my home. Never! Since you are attached to him, you will stay only as long as needed to speak with my cousin and then you, too, will be gone from here."

"Well, I never!" Lydia huffed.

"I imagine not," Richard whispered loud enough for all to hear.

"What do you want, Lydia?" Darcy stood with his arms crossed over his chest.

"We need money to live on and we need enough to set up a house, buy a wedding ring due a woman of my position, and a horse and carriage so I can make social calls. My husband and I both could do with new clothing, and I insist on a woman to cook and clean." She didn't bat an eyelash. "I do believe that is all."

"You believe so? Hmmm." Darcy didn't flinch as she stated her demands. "Well, Lydia, let me tell you how it will be. Neither you nor Wickham will get one cent from any of us. Your husband is now solely responsible for your care. You need to take your desires up with him."

"How could you do that to your wife's little sister? I thought you loved Lizzy. If you did, you would do anything to keep her from knowing how much I suffer." The tear appearing in the corner of her eye was clearly forced, a move he had seen more than once from Caroline Bingley.

"My marriage has nothing to do with yours, Mrs. Wickham. Neither does Bingley's."

Bingley nodded without hesitation.

"Well," Lydia huffed. "We shall see about that. I'll write to my sisters and you will see. You just wait."

"With what? What are you going to write with? Can you afford paper and pen? Can you afford the postage? Or did you think either one of us would carry such a tale to the women we hold dear to our hearts?"

"It's all your fault, Will Darcy," Lydia blurted, ignoring his questions. "Had you given George his share of Pemberley, I wouldn't need to be here begging for help."

"His share?" Darcy had heard it before—many times. He refused to raise his voice. "There never was a share for Wickham. Ever. He was a hired hand and nothing more. He was fired from Pemberley. He was fired from Netherfield as well. You, Mrs. Wickham, have tied yourself to a liar and a cheat; the most worthless man I know."

"How can that be?" Lydia clutched her hands to her chest, and for the first time Darcy saw her age. "He gave me all the details of how you cheated him and how we would make you pay. He loves me. He wouldn't lie to me!"

"And I would?" Darcy fought to keep the anger out of his voice. Deep down he felt sorry for Lydia, as he would for any female who encountered Wickham.

She dropped her eyes to her lap. "I don't know."

"What we will do for you and your husband is provide transportation back to Baltimore where you can join your parents. Once there, a sum of money will be available for you to access with the help of your uncle Gardiner."

"How much?" Her head snapped up.

"Enough." Darcy bit his tongue.

"I want a wedding ring. With a diamond."

"Then you will need to discuss this with your uncle."

"I want my money now."

"You will only receive it when you arrive at Baltimore."

"George isn't going to like this." Lydia pressed her lips together, her eyes focused on some far off spot. "But I can show him off to all my friends if we head east. They will be jealous and wish they were me." She laughed. "It's a good plan, Will. We accept."

"I'll make arrangements today."

When Lydia stood, she held out her hand, her palm up, and her foot tapping on the floor.

"No. I meant what I said. You get nothing."

"I don't see what Lizzy sees in you, Will Darcy. You are a selfish old bear and I hate you," Lydia whined. "But…I love your money and your plan, so I'll return this afternoon to see when we need to be at the wharf."

She walked to the door. "Don't bother seeing me out and don't bother giving my greetings to my sisters. They mean nothing to me now."

She slammed the door behind her.

Silence filled the room, each man dumbfounded.

"And you mean nothing to me as well," Darcy spoke into the air.

Chapter 20

Two weeks after Darcy left Pemberley, he returned with Bingley at his side. Their horses trod through the rain and mud as the wind threatened to blow them off their mounts. Tree branches whipped back and forth on each side of them.

Darcy had one thought—get home to his Elizabeth.

The pounding raindrops muffled the sounds of their arrival so no one was on the porch to greet them. It was expected, though it felt like an abandonment all the same.

Elizabeth had received a note from Darcy the first week they were gone, briefly reporting how they had located Lydia. In the nine days since, there had been no word at all. She knew better than to believe that 'no news was good news'. This was her youngest sister, after all.

The stomping of the men's boots on the wooden steps at the front of the house was the first clue they were home. Pulling the skillet off the stove, she grabbed a towel to wipe her hands as she rushed to the door.

He was soaked to the skin and she didn't care. Before he could hang his hat on the peg by the door, she had her arms tucked under his jacket and wrapped around him. In one smooth move, she was up on her toes to meet his mouth half way. She cared not for Bingley and Jane. Ignored were Mary, Kitty, and Georgiana. Her Will was home.

Without moving his lips from hers, Darcy shrugged out of his coat, leaving it in a pile behind him. He never wanted to let her go. She tasted of hope and dreams and of everything good. Feeling her hands run over the softness of his cotton shirt, she pressed between his shoulder blades, holding him to her as tightly as possible, and he felt how her need for comfort equaled his own.

Unmindful of their guests, he bent and, in a motion as old as time, scooped behind her knees until she was nestled in his arms. He felt her breath on his neck and it weakened his knees. Without looking back, he climbed the stairs and kicked the master bedroom door shut behind them.

312

"We are terrible hosts," Elizabeth giggled softly. That same spot on the bottom of her foot itched so she rubbed it against his leg. Kissing the edge of his jaw, she took a deep breath and let it out slowly. When he did the same, she knew it was time to talk.

"Would you tell me about Lydia?" She softly stroked the side of his face, running her hand into his hair and then pulling it back down to gently tug on his earlobe. She kissed his jaw again. "Please?"

Will captured her left hand in his own and brought it to his mouth to plant a kiss on the inside of her wrist, before entwining his large fingers with hers. He cleared his throat to speak.

"When your sister came to Fitzwilliam's house in town, she appeared to be unaffected by how her marriage put her in harm's way. She was bold and demanding."

"What did she want?"

"Money," he huffed. "And a wedding ring."

"Of all the foolish things," Elizabeth whispered to herself.

"In advance, I had decided to pay for travel for the two of them back to Baltimore and settle some funds with your uncle so they would need to go through him to gain access."

"A good plan."

"Yes, so it seemed." Darcy paused and she felt his hand tighten on hers. "Lizzy, I thank the heavens that Richard was there through the whole of Lydia's time in that room."

Elizabeth leaned up on her elbow so she could look him in the face. "Why?" Her hesitation to ask, and his hesitation to continue, worried her.

"He recognized certain tells while your sister was speaking that both Charles and I failed to see."

"What do you mean? Lydia is and always has been pretty straight-forward."

"Yes, but this was different." Darcy again kissed her hand. "Richard was able to read her like a book. He noticed how she refused to make eye-contact with any of us. He caught a tremor in her hands and how her fingernails dug into the arm of the chair each time she spoke. He even caught how, at one point, she stared off like she was trying to recall the exact words she was supposed to say."

"What does this mean?" He was right. This didn't sound like Lydia.

"He believes Wickham spent the first days after their marriage filling her head with lies. Then he coached her with what to say and how to act. Once Rich told me this, I went back over the conversation and I could hear Wickham in each and every word she uttered."

"Do you think she was afraid of him?"

314

"Yes!" Darcy shuddered. "And we were right to be concerned."

"Oh, no!" Elizabeth sat up, facing him. "Tell me."

"Lydia had no money so she walked back to the tavern where they were staying. The three of us followed at a distance and were easily able to hear the argument that followed." Darcy sighed. "Wickham called your sister names a female should never hear when she returned empty-handed. He told her she would have to go downstairs and offer to work for the owner of the facility in any capacity available so he could have money to pay for their rooms. When she told him she would not, he... he slapped her."

"No!"

"Yes, Lizzy." Darcy scooted up so he leaned against the headboard. "When we came to her aid, Wickham... he became even more aggressive in his words to her, blaming first me and then his wife for being in reduced circumstances. She looked so lost and hurt, every one of her young years. I didn't know what else to do, so I stepped between them and turned my back to Wickham. I pulled her to me and covered her ears with my hands. Lizzy, she shook so badly I had a hard time standing still."

Elizabeth could no longer hold in her tears. She cried for the pain her sister had suffered and for the ignorant loss of her innocent youth. Her heart ached at what her husband endured at the hands of two foolish souls.

"Tell me. What has been done?" Elizabeth had been aware enough to realize her sister had not entered Pemberley with the two men. She had no idea where Lydia was.

"There's only one thing that will move Wickham and that's the opportunity for seemingly easy money. Richard had heard of a gold strike on the Fraser River area of Canada and when he shared it with Wickham, it was quickly decided that Bingley and I would buy passage for him as well as give him a stake for his supplies. I'm sure you wouldn't be surprised that he wanted more, but the promise of gold made him much more malleable than we had hoped."

"Did Lydia go with him then?" Elizabeth hoped not.

"No, she did not." Darcy gave a gentle tug on her hand so she leaned into him. "Wickham clearly stated that he had no intentions of taking her along. He told her he regretted marrying her as he did the others he'd wed."

"What?"

"Yes, apparently he's been married before and has made it his habit to do so and then walk away when something new comes along."

"Then their marriage isn't legally binding, is it?"

"Richard doubted it, though there would need to be proof."

"Oh, good heavens!" Elizabeth shook her head. Of all the stupid things to have happen. "Then where is Lydia?"

316

When he rolled his eyes and looked to the ceiling, Elizabeth knew she wouldn't like what was to come.

"It seems your sister was more in love with the idea of being married than actually having a husband. After a few day's search, Rich found a family traveling back east who were willing to escort your sister to Baltimore. They are an older couple who are deeply religious. Your sister will be well looked after. I wired funds to your uncle to see a small home purchased for her. She agreed to take in your parents."

"At great cost to you."

"To us, my dear." He kissed her at her temple. "But she was happy at the decision. She was perfectly willing to keep Wickham's name despite the fact that she would most likely never see him again. Should there be a child, the pretense of being wed will give it legitimacy."

"Is that all?" Elizabeth hated to ask as Will had already done so much.

"She had one demand only that I found confusing, but easy enough to fulfill."

"I cannot imagine."

"She wanted a diamond on a wedding band so she could show it off to all her friends." Darcy chuckled. "To my surprise, Lydia chose a modest ring and was so pleased with it that she couldn't take her eyes off it. Of course, this meant she kept walking into things before we jumped into a carriage to return to the Fitzwilliams. By the time Bingley and I went back to the saloon to pack up the few items she'd brought with her, Wickham was gone. Charles and I stayed to see Lydia off with the Wilson family, and then we came home."

"I love you, Will." She put her head on his shoulder and held him tight. "I love you so much for so many reasons."

Again, he was reminded of the differences between the sisters. And, again, he was so relieved it was Elizabeth who was his wife.

"I love you as well."

The next morning, Darcy and Elizabeth didn't stir until the smell of coffee and frying bacon wafted upstairs into their room.

"Lizzy?" Darcy mumbled into her hair.

"Mmm?"

"Who's cooking breakfast?" His empty stomach rumbled while he spoke.

She giggled.

"Are you hoping it isn't Maggie?" she murmured into his ear. "Much has changed in the two weeks you were gone. When Mr. Thornton came to call on Mary, she decided to learn as much as possible from Maggie and me so she would be able to keep a good home should he ask her to be his bride. Georgiana and Kitty decided it was time to learn as well."

"What a great idea." His smile was delighted.

"Yes, I'm very proud of the girls." Elizabeth was pleased with each of them. "At first, their attempts were a challenge for them to cook and for Jane and I to eat. Nonetheless, they kept after it and have proved to be good in the kitchen."

"Which young lady is cooking this morning?" He worried he would not be able to pretend the chef was Georgiana and the meal wasn't palatable.

"They all are."

She threw back the covers and jumped from the bed. "I'm hungry too."

"Where are Charles and Jane?" Elizabeth asked Mary, who was carefully placing the plates and forks in their proper position.

When her younger sister looked up and lifted her brow without reply, a blush started up Elizabeth's neck. She looked over to see the same brilliant red creeping up Darcy's cheeks in almost a mirror image of what she supposed hers would be.

Before either could speak, Kitty stepped to the table to place a bowl of fried potatoes and onions next to the scrambled eggs.

"I can't imagine why you didn't realize you were sleeping in the bedroom Jane had been staying in. In spite of her tidiness, surely you figured out you had displaced her at some hour of the night."

Georgiana moved alongside Kitty with a platter of biscuits. All three girls were struggling to contain their mirth.

"I...I..." Was all Will could add as a reply.

His discomfort was all the catalyst they needed to burst into merry laughter. Finally, both Darcy and Elizabeth joined in. The relief this expression of emotions provided was immense.

Once seated around the table, Kitty inquired about Lydia. Elizabeth thought it the path of wisdom to allow her husband to address the subject.

"Your sister was given a choice as to what her future would be. She was happy to return to Baltimore with a family traveling that direction. She will be able to provide a home for your parents."

"But her husband. What about Mr. Wickham?" Kitty was relentless, which was understandable due to their familial closeness.

"Wickham left for the gold fields of Canada. I sincerely doubt she will ever see him again."

The girls looked at one another, confusion on their faces.

"Sisters," his manner of address pleased Elizabeth. It was the first time in her hearing he had done so. "Once Lydia realized the caliber of man she had married, she decided distance was the best choice for her. In the future, should she decide to seek another husband, steps will be taken to dissolve the marriage. For her, four days of being Wickham's bride convinced her beyond measure that being a wife to an immoral man was the worst sort of life. She has vowed to both Charles and me that she will never marry. Whether or not she continues on that path remains to be seen."

"Was it that bad?" asked Kitty, hesitantly.

"I'll be honest. It was worse than bad." Darcy shook his head as his eyes met each of his sisters'. "So allow this to be a lesson to all three of you. Once you tie yourself to a man, you could either be the happiest woman on earth or the most miserable. I'd advise you to get to know him well before accepting any offer to wed."

"Like you and Lizzy?" Georgiana's smile was mischievous. "Let's see, you knew each other fewer than twenty-four hours when you married, didn't you?"

Again, Darcy blushed. Elizabeth reached over and laid her hand on his arm.

"You are both right and wrong, Georgie." Elizabeth's smile softened her words. "Despite the fact that I'd only set eyes on him the day before, I loved your brother for months. Each heartfelt letter he wrote revealed a kind, gentle man who had the same appreciation for his surroundings as I did. I knew that with each word, he was telling me he would care for me and eventually love me."

"But Lizzy said she hated you when you first married," Mary blurted, ever forthright.

"She is correct." Darcy draped his fingers over where Elizabeth's hand rested on his arm. She felt his gentle squeeze. "We had a rough start, but Lizzy's right. The letters she wrote in reply captured me to such an extent that I wanted the author by my side, and no other."

"The problem was when we realized it wasn't Charles and Jane who had written the letters, but ourselves. By then, your brother had offended me and I'd responded with a sharp tongue." Elizabeth was grateful they could both smile at the memory. "However, while the letters attracted us, it was the day-to-day working together for the same goal that finally united us. We were forced to come to discern both the good and bad in each other, and we learned to love each other deeply in spite of our flaws."

Darcy injected. "Our love has been tested and is now something I value higher than gold."

"Well," Kitty said with a snort, "apparently Mr. Wickham decided gold was more valuable than Lydia."

"Yes, which means they both lose, doesn't it?" Darcy answered.

"I guess." Kitty shrugged, as did Mary and Georgiana.

"Then I suggest we enjoy this meal you worked so hard to prepare." Darcy handed the platter to his wife. "Someday you will meet the man of your dreams. When you do, you will be proud to bear his name. There will be no one else you will want to spend forever with."

All three girls sighed.

"I don't think I'd want to be a mail-order bride," Kitty proclaimed. The others nodded their agreement.

"Smart girls," Darcy mumbled. Elizabeth heard. She smacked his arm and then chuckled. *How she loved this man.*

The rain had slowed to a heavy mist, blanketing the property and hiding the river from their view. Elizabeth shrugged into one of Darcy's old jackets and joined him as he leaned against the porch railing. As she had done before, she wrapped her arms around him from behind and rested her head between his shoulder blades. She felt the tension leaving him as she squeezed him tightly.

"What's on your mind, Will?" she murmured into his back, the wool of his coat scratching her cheek. Elizabeth moved to stand at his side, her arms never leaving his torso.

He encircled her and pulled her close, dropping a brief kiss to her temple. "Do you regret being a mail-order bride?"

She could feel the irregularity of his breathing as she considered how best to answer.

"No matter how it came about, I can say with honesty that am happy I am your bride. I love you, Will Darcy, with my whole heart, soul, and strength."

"You do, huh?"

She felt his smile against the side of her face. "I do."

"In spite of the troubles and the way things started out for us," he continued, "I will forever be pleased I took the plunge and added the note offering you marriage in Bingley's letter."

She nodded, happy as well. "It was rather out of character for you. I've watched you carefully consider almost every decision you've made. To know our marriage was a matter of impulse amazes me."

"Me too." He turned to her. "I know I am four months too late, but will you?"

"Will I what?" She tilted her head in confusion. When he dropped to his right knee without breaking eye contact, a notion of what he had in mind made her smile from ear to ear. "Oh, Will," she sighed. Her heart started pounding as a tear of joy trickled down her cheek.

"Will you marry me? Will you be my bride?"

His eyes brimmed with love and goodness, and she had never felt as overcome as she did at that moment. She longed to hold him and have him hold her more than she wanted her next breath.

"Yes, Will. I will marry you."

As soon as the last word was uttered, he whooped. Grabbing her around the waist, he lifted her and spun her in circles until his face drew so close it was impossible to do anything other than kiss him senseless.

Three young faces pressed up to the living room window, smiles on all of their faces.

"I want what they have," Georgiana declared to the nods of the other two. Stepping back, she held her hand out between the girls. "Then shake on it. We promise not to marry until we can find a love like Will and Lizzy. No mail-order. No running off in the night. Promise?"

Each girl took a turn extending their hand in commitment. "Promise."

Epilogue

Jim Thornton asked Mary to be his bride less than two weeks after the promise. In spite of the teasing from her sisters, Mary said yes.

Georgiana was the next to wed, though it was years later and she was twenty-one when she accepted the son of a man known since childhood to her Fitzwilliam family. He was the youngest attorney to be made partner in Richard's law firm. His specialty was business law. It was love at first sight. They married only 28 days after becoming reacquainted.

By the time the wedding took place, the Bingleys had three strawberry blonde-headed daughters and Jane was expecting child number four.

Harald and Cynthia Pedersen added two more children, one son and one daughter, to their family—though they were not twins.

It was Darcy and Elizabeth whose first pregnancy ended with one child of each sex. They did the same the second time she whispered into her husband's ear that they might want to start building an addition to the family home. When the eldest twins were five and the next set were three, Elizabeth realized she was again expecting to add to their family.

Darcy took her seriously and added two more bedrooms, indoor plumbing throughout the house, and increased the kitchen and dining room floor plan. Miss Rose Anne Darcy became the youngest sibling to twins Matthew and Madeline and Alexander and Amelia.

Shortly before the arrival of Jane's first daughter, Clementine, the Gardiners moved to the Goulding Ranch, bringing news of Lydia and the Bennets. There was an unsteady peace between mother and daughter. Mr. Bennet kept to his bookroom as was his usual habit.

True to her word, Mrs. Lydia Wickham rejoiced in flashing her ring to anyone who would notice. She became frugal with her mother so none of what she considered 'her' money was spent in a manner she did not directly approve. She kept her parents in the small cottage Darcy had purchased for her until her father died of pneumonia in 1874.

In 1875, at the age of fifty, Mrs. Frances Bennet replied to an advertisement placed in the matrimonial column of a Baltimore newspaper by a thirty-eight-year-old man seeking a wife for his home at the mouth of the Columbia River in Astoria. Within a month she was on the train to the west coast. The new Mrs.

Horace Thompson flourished living with a man who clearly adored her. Once a year the couple would travel upriver to Oregon City to visit with their grandchildren.

Elizabeth was completely surprised when she met her new father-in-law. He was just under five-feet-tall and probably weighed under one hundred twenty pounds soaking wet. The former Mrs. Bennet worshipped the ground his small feet walked on and he called her his Sugar Plum.

Gratefully, the visits were shared with the Bingleys. Each time they came, the main theme of all conversations started by Francis Thompson was the need for Kitty to find a husband. Each time Kitty dug in her heels and staunchly refused. It was a battle they were both determined to win.

Kitty met the man of her dreams at Sunday services. He was a quiet man who was there to see to the needs of his elderly mother. Eight months passed before he could convince Kitty to give up her single state. On the day of her marriage, she admitted her fears to Elizabeth, but on their one year anniversary, she confessed she was the happiest woman on earth.

The following year, word trickled down from Canada that George Wickham had been caught cheating at cards. Frontier justice was swift and Lydia became a widow days before her twenty-second birthday. With no family remaining on the East Coast, and most of her friends married, she sold her cottage for a good sum and returned to Oregon City in 1877.

With Darcy's help, she purchased a house on the main street of town. The income from her Baltimore home was invested in an up-and-coming woolen mill that met with large success. Within the next ten years, she was an independent woman in her own right who lived to flirt with the perpetually unmarried Richard Fitzwilliam each time he came to town.

"Sweetheart." Fitzwilliam Darcy hugged his wife to him as they stood at the railing, their favorite spot on the porch. It had been eleven years since their marriage.

"Yes, dear." Elizabeth loved her thirty-eight-year-old husband's gray sideburns and the streaks of the same color in his mustache. His attitude had softened with each child born, though his body was as vital as it was when they first wed.

"Little Rose told me she wanted to marry me when she got bigger."

"Oh, she did, did she? And what did you reply?" Elizabeth chuckled at her precocious child. Both sets of twins were a blend of their parents. In the nature of those of multiple births, they were exceedingly close to their partner from their mother's womb and didn't seem to need the company of anyone else. Rose? She was her mother's daughter and had her father wrapped around her little finger from her first breath.

"I told her that being four, she had plenty of years to worry about who would be her husband and, besides, I already had a wife."

"That was a sensible answer, husband." Elizabeth leaned into his side and jabbed him with her elbow. "Now tell me, what did you really want to tell her."

The words poured from him like water over a dam. He placed his hand on his chest and rubbed.

"I wanted to insist she promise me she would never marry, that she would never want to leave home, and that she would never love a man like she loves me."

"You dear, dear man." She clasped his fingers and kissed the back of his hand. "Do you remember the first letter you wrote for Bingley? You spoke of how quiet it would be living here if we didn't listen for the sounds of nature. You wrote of twin fawns eating and playing by the honeysuckle arbor. Do you recall?"

He gazed out over the land and pulled her tighter. "I do."

"My love, you have taught each one of our children to hear the sounds, to see beyond the obvious to what exists beyond their small circle. You have set an unparalleled example for our sons of what it means to be a good and responsible husband and father. And you have set a standard for the kind of man our daughters should look for in a mate." She reached up and kissed his cheek.

"Do they have to grow up, Lizzy? Alex is already almost as tall as Matthew and he's only eight. Madeline is helping more and more in the house and Amelia plays with her dolls like she can't wait to have her own family. I am not ready for this."

She smiled into his neck.

"Matthew and Maddie are only ten, Will. You still have a few years yet."

"It goes by so fast."

"That it does." Daily she noticed her eldest son becoming more skilled at the chores his father assigned him, and Maddie already knew more about keeping a house than Mary, Kitty, and Georgiana did when they arrived in Oregon back in 1869.

They both sighed in tandem.

"I'm glad you answered my letters." Darcy spoke into her hair.

"And I'm glad you wrote them in the first place." Again, she smiled.

"I'm glad you were *my* mail-order bride."

"Me too."

Occasionally over the years, they would tease each other about the attraction they felt to who they thought had written the letters. Neither of them had any regrets.

Bingley and Jane were perfect together. They never allowed Caroline back into their home, and she never once came to visit them or acknowledge the birth of their children.

Bingley was the sole male at Netherfield Ranch. The fourth and fifth pregnancies gave them Charlotte and Claire to add to Clementine, Clarissa, and Cassandra. All five girls were fair-haired with blue eyes and had the sweet nature of their mother and the amiability of Charles.

When the men were cloistered in the study with a bottle of whiskey and no females, the conversation often turned to the future.

"Would you ever let your daughters marry someone they knew only by letter?" Bingley would inevitably ask.

"Never!" Darcy would always reply.

Jane and Elizabeth would have variations of the same conversations with, pretty much, the same results.

Late at night, when the children slept, Darcy would invite his wife to their spot on the porch. It was their time for reflection of the day and a sharing of plans and dreams for the future.

On this night, their twelfth anniversary since the day they were married before the Justice of the Peace, Darcy didn't speak.

Instead, he handed her a folded piece of paper with a single white rose balanced across the top.

She moved to the rocking chair and turned the wick up on the lantern. Putting the rose to her nose, she inhaled the sweet fragrance. Laying it on the table next to her, she waited for him to settle back at his post, leaning against the railing. He refused to look at her. Instead, his back was to her as he gazed into the darkness beyond. She noted the stiffness of his shoulders and knew he was reining in his emotions until he knew her response. It was his way.

July 1, 1881

My dearest Elizabeth,

I clearly remember the night I added my note to the bottom of Bingley's letter asking you to come to Oregon to be my wife. Above all things, I desired a woman who would turn my house into a home; a woman who would share my fears and joys, who would want to rise in the morning with me to face each new day and yearn for the comfort of our bed each night.

In you, Elizabeth Darcy, every one of my dreams has come true. You are my heart and soul. You are my life and my love. If I have failed to adequately express my appreciation for your taking a chance on a stranger, I beg you accept my sincerest thanks now.

Although we were not in love the day we wed, I know from my heart that I started falling for you the very next day when you bravely tended my wound and fearlessly gave commands to men far taller and stronger than you to see to my care.

I will love you, my mail-order bride, until we take our last breath on this earth. You are the only woman for me. I promise.

Will Darcy

Elizabeth clutched the letter to her heart. She would fold it and place it with the other four he had written for Charles. Finally, she set it next to the rose and stood to walk to her husband. He turned as she stepped near.

"You are the only man for me." Putting both hands to the sides of his face, she kissed him with all the passion she felt bursting inside her. "I promise."

The End

About the Author

Joy Dawn King started telling stories from an early age. However, she did not write any of them down until she was 57 years old. While living high in the Andes Mountains of Ecuador with her husband and family, she read Jane Austen's Pride and Prejudice for the first time. It was love at first page. After she was done, she longed for more.

When searching for another copy of Jane Austen's writings, she happened upon several books that offered alternative paths to happily ever after for Mr. Darcy and Elizabeth Bennet. She purchased and read as many as she could find. Finally, in early 2014, she had an idea for a story about the couple that would not go away. Thus, her first book, *A Father's Sins: A Pride and Prejudice Variation*, was born.

Since then, Joy and her husband moved back to the U.S. and plot bunnies kept hopping in and out of her imagination. Now, it's all she can do to keep up with them. But, she tries.

Bonus Preview:
Love Letters from Mr. Darcy:
A Pride and Prejudice Novella

by J. Dawn King

Excerpt from Chapter 2

"Mr. Darcy." She stood and walked to him, the room suddenly silent as she did so.

What was she about? Was she going to refuse him as she had done in this very room only two nights before? He felt perspiration on his palms and wanted to wipe them on the sides of his trouser legs. Finally, after what seemed like an hour, or a half a day, he responded.

"Miss Elizabeth, might I be of assistance?"

"I thank you for your offer as yes, it is your help I seek." She turned to her friend to satisfy her curiosity as she pulled a letter from her pocket. "Charlotte, I happened upon Mr. Darcy yesterday in the glen and we spoke of a situation at Longbourn where the gentleman's experience in estate management—in particular, that of removing unwanted pests—would be of immediate benefit. Last night, I endeavoured to pen the information to my father and fear I may not have the details entirely correct."

"Oh, no! Cousin Elizabeth, it should have been Lady Catherine you should have petitioned for there is not another more knowledgeable soul in all of England when it comes to making decisions as to the proper running of a property. I do surmise, Cousin, that had your father accepted willingly the recommendations I passed on from my benefactress, the estate to which I am entitled to inherit would be in a far better financial condition than it is currently and it certainly would not be overrun with rodents."

"Mr. Collins!" Charlotte implored him to remember his manners and stopped him from speaking further.

Elizabeth's face reflected horror and embarrassment at his crass sharing of such personal information.

Miss Maria Lucas had her chin to her chest as she worried her skirt fabric between her fisted hands, and Colonel Fitzwilliam looked on the scene with seeming pleasure. Then he stared directly at the parson.

"Is that right, Mr. Collins? You believe Aunt Catherine to be an advisor to Darcy who is in possession of an estate more than twice the size of Rosings Park?" He paused, acting confused. "Why do you think it is that Darcy is required to come twice a year to survey the property and balance her account books? If it was as you claim, would it not be my aunt who would be doing such to Pemberley instead?"

"But..but..." Mr. Collins sputtered.

"To ease your mind, sir, might I recommend that Darcy read Miss Elizabeth's letter. Should he have any concerns that he could not supply the exact information needed for Mr. Bennet, he could take up the matter with our aunt."

Mr. Collins was quick to agree. "Yes, Cousin Elizabeth, please read your letter aloud."

Darcy spoke up before either the colonel or Miss Elizabeth could do so.

"I do not believe it to be necessary. Should she have phrased the matter incorrectly, I would not want Miss Elizabeth to suffer discomfort from having her family and friends know of her error. As it happens..." he reached into his own pocket and pulled out a letter of his own. "I, myself, have written to Mr. Bennet for the same purpose. Does your letter include greetings for your family?"

"Yes, it does." He could see the gratitude on her face.

"Then I will include yours with my own. If I might add a post script so Mr. Bennet knows how I came into possession of his daughter's letter, we can arrange for an express rider to send them on their way."

Charlotte moved to a desk in the corner and opened the ink well, placing the sharpened quill carefully at the side of the writing surface. Mr. Darcy wrote quickly, sanded the newly inked parchment. He then folded and sealed the two letters together. Yet, when he moved away from the desk, there was not one missive in his hands, but two. *Odd!*

Mrs. Collins watched him carefully as he walked back to stand next to Elizabeth. As quick as a breath, the second letter was dropped into her friend's pocket. Charlotte's brows went up and her hand went to her mouth. Her eyes swept around the room to find that the only one other than herself who noticed was the colonel. When Darcy's cousin slowly shook his head "no" and the corner of his mouth lifted, Charlotte knew not to make mention of the matter.

Elizabeth Bennet had, against all the rules of propriety, received correspondence from Mr. Darcy. *How shocking!*

J. Dawn King

http://JDawnKing.com  J. Dawn King @jdawnking

Yes, Mr. Darcy

In *Yes, Mr. Darcy* our hero is honorable, tender, and entirely swoon-worthy (sigh!). Elizabeth is compassionate, intelligent, and empathetic. This story explores what happens when their attitudes and faults do not get in the way of their relationship. A sweet, happily-ever-after.

One Love, Two Hearts, Three Stories
A Pride and Prejudice Anthology

The Library

What happens when Fitzwilliam Darcy and Elizabeth Bennet are alone in the library at Netherfield Park and they decide to talk instead of ignore each other?

Married!

Fitzwilliam Darcy needs a wife! Elizabeth Bennet needs a husband! What results when two strong-minded, kind-hearted strangers unite in this most sacred state? Will love grow?

Ramsgate

When Miss Georgiana Darcy stumbles upon her beloved George Wickham willingly wrapped in a passionate embrace with someone else, the elopement is off. Running to her new friend, Miss Elizabeth Bennet, she involves her in a plan to get help from her brother, Fitzwilliam Darcy, and bring Wickham to justice. Enjoy this alternate path to our favorite couple's happily ever after.

Available in Trade Paperback, eBook, and Audiobook format from the following retailers:

J. DAWN KING

A Father's Sins

How do Fitzwilliam Darcy and Elizabeth Bennet overcome the consequences of poor decisions made by their fathers when Darcy and Elizabeth were young? Will love have a chance?

Also Available in Spanish
También disponible en Español

The Abominable Mr. Darcy

Mr. Darcy was an enigma…
until he spoke. Then, he was the enemy.
Miss Elizabeth Bennet's eyes are instantly drawn towards a handsome, mysterious guest who arrives at the Meryton Assembly with the Bingley party. The gentleman destroys her illusions by delivering an insult that turns him from Mr. Divinely Attractive to the Abominable Mr. Darcy.

Compromised!

Fitzwilliam Darcy's heart was crushed and weighed down by the consequences of his sister's actions. Elizabeth Bennet, knowing the rules of propriety would be broken if she offered him human kindness and comfort, made a decision that would change both of their lives. Permanently!

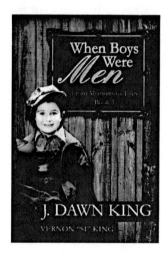
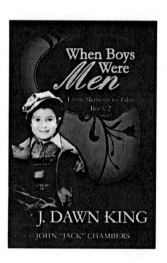

J. DAWN KING

Love Letters from Mr. Darcy:
A Pride and Prejudice Novella

How much power is in the written word?
Mr. Fitzwilliam Darcy is determined to find out.

Crushed beyond measure at the rejection of his proposal, Darcy struggles to explain both the facts and his feelings by letter to the only woman he will ever love. Can such a reticent man find the words to enable Elizabeth Bennet to know the man behind the mask? Will she read his carefully crafted epistle once he delivers it into her hand? Will he catch even a small glimmer of hope?

Affection and respect. Two magical words Miss Elizabeth never expected to hear from the last man in the world she would ever marry, yet they undeniably appear before her eyes in black and white. Devotion and adoration. Humph!

Follow literature's most beloved couple during the weeks following the disastrous proposal as a series of heartfelt missives has created such havoc in Elizabeth's heart that she is finally moved to write him back. Will hers be a letter of love as well?

In this sweet novella-length variation of Jane Austen's Pride and Prejudice, we will see love bloom and grow. This is a Regency historical romance from bestselling author, J Dawn King.

Mr. Darcy's Mail-Order Bride:
A Pride and Prejudice Variation

Jane Austen's Pride and Prejudice
meets the Wild, Wild West.

Available in Trade Paperback, eBook, and Audiobook format from the following retailers:

CPSIA information can be obtained
at www.ICGtesting.com
Printed in the USA
LVOW12s1646090217
523759LV00002B/585/P